THE BREACH

A Thriller in the Age of Climate Change

The Second Book in The Dome Series

W.F. VAN DER HART

This book is a work of fiction. Names, characters, places and incidents are the product of the author's imagination or are used fictitiously. Any resemblance to actual events, places, or persons, living or dead, is coincidental.

First published in 2021

Copyright © W.F. van der Hart, 2021

The right of W.F. van der Hart to be identified as the author of this work has been asserted by him in accordance with the Copyright, Designs and Patents Act 1988

All rights reserved. No part of this book may be used, reproduced, distributed, or transmitted in any form or by any means, or stored in a database or retrieval system in any manner whatsoever without written permission from the author.

First edition, 2021

Cover and interior book design by W.F. van der Hart

ISBN 9789464007367 (paperback)
ISBN 9789464007374 (hardback)
ASIN: B09L64DTN3 (eBook)

To my wife, the love of my life

THE BREACH

1.

The waves were bigger out here on the high seas. Every time a wave hit the bow, a large splash of water sprayed over the people packed together in the open boat. The refugees wore a life vest and most of them did not know how to swim. The smell of dirty, sweaty bodies mixed with the fresh sea air. Underfed men sat crammed together in the boat, next to their crying children and anxious wives. They had all waited a long time for this and felt equal, part excitement and anticipation. Most of them spent years saving to pay for this trip. Some of them had traveled long distances over the African continent to get here. Some were running away from war or anarchy, while others were hoping for a better and healthier life. They all entrusted their lives to him, a tremendous responsibility.

Looking at the dark clouds on the horizon through his binoculars, Maheer had a bad feeling about the whole expedition. For months he had been preparing everything for this journey, testing his jamming equipment extensively, but still, deep down, he worried. His brother had told him not to go, but he did not want to wait any longer in this godforsaken place. They had traveled a long time to get here and his brother had emphasized that he had to be patient, but he was tired of being told what to do and after another argument with his brother, he left.

Six boats on their way to cross the border and enter Europe. The coastline behind him had disappeared slowly out of sight. Wherever he looked, he saw only ocean. He stared at the screen on the control panel. It clearly showed the border on the electronic map. At their current speed, it would take them about half an hour to reach it. He peered at the other boats on his left and on his right. Earlier that morning, he had gone over all the details with the other captains and they all knew what to do. Everybody was quite nervous, nevertheless they were all very motivated to cross. Two weeks before, they had tested the jamming equipment on different types of drones in a field not too far from the village. The successful test convinced them the plan would work, and they wanted to leave as soon as possible.

The sea was relatively calm, although the waves were much bigger out here in the open sea. The boat was hanging low in the water under the weight of the more than fifty people crammed inside, making the waves look even more impressive. He looked at the people in front of him. They all had a story. One more shocking than the other. But Maheer had been through a lot as well, and he did not care about the others. They were merely there to finance his mission. It was hot, and he tried to stay as much in the shade as possible. Looking at the sweating people in front of him, he realized he should have arranged for something like a cover on board to create some shadow for everyone. Too late now, but since they did not have to travel such a long distance, he figured they would probably survive the sun and the heat.

They advanced toward the border with the six boats, all next to one another in one line. Maheer had instructed the other captains to steer in this formation at a distance of several hundred meters between each boat. He had strategically chosen the position in the middle of the formation. He figured this way he had the highest chance of passing the border alive. Looking at the boats on his left and on his right, he felt slightly reassured not being the only one on this risky endeavor.

Out in the open sea, the air was less dusty than on land, and his breathing was less painful. He wore a respo. Even though he had not replaced the filter inside for a long time and the effectiveness had decreased, it was better than the masks worn by most of the other passengers in his boat. Together with his brother's gang, they had attacked a trade ship several months before and they had stolen a large batch of respos. Only the closest circle of his brother had gotten one, the privilege of the top members of the organization.

Suddenly, one of his men rushed toward him and passed him the binoculars.

"I spotted a drone, sir!"

Maheer peered through the binoculars, and on the horizon, he spotted a small gray dot moving through the sky. He checked the control panel. They were close to the border. He carefully followed the drone's movement through the sky. It seemed to continue on the right, moving away from them. He could not see any others. They moved further through the water, while the drone slowly disappeared on the horizon on the starboard side. A moment later, he warned the other captains through the onboard radio.

"Attention! We're approaching the border. Prepare the jammers!"

On either side, he saw how the crew on board the other boats began their preparations. On board of each one, one of the crew members was peering through binoculars. He looked one more time starboard, but the drone had disappeared out of sight. Then he spotted one of the security buoys on port side. They were about to cross the border and soon the buoy would detect them. As he did not spot any other drone in the sky, they continued ahead. He looked at the control panel as they crossed the border. No drones yet, and they continued at full speed. People on board were quieter than before. The only noise they heard was that of the engines and the waves banging against the hull. He could feel the tension rise.

Several minutes later, Maheer was startled by someone yelling on board one of the boats on his port side. He heard the captain of the boat furthest from him shout frantically through the radio.

"We signaled a drone approaching on port side. Prepare your jammers for interception!"

He peered nervously through his binoculars on port side. After searching left and right on the horizon, he suddenly spotted the approaching drone. He felt the adrenaline rushing through his body and yelled at the crew member next to him, who was holding the jammer.

"Amir, look on port side behind the last boat! A drone is approaching. Fire your jammer as soon as it gets within reach."

"Yes, sir!"

Amir looked through the visor of the black, tube-like weapon until he spotted it.

"I see the drone, sir. It's still out of reach."

Maheer looked at the boat closest to the drone and noticed one of the crew members aiming at it. It flew closer and closer. Unexpectedly, a loud announcement came from the sky.

"Warning! You're entering European waters. Please return immediately or we'll have to shoot! Attention! Vous entrez dans les eaux Européennes! Veuillez reve…"

The announcement continued in different languages, and he noticed how the people on board were getting nervous. The drone came closer and seemed unaffected by the jammer. He felt his heart pounding in his chest. Then, all of a sudden, it started moving down and back up. Maheer felt a slight relief when they finally got a lock on the drone. The humming noise of its propellers stalled from time to time and the engines faltered. It started dropping, but then rose back up in the sky, after which it dropped again. It was still about ten meters above the water when suddenly it fired a shot in front of one of the boats. The explosion caused a tremendous splash of water. That was a first warning shot, Maheer thought to himself. He knew that the next one would target the boat itself. He started doubting his plan as he looked at the drone rising and falling.

As it got closer, the jammer on the second boat also seemed to get a lock on it as it suddenly dropped faster. Seconds later, a wave hit the drone, and it crashed into the sea. A loud roar sounded all around him as the more than three hundred people cheered. Some stood and raised their fists in the air. He looked at the drone floating in the water. It seemed to have stopped working. His moment of relief stopped abruptly when he heard one of the captains through the radio.

"Attention! Another drone approaching on starboard side. Prepare your jammers!"

He turned his head to the right. This time, he did not even need his binoculars as he immediately spotted it approaching fast on the horizon. He looked at the control panel and they were almost one kilometer behind the border. They kept going at full speed. The cheering stopped and everybody peered toward the approaching drone now. This one did not make any warning announcements, but immediately fired in front of the first boat, causing quite a panic on board. The drone came closer, and the jammer seemed to have locked in on it. They could hear the propellers falter.

As it started vacillating down, it fired another time. This time, it hit in the middle of the crowd sitting on the deck of the first boat. The explosion killed a dozen people instantly, and it injured many more. He watched a man screaming and trying to get out of the crowd. He was missing his arm. Some people jumped overboard. The smell of burned flesh filled the surrounding air. The sight of the panic on board was horrifying. The crew member holding the jammer continued firing at the drone, and the boat next to it also got it within reach. It fell down faster now, crashing into the water a few meters away from the bow.

Again, the masses on the boats cheered, although shorter this time. The sound of the moaning victims soon overtook the cheering. Maheer could hear the captain on the severed boat yell at the crowd, and he noticed how they started throwing the dead bodies overboard. There was crying and moaning all around, and some people were taking care of the wounded.

While they continued further, he peered through his binoculars at the horizon and contemplated what just had happened. He had expected every drone at first encounter to announce a warning, but the second one had not done that. This puzzled and worried him, since it meant this could get more difficult than he had anticipated. The voice of one of the captains on the radio interrupted his thoughts.

"Another drone approaching on port side!"

He scanned the sky with his binoculars until he spotted the oval-shaped drone. It was different from the previous two, bigger. It came closer and closer. His heart beat faster as it approached. He did not like the look of it. It was flying much higher than the other ones. They all looked at the drone coming closer until it was flying high above their heads. Still, they could not hear a thing. No humming noise from the propellers. It stopped moving high in the sky above them. Maheer yelled anxiously at Amir, who was aiming his jammer at it.

"Are you firing with that jammer?"

"I am, sir! I am, but it's too far!"

Maheer nervously glanced up at the gray shape hovering above them. Realizing the drones were all linked and that they probably used some sort of artificial intelligence, he felt as if someone swept away the earth under his feet. He peered through his binoculars to have a closer look and became paralyzed with fear. Several missiles were coming from the drone. In a brief moment of disbelief, he looked at the horizon. Before he could say anything to the rest of his crew, an enormous explosion blew away one of the boats next to them, followed instantly by more explosions. Within minutes, there was only rubble floating on the waves.

2.

The elevator doors opened and Dylan peered into the dark hallway. He scanned the hall for movement, but saw nothing. It was humid inside. He walked slowly through the corridor, checking every door carefully. The elevator doors closed behind him and he felt drops on his head. He heard water dropping around him and a low humming sound further away. He must have advanced about ten meters into the corridor when he heard the electronic bell of the elevator arriving. He turned around and aimed his gun at the doors. He had to be careful. It could be a trap, or maybe his friend had finally made it to the elevator.

He looked one more time behind him to ensure no one was sneaking up on him, then put his finger on the trigger while the elevator doors were opening.

"Hakim! You've made it. I thought I wouldn't see you again."

"Yeah, I fell through that hole in the floor when I was walking behind you. It took me a while to find the way back. What the f…"

Hakim aimed his gun at him and fired. Dylan was startled, but when the shots missed him, he turned around. A few meters away, he saw a mutilated man falling on the ground, moaning with pain and green slime drooling from his mouth.

"Phoe… that was close, Dylan. Let's keep going! We have to get to the roof as fast as possible!"

Dylan followed him down the corridor. He did not hear any sounds around them until he passed an open door on his right. Out of nowhere, a mutilated creature jumped on Hakim, screaming awfully. Dylan saw how he raised a large machete above his head. He didn't waste a second and fired his gun at the man on top of Hakim. With a big splash, his head exploded, and the body dropped onto the floor. Hakim turned his head and, with his face full of blood spatters, smiled at him.

"Thanks!"

There was a staircase at the end of the corridor, and he followed Hakim upstairs. It was darker here. He switched his goggles to night vision. Hakim was now all light-green and the surroundings were dark. In the darkness, he heard someone panting behind him, and he turned to have a look.

"Hakim, we have visitors. Behind us!"

He fired his gun at the light-green silhouettes. One by one, they shot them all down until the corridor was empty again. They continued climbing the stairs until he heard Elizabeth's voice.

"Dylan! Dylan! That's enough! Dinner is ready."

He hit a button and in front of him the words 'Game paused' popped up.

"Sorry Hakim. I've got to go."

"No problem. I'll see you later."

Dylan took off his mask and was back in his room. He looked over his shoulder and Elizabeth looked annoyed through the door opening.

"I thought you were going to help me prepare dinner? Well, everything is on the table already, but tomorrow it's your turn to cook."

"Sorry, but this Zombimasters is quite addictive."

"Yes, I've noticed."

Dylan took off his white full-body haptic suit, hung it up on a hook on the wall and continued to the kitchen. Since his quest to find his biological parents had ended, he had much more time available and started playing games on his new virtual-reality console. After the rather disappointing meeting with his biological father, he had moved on with his life. He discovered that his biological mother died a long time ago and sadly that his father was a cold person who had no interest in his son. It was what it was, and he had found peace with it. Back in Ikast, he focused on his job and enjoyed his life.

In the kitchen, Elizabeth had set the table already, and she was serving the delicious meal she had prepared. She had her long brown hair tied in a knot up in the back of her head. She looked at him with her penetrating eyes and made him feel like a schoolboy who got caught doing something naughty.

"I thought you had promised to play less with the VR console?"

"Yeah, I know. I'm sorry, but Hakim sent me a game invitation this morning and I couldn't resist."

He took her in his arms. She tried to look upset at him, but she couldn't suppress a faint smile. They kissed, and it felt good. Since their trip to Greenland, their bond had become stronger, and his admiration and affection for her had only grown further. She had been so supportive in his search for his biological parents. He felt they belonged together, like Ying and Yang, with an incredible charge between them that never seemed to stop.

"I'll prepare your favorite Indian dish tomorrow."

"Mmm, that would be nice. Who is this Hakim, anyway?"

"He works here at Enviro in some department in the Security division. I met him a month ago at lunch when I was talking to a colleague about our new VR console. Hakim had just bought the same one, and that's how we started talking about gaming. We joined today on a mission to destroy the zombie master. It's really amazingly realistic."

"There's quite some controversy around this Security division. A lot of their products get people killed. What does he do there?"

"I believe he's working on some software projects, although we didn't really talk much about work. Just when I told him how the police had rescued you in New York, he explained that the Security division makes those reconnaissance drones they had used in the rescue mission."

"Really? I thought they only produced horrible weapons and this inhumane border security system in the Mediterranean."

"Ah, come on. I know it's a cruel system, but a very necessary one, otherwise Europe would be flooded with refugees. We would risk losing our standard of living and our social security system would collapse."

"Jesus, you sound like Matteo."

Dylan did not want to get into this discussion, knowing how she felt about the security wall. She was clearly getting upset, and he quickly changed the topic.

"By the way, any news from your mother?"

"She's still in the hospital. It looks like her condition is getting worse. She's refusing a lung transplant and there's not much else the doctors can do for her. She's getting pain medication and oxygen."

Elizabeth's mother suffered from chronic obstructive pulmonary disease, the same disease that killed Dylan's mother. He knew that without a lung transplantation, the outlook for her mother would be grim.

"How is your father holding up?"

"He spends a lot of time in the hospital and seems to hold up, but I think it's very difficult for him. Matteo checks up on him regularly and they often go together to the hospital."

Dylan had visited her mother in the hospital in Lausanne a few weeks ago together with Elizabeth, and last weekend she had gone there alone. He encouraged Elizabeth to go and visit as often as possible. At the time, he had spent quite some time with his mother in the hospital, and it had helped him cope with her death.

"Maybe you should take some time off to be with your family?"

"Yes, I thought about it already, but it's quite busy at work now."

"Well, if your mother is getting worse, I think you'd better spend time with her now, before it's too late. You could always try to work from Switzerland."

"I guess you're right. I'll tell my boss tomorrow."

"I'm sure she'll understand."

3.

His phone rang while Marco was walking through the large warehouse. It was dark outside, and he had just ordered his men to prepare a shipment. He put down the box he was carrying and answered the call. He got shivers down his spine when he recognized the voice of his boss. He knew what he was capable of, and any contact with him always made him nervous.

"How is our friend coming along with the information we requested?"

"I spoke to him yesterday. He apologized for the delay, but insisted that he needs more time to copy all the information."

"What!? More time!? Does he think he can play around with us like that?"

"I've repeated our threat, but he sounded sincere. Apparently, he has to copy a lot of files and the security in his company is quite tight, so he has to be careful not to get caught."

"It shouldn't take that much time. What a bullshit!"

His phone felt warm against his ear as his palms began to sweat. He knew he had to thread carefully with his boss.

"That's what I told him as well, boss. He got all nervous and explained that the security in his company is so tight that he can't copy files without setting off some alarms."

"Sounds like he's just looking for excuses. Maybe we should send him another message from his sister."

He switched the sweaty phone to his other ear now as he tried to reason carefully with his boss.

"I threatened him already, although I've the impression that he's telling the truth. The guy explained that if he just makes an electronic copy of one of the requested files, the security officers in his company would immediately show up at his desk and he would be in trouble. He's actually taking pictures of his computer screen to copy everything. So, he needs more time than expected. He could hand us over the files on Friday."

"Friday, huh? Well, I guess we don't have much choice. All right, then. Tell him he has until Friday. Explain that if he doesn't have the requested information by then that we'll cut something off his sister and send it to him. Is that clear?"

"Yes, boss. Very clear. I'll tell him."

"All right. And you know what to do with him on Friday, right?"

"Of course! I'll take care of it. I don't think he suspects anything."

"Good! Call me when the ship leaves the harbor!"

"I will, boss!"

4.

After a long day at work, Dylan entered their apartment at the Enviro compound in Ikast. Elizabeth had gone to visit her mother in the hospital in Lausanne, and the silence inside was quite a contrast to usual. He had become so used to her presence every day that it felt weird when she was not there. He was glad, though, that she was visiting her mother, since it looked like her condition was deteriorating every day. He knew as no other how important it was to spend extra time with a dying loved one. Still, he missed her.

After a quick dinner in the kitchen, he checked his messages. Hakim asked him to join in the Zombiemasters game. That afternoon, he had run into Hakim in the office, but since he seemed very nervous, they had barely talked. It would be good to catch up with him. He entered the room they used for his VR console and put on the haptic suit and then his mask. A few seconds later, he was standing in a deserted building, and he changed his weapon while looking around. After entering the next room, he ran into Hakim.

Two hours later, he felt exhausted from gaming so intensely and said goodbye to his friend. While taking off his mask and suit, he thought back to the game he had just finished. He had never seen his friend play this fanatically. He clearly had to blow off some steam. They had broken some new records, but he felt like relaxing now. Normally he would not game that long, but with Elizabeth in Lausanne, he had lost track of time. He prepared some tea and then at eleven he called Elizabeth. She was still in the hospital.

"How is your mom doing?"

"It doesn't look good. She sleeps most of the time and in the brief moments she's awake she gets tired quickly."

"Ai. It sounds like she's getting worse. How is your dad coping?"

"He's with me in the hospital, together with Matteo. I've the impression he's trying to be brave for my mother, but I think he's scared of losing her. The prognosis from the doctor isn't good. They told us it's a matter of days now."

"That bad? Last week they didn't sound so negative?"

"Yeah, these last days everything deteriorated."

"Okay, Elizabeth. I'll look for a ticket for the first hyper-loop to Bern. It's probably too late to catch the last one tonight, but I'll take the first one tomorrow morning."

"Dylan, don't feel obliged."

"Don't be ridiculous! Of course, I should come over. It doesn't sound good, and your parents have always been there for me. No, I'm taking the first hyper-loop out there."

"You're nice."

"On top of it, I miss you!"

"Yeah, me too."

"I'll check the availability right away and call you back."

He hung up and checked the website of the hyper-loop service. The earliest times were all fully booked, but he managed to book a seat on one for eleven o'clock. He called her back.

"I've just sent you my schedule. I should arrive around noon in Bern, and then I'll come with a taxi to the hospital in Lausanne. With a bit of luck, I should be with you before one o'clock."

"Great! I'm looking forward to it!"

"I'll call my boss tomorrow morning to tell him I'm taking some days off. I hope he won't make a fuss."

"Nah, don't worry. Your boss is quite cool. I'm sure he'll understand."

"I hope you're right."

They said goodbye, and he ordered an air taxi to Copenhagen for the next morning. While brushing his teeth in the bathroom, he thought of his own mother and how he had spent so much time at her side in the hospital. Later, in bed, he felt good about joining Elizabeth. She and her family could use all the support, and he wanted to be there for them. Soon after, he dozed off, completely unaware of how difficult this trip was going to be.

5.

Amos was sitting at his desk in his office and stared apathetically at the gray wall in front of him. He still could not believe the message he had just received. How could this be possible? A few weeks ago, he handed in his report and it explained the whole intrusion event meticulously. He had made sure to write the full report himself without involvement of anybody to avoid any awkward questions.

Since the intrusion, he constantly felt depressed and down. In his mind, he kept replaying the whole event over and over. Feelings of guilt and shame overwhelmed him almost every day. He slept badly and was suffering from nightmares. He woke up often at night soaked with sweat. After sending his report to the Council, he had hoped that he would feel better and that he could leave things behind him and continue with his life. Unfortunately, life was never that simple, and he sank deeper into a depression.

After the night that Dylan had reached the dome alive, Amos tried to shut off all his feelings and focused on his work. He avoided the questions from his son, although it was clear to him that Elliot would not let go. He tried to keep the intrusion a secret and even instructed his staff members not to disclose any information. His ignorance got crushed quickly after, as rumors about the intrusion started circulating. Soon after, several Council members asked him questions, and he promised to explain everything in his report.

At the same time as he started writing the report, he also started implementing a solution to prevent a new intrusion in the future. He ordered his people to install a gigantic minefield in between the two walls around the dome and pushed them to the maximum to ensure that they would complete it before he would hand in his report. He had it all planned out and wrote the report all by himself, without involving anyone else. He described in detail what had happened and how the intruder had succeeded. He presented the measures he had taken to upgrade the security to prevent an intrusion like this in the future. Driven by fear and shame, he left out some delicate details. He sent out the report feeling satisfied and relieved, hoping that the whole thing would blow over.

But today a message from the Council shattered all his hopes. They had initiated an independent investigation into the intrusion. Conan, the head of Internal Affairs, was going to lead it. He knew him and his reputation. Everything would come out. It felt like someone had swept him off his feet. He knew it was only a matter of time before they would find out what he had done. They would discover that some guards had noticed that the intruder looked like Amos and that he had not ordered the guards to terminate him according to protocol, but to release him alive. How was he going to justify all this? He felt the room turning and rushed out of his office in panic.

6.

The buzzing sound of Dylan's alarm clock woke him up the next morning. He took a quick shower, dressed, and had some breakfast. He checked his luggage a last time to ensure he had everything for his trip. Then he looked for his phone to call Olav Sorenson, his boss. He hesitated for a moment, since he was not sure how many days he would need in Lausanne. At least this Friday and maybe two or three days the next week, possibly longer. His boss was sympathetic though and told him to take as much time as needed.

After receiving a message that his air taxi had arrived, he took his travel bag and left the apartment. When he walked through the large entry hall, he recalled his first look at the Enviro compound. He had been so impressed by the humanoid robots. Outside, he rushed into one of the white driverless vehicles in front of the entrance. It drove him to the landing platform where his air taxi was waiting.

Several minutes later, the humming sound of the propellers above the cabin increased as the taxi lifted off. It moved upward, then sideways, and accelerated away from the platform. He had a magnificent view through the windows all around him. He looked down upon the Enviro headquarters, as it became smaller and smaller, a massive black star-shaped building surrounded by an enormous private terrain. The town of Ikast disappeared, and he tried to enjoy the magnificent view illuminated by the rising morning sun.

The air taxi landed about an hour later on one of the platforms of the immense sky port in Copenhagen. Once inside, he descended to the lower level. Then he put his respo on his face and went outside. It was hot and sunny. He scanned his passport in the taxi departure area. A white driverless taxi in front of the row opened its doors and Dylan took a seat.

"Good morning, Mr. Myers. Where would you like to go?"

"To the hyper-loop station, please."

He took off his respo as soon as the hissing sound stopped and the green light switched on. It was relatively calm in the streets and he arrived seven minutes later at the station. He entered the main hall and looked at the large screen. The hyper-loop to Bern was scheduled to leave at 10:55 and he still had to wait for one and a half hour, enough time for a nice cappuccino at the brasserie next door. A few weeks ago, he had waited with Elizabeth in that same brasserie. It was a great place to relax and observe people along the busy street. He took a seat close to one of the large windows and ordered.

While enjoying his cappuccino, he read an article about an unfolding disaster in the south of India. Since his visit to his homeland during the quest for his biological parents, he paid much more attention to any news about India in the international press. He felt a strong connection with his country of birth, even though he had lived almost his entire life in Europe and in the United States.

Because of specific weather circumstances, an enormous brown cloud hung low above the ground in a large region northeast of Bangalore. The highly polluted air caused many people to flee the region. The article showed a picture of long lines of cars driving through a brown smog cloud. The government deployed the army to help evacuate them, but still, this toxic cloud already had killed about two hundred thousand individuals. The many people with acute respiratory problems overwhelmed the local hospitals. Despite the constant flow of climate-change related disasters in the news, this one touched him more than others. He had seen with his own eyes how climate change struck India. The country, and especially the poor, were paying a high price for decades of negligence.

For a moment, he stared out of the window and thought back to the poor people he had seen in New Delhi. Life circumstances in India were much harder than over here in Europe. Out of the blue, he noticed a heavy-set man running outside who looked familiar to him. The man passed right in front of his window and then he recognized him. It was Hakim. What was he doing in Copenhagen? He waved at him, and Hakim noticed him as well. He had a strange, terrified look on his face that he had not seen before. He continued running and disappeared out of sight.

Dylan continued reading his article, but a few seconds later, he got startled. Hakim appeared out of nowhere at his table and looked anxiously at him. Dylan had to look up at him, since he had approached his table closely and was towering above him with his large, slightly obese body. He was sweating and completely out of breath.

"Hi Hakim! What are you doing here?"

"I… I… I'm… in trouble," he muttered.

He looked outside and behind him, clearly frightened. Then he looked nervously at Dylan and took his hand. With his sweaty hands, he put something in his palm.

"Please, bring this back to Enviro. It's really important. Don't let anybody else take it!"

Dylan stared at his closed hand and under the table he opened it.

"What's this?"

But Hakim had rushed out already. He looked outside to see if he could spot him somewhere, but he had vanished as quickly as he had arrived. He opened his hand again under the table and glanced at the tiny memory stick. Flabbergasted, he tucked the memory stick away in the pocket of his jacket. He had no clue what to think of this strange encounter, but decided he would bring the stick back to Enviro after his trip. He ordered another cappuccino and continued reading.

7.

The hyper-loop was about to arrive in Bern. Dylan had dozed off in the comfortable chair quickly after leaving Copenhagen. The hyper-loop decelerated, and he woke up as he got pushed forward. The five-point harness he wore kept him in his seat, but his head felt heavy. Not the most pleasant way to wake up. It instantly reminded him why he disliked traveling with the hyper-loop. Still, it was fast and secure and had out-competed other means of transportation like planes or trains on connections like this one. In addition, it was a sustainable option that did not emit greenhouse gases.

Carrying his luggage, he walked toward the exit and bought a sandwich at one of the food counters. He took his respo out of his bag and put it on. He left the station and walked toward the taxi stand. The sky looked threatening and dark. Inside the driverless taxi, he announced his destination and drove away. As soon as the green light went on, he took off his respo and called Elizabeth.

"I arrived in Bern and should be in Lausanne in about an hour."

"Great. I just arrived with Matteo at the hospital. My dad slept next to Mom last night."

"I'll first pass by the compound to drop off my luggage and freshen up a bit, and then I'll join you."

They said goodbye, and Dylan looked outside. The sky had gotten darker, and it started to rain. After the death of his mother, he inherited the apartment in the compound in the north of Lausanne. His friends advised him to sell it, but he decided to keep it. Secured, high-tech compounds were scarce on the market, and with Elizabeth's parents living next door, he found it convenient to keep it. Besides that, he would not know what to do with the money, anyway.

The rain got heavier and, looking at the dark sky, it would probably increase even further. He had rushed so much that he had not bothered checking the weather forecast. He checked it on his phone now and saw that they predicted heavy rain storms all day. Last week it had rained heavily all over Switzerland and he had read an article about a large mudslide in the Swiss mountains.

Over the last thirty years, the permafrost up on the mountains had been gradually thawing. Initially, just the lower parts, but later also at heights above three thousand meters. It had started with the thawing of the surface, but with increasing temperatures also the deeper grounds thawed, rendering the slopes unstable. Heavy rain regularly caused large mudslides. Last week, heavy mud streams came down from a high mountain range and crossed a busy road, wiping away several cars from the road and killing dozens of people.

The noise from the rain on the roof of the car increased further now the rain was pouring down. At least there were no steep mountain slopes next to the road from Bern to Lausanne, he thought. The story of the mudslides scared him, nevertheless. The visibility outside decreased tremendously, and he could no longer see the car in front of him. He still saw some headlights behind him. He felt less and less comfortable in the driverless car. A moment later, he got startled when the car abruptly got pushed back. He looked behind him and noticed they had passed through a stream of water flowing over the road.

Looking to the front, he noticed there was so much rain that it inundated the road. The noise on the roof of the car became deafening, and he felt frightened, all alone in this car. The rain storm triggered childhood memories of that dreadful day in Augusta, Georgia, when he lost his father. He vaguely distinguished a river in front of him on the left side. The water floated wildly through the river as it passed under the road. When they crossed over it, he noticed the water was much higher than usual.

Suddenly, the car got pushed back again, but this time it slipped on the road. He could feel how the tires lost their grip, and the car slid a few meters over the road before gaining traction. They had passed through another stream of water. He looked behind him and saw the headlights of the car behind him. Then, just at the moment the car passed through the stream of water, he saw it slip. It swirled for a second left and right, and then a few seconds later, the car slipped off the road and flipped on its side. His taxi just continued driving. He saw how another car slowed down and stopped next to the crashed car. Both cars quickly disappeared out of sight. He turned to the front, realizing how close he had been to an accident. He felt sorry for the poor people behind him. The whole rain storm freaked him out, and he felt lonelier than ever before. He looked at the time and asked, "How much time left before arrival?"

"Fifteen minutes until arrival at our destination, sir."

Fifteen long minutes still, he thought. The rain continued pouring, and he tried to think of other things. He thought of Elizabeth and her sick mother. Then of his own mother and how she died in that same hospital the year before. Gradually, the rain became less intense, and he felt relieved when they left the highway. The noise in the car decreased. He had almost arrived and began to recognize the streets. He lived for more than ten years in this neighborhood. It felt like home.

A moment later he spotted the gray bunkerlike shape of the compound at the end of the road; he had arrived. What a trip, he thought to himself. He thought back to the strange encounter with Hakim earlier that morning. He checked his pocket and felt the memory stick inside. He wondered why Hakim had looked so terrified.

8.

The entire morning Hakim had been stressed and tensed. He knew he had no choice. Still, it felt like a betrayal. It took him quite some time to prepare what they wanted. He knew better than anyone how tight the security at the company was. He landed with the air taxi in Copenhagen and took a driverless taxi to the meeting point. The closer he got, the less comfortable and less convinced he became. Maybe he should not give them the information. Deep down, he felt nothing good would come from it, and that he was going to regret it. Then the image of his frightened sister, Aisha, came back to him. No, he had to do whatever it took to get her to safety.

It had only been a few weeks since he had received this horrible message. After seeing the video of his sister, he freaked out completely. She looked so terrified, and the images appalled him. He had never seen her so afraid and she was crying the whole time. Right after that, he called her. A stranger answered her phone and shattered his hopes.

"Hello Hakim. I guess you've seen the nice video we've made of your pretty sister?"

"Who are you?"

"My name is of no importance to you. More important is what we want from you."

"What do you mean?"

"We want you to provide us with some information."

The man explained what they wanted from him. They were looking for highly sensitive and classified information from the Enviro Security division. He tried to explain that they protected this information with the most stringent security protocols and that he could not just make a copy like that. They would immediately notice the breach and stop him.

"Hakim, you're a smart man. I'm sure you'll find a way to get it. If not, we'll kill your sister!"

"But… I can't…"

"Get us what we want and we'll let her go. Her life is in your hands now."

"Please don't hurt her! I'll try."

"Wise choice, Hakim, and don't involve the police, or we'll cut your sister into pieces! You've got one week."

The taxi arrived at the restaurant where the man had told him to meet. He was ten minutes early and entered nervously. Inside, he took off his respo and walked all the way to the back. He passed a table, and a man looked up at him. His heart was pounding in his chest as he looked around. The man continued talking to the woman in front of him. Hakim walked to a table in the back. A waiter came to take his order. After he left, Hakim got up and walked further into the corridor in the back, toward the restrooms.

After passing the kitchen, he entered the men's room and looked in the mirror. He felt nervous and his hands were trembling and sweaty. He washed them, but it didn't help much. The whole thing felt wrong. What the hell was he doing here? Maybe he should have involved the police? Then he thought back to his sister and returned to his table. He tried to drink his tea, but his hands were shaking and he spilled some tea on his trouser. A man entered and Hakim looked at him to check if it was whom he was supposed to meet. The man glanced his direction for a moment, but then turned his head to the other side and took a seat at a table next to the window.

A couple of minutes later, he noticed a dark van parking in front of the restaurant. A man with a shaved head stepped out and entered. The driver remained in the van. After passing through the airlock, the man took off his respo and looked around until his eyes met Hakim's. Without hesitation, the man came toward him and he felt the adrenaline rushing through his body. The broad-shouldered man sat down in front of him and grinned.

"Hello Hakim. Nice to meet face to face at last. Did you bring what I asked for?"

Hakim looked at the muscular man in front of him, who was wearing a tight shirt emphasizing his broad torso and muscular arms. On his hand he had a tattoo of a snakehead, which appeared to crawl over his arm and out of his sleeve. His nerves were getting to him and he muttered, "Wh... wh... where's my sister?"

The man grinned, and Hakim noticed the large scar on the man's neck.

"She's safe. Did you bring the information?"

"Yes."

"Okay, show me!"

He slowly took the memory stick out of his pocket. The man grinned again and tried to grab it, but Hakim quickly pulled his hand away.

"First, I want to see my sister."

He stopped grinning and replied calmly, "Of course! We'll bring you to her."

He pointed at the dark van in front of the restaurant.

"Is she far away from here?"

"No, not so far."

Hakim did not like the look on the man's face. He had a bad feeling.

"How long a drive?"

The man seemed to get slightly annoyed now and moved in his chair before answering.

"Not far, maybe an hour's drive."

"Okay, I'll come along, but I'd better first go to the bathroom."

He walked away from the table toward the restrooms. The whole thing felt wrong. Aisha lived in Damascus in Syria, and to get someone into Europe was extremely difficult. Anyone from outside the European union needed a special permit to enter, and those were nearly impossible to get. No, it felt like a trap, and he had to get the hell out of there.

In the corridor, instead of opening the door to the men's room, he opened the one to the kitchen. He hurried through the kitchen. A cook told him to go back and tried to stop him. He pushed the man out of the way with his heavy body and rushed to the back door. In the alley outside, he ran toward another street parallel to the main street where the van was parked. He dashed through this street and took another, leading him further away from the restaurant. He checked if anyone was following him, but there was nobody behind him.

He got startled when his phone rang and answered while running.

"Hakim, that's not nice of you to sneak out like that. It's no use running away."

The call freaked him out, and he hung up. He thought he should go to the police station and continued running in that direction. The dark van came around the corner in front of him. They had found him already. He ran back into the street where he had just come from. The van followed him into the street. He rushed into a small alley and heard it stop and turn with screeching tires behind him. The alley led him onto another large street, and he ran as fast as he could. He passed the restaurant of the hyper-loop station, and in a blink, he noticed his friend Dylan sitting inside.

That was the best solution he could think of, and he dashed into the restaurant. Dylan was astounded to see him arriving this abruptly. While perspiring heavily and out of breath, he handed the memory stick to him and rushed out. Outside, he saw the muscular man with the shaved head coming toward him, and he ran away. At the end of the street, he turned right and saw the police station in the back. He tried to speed up, but his legs were too tired. The weight of his heavy body was holding him down. He had to cross one more street before arriving at the police station.

A few seconds later, he was about to cross when the dark van halted right in front of him with squealing tires. The side door opened and two heavy men jumped out. They dragged him in and closed the door. One of the men pulled a black cloth bag over his face, and then he felt a blow on the back of his head. He fell unconscious on the floor.

9.

As Dylan opened the door to his apartment, a wave of memories crashed through his head. He had lived here from the age of ten and shared the spacious apartment with his mother until she passed away last year. He looked at the picture on the table in the hall. He was standing between his adoptive father and mother, with his dark face and big smile, exposing his white teeth. He must have been nine in the picture. After the disappointing meeting with his biological father, he realized how lucky he had been with his two wonderful and loving adoptive parents. He cherished his memories of them.

He unpacked his travel bag and opened a bottle of water from the fridge to lessen his thirst. Then he ordered a driverless taxi. Ten minutes later, he rushed out of the apartment to go to the hospital. The rain was less intense, though there were many puddles of water. Driving through Lausanne triggered lots of memories. He had enjoyed a relatively pleasant youth here and a great university time. While arriving at the hospital, he reckoned he should try to meet up with his friends and with some professors from the Swiss Federal Institute of Technology where he had graduated.

In the hospital, he went straight to the palliative care department on the first floor. The door to Elizabeth's mother room was ajar, and he stepped inside. Her mother seemed to be asleep and was breathing through an oxygen mask. She looked even more aged and tired than last time. Elizabeth, Matteo and their father were sitting next to her bed. Elizabeth got up the moment she noticed him. She gave him a big hug and a kiss.

"I'm happy you're here."

Her brother came to hug him, and he slapped his brawny arm on Dylan's back. In a low voice, he said, "Good to see you, buddy!"

"Hi Matteo, have you been working out again? It looks like you've gotten even more muscular?"

"Yeah, I'm following an advanced martial arts training. I'm in top shape at the moment."

Dylan hugged Elizabeth's father, and in a low whisper he asked, "How are you holding up?"

"Good to see you, Dylan. I'm okay. Those hospital beds are not too bad."

"How kind of them to let you sleep in the hospital. How is she doing?"

"She sleeps most of time and when she's awake, her breathing is difficult. They're giving her pain medication, but the last few days her condition has deteriorated further."

Dylan noticed the tears on his face. He was clearly having a hard time, and he did not really know what to tell him. What do you tell a man whose love of his life is dying? He held him in his arms for a moment until Elizabeth intervened.

"Okay dad, let me get you some coffee, or do you want something else?"

"A cup of tea, would be nice."

Her father sat down on the chair next to the bed. Elizabeth took Dylan's hand, and they walked out together.

She explained that her mother had been awake only for a brief moment today. They had asked the doctor the day before for a prognosis. Though he could not be sure, he indicated it could be more a matter of days rather than weeks. There was not much more that the doctors could do for her, except to make it less painful.

When they returned with the drinks, her mother was awake. She turned her head, and it struck Dylan how tired she looked. Her eyes had become hollow, and she had a pallid face. It reminded him of his own mother during her last days, which did not bode well for Elizabeth's mother. It touched him deeply to see the happiness in her eyes the moment she noticed him.

"Hi Dylan. So nice of you to come and see me."

He kissed her, and she held his hand for a moment. Elizabeth's mother had always been fond of him, and she was so happy when they finally moved in together in Copenhagen. They talked for a moment until, at some point, she got too tired. He went for a walk with Elizabeth and Matteo, while Elizabeth's father stayed with her mother.

Downstairs in the hospital's restaurant, they ordered some drinks and sat down at a table. They talked about all kinds of things, and it felt great to be reunited again. The three of them had lived through many adventures together. Soon after, they were exchanging anecdotes from the past.

That evening, they had dinner in that same restaurant. After dinner, Dylan returned to the apartment, while Elizabeth and Matteo stayed a bit longer with their mother. In the driverless taxi on the way back, Dylan watched the dark sky. Seeing Elizabeth's mother today, he felt happy that he had come over immediately. It all reminded him of his mother's last days.

10.

After the kidnapping in Copenhagen, they drove non-stop southward. Hakim remained unconscious until late in the evening, when they had already entered France. Normally, Marco would let his men take care of it, but he knew very well how important this information was for his boss. As soon as Hakim regained consciousness, Marco drove the car into a deserted parking lot along the highway. There was only one truck there, and they parked on the other side of the parking in a dark area.

Hakim sat against the side of the van and felt dizzy. They had tied his hands and feet with tie wraps, and he still had the black bag over his head. They stopped moving. He heard a door sliding open, followed by footsteps, and then a voice.

"Frisk him!"

Two men started searching his pockets and pushed the heavy-set Hakim from left to right. One of them took his wallet and handed it to Marco. He checked the contents and then discarded it. After the search, Marco got nervous. They had not found the memory stick. He wondered how the hell he was going to explain this to his boss. His ruthless boss would not be pleased.

"Where's the memory stick?"

Hakim tried to sit back against the side of the van.

"Where are you taking me?"

Marco nodded to one of his men, who kicked Hakim very hard against his upper leg. He moaned from the pain.

"Where's the memory stick?"

"What memory stick?"

He nodded again to his men, and this time one of them lifted him up and then another kicked him very hard in his chest. Hakim fell sideways on the floor, grasping for his breath.

"Stop playing around now. Where is it?"

Hakim was still panting on the floor and did not answer. One of the men put his heavy boot on his chubby hand and pushed until he cried with pain. Still, he did not speak. Marco's phone buzzed, and he took it out of his pocket and looked at the screen. It was the boss. He stepped outside and answered with his heart pounding in his chest.

"Hi boss, I was about to call you."

"Do you have the memory stick?"

"Well, uh, not yet. He had it on him when I met him, but after taking him for a ride, we couldn't find it on him. We're interrogating him at the moment."

"What!? What do you mean, you don't have it!?"

"Well, uh, we haven't found it yet, even though he showed it to me in the restaurant. He was unconscious until now, so we've just started interrogating him. I'm sure it'll show up."

"It'd better show up, or you're in big trouble! Did you copy all the data from his phone and throw it away?"

"Well, I've made a copy and took out the sim card."

"Did you throw away the phone?"

"Uh, well, not yet."

"You idiot! They can trace you, even if you remove the sim card. Throw it away immediately before you have cops all over you."

"Okay, right away, boss!"

"Oh, and one more thing. I heard a rumor that all Enviro employees have a chip implanted in their right arm. Apparently, they can use it to trace people. So, if he cooperates, you can remove the implanted chip with a knife and stitch him up nicely after. If he doesn't, there's another way to disable the chip by frying it for ten minutes at high temperature. That should make the bastard talk."

"All right boss, I'll get to it right away!"

"Oh, and one more thing. Don't kill him. I need him alive."

"Sure, boss. No problem. I'll keep you posted."

He hung up and returned to the van. He took Hakim's phone from the dashboard and threw it in a bin in the parking lot. As he returned to the van, he noticed two cars arriving and coming their way.

"Start the van! You drive while we continue questioning this bastard here in the back. We have to make him talk or the boss will deal with us. Let's go!"

11.

On Sunday morning Elizabeth and Dylan went next door to her parents' apartment to have breakfast together with Matteo. Elizabeth's father had slept in the hospital again. After preparing the table, they ate together and talked about their evening the night before. They had invited several friends over for drinks and it had been like the old times, a wonderful evening together.

Elizabeth was teasing her brother as he had spent most of the evening talking to a longtime friend of hers. About a year ago, Matteo's relationship with his girlfriend broke off. They had lived together for about four years and since the break-up, he had not been dating much. Elizabeth would love to see her brother happily in love, and she actually thought her friend might be a suitable match.

The conversation got interrupted when Elizabeth's phone rang. It was her father. They all looked worried while she was talking. Apparently, her mother had weakened further, and she had just asked if they could all come to the hospital to see her. They ordered a taxi and rushed with their respos outside. Elizabeth was all stressed out and feared her mother would die before they would arrive. Dylan and Matteo tried to calm her down.

At the hospital, they rushed to her mother's room and when they opened the door, her father was sitting next to her, holding her hand. Her face was slightly yellow, caused by the liver failure she had suffered the day before. She turned her head slowly toward the three of them and smiled faintly. They kissed her and sat around the bed. Elizabeth looked at her and noticed how a tear slowly formed and dropped from her eye. She held her hand. Her father, who was sitting on the other side of the bed next to Matteo, was holding her other hand.

A moment later, her mother sighed deeply, after which she lay there, quiet. Elizabeth's father closed her eyes and hugged her one more time. Then he turned away, and Matteo held his father in his arms. Elizabeth gave her mother a kiss on her forehead and turned to Dylan, who hugged her as she cried in his arms.

12.

Elliot arrived home early. The day before, he and his team handed in their proposal to implement a change to the nuclear fusion reactor, which would increase the energy production by more than ten percent. Today he did not have much work, as they were awaiting the reaction to their proposal from Elias, their boss.

In the apartment, he remembered that coming Saturday it would be the annual commemoration of his mother's birthday. This year she would have turned fifty-five. He started preparing the table in the corner of the apartment. He wanted to make an extra effort since fifty-five was a special age. He put several frames with photos on the table. Meanwhile, he thought back of the photos he had seen in his father's room, when he had sneaked around there. He thought some of those photos would be great for the commemoration.

Since his father had caught him at the time, he thought he could just ask him about the photos when he would come back from work. To please his father, he thought it would be nice to surprise him with dinner. He checked the fridge to see if he had all the ingredients for his father's favorite dish. Two nice large zucchinis, several tomatoes, onions and garlic and a can of lentils. About thirty minutes later, he put the prepared dish in the oven and hoped his dad would not be late.

His father entered the apartment just when Elliot was taking the dish out of the oven. Amos smelled it immediately at the door. He still felt horrible, but the aromatic smell distracted him. He walked into the kitchen, and Elliot smiled at him, showing the oven dish with the stuffed zucchinis in his hands.

"I was home early today, so I prepared your favorite dish."

Elliot looked at his father and noticed something was wrong. He even thought his eyes looked watery, as if he was about to cry. Just when he was about to ask him what was wrong, his father spoke.

"Oh Elliot, that's really nice of you."

He tapped his son on his shoulder and took a glass of water. Then he went to freshen up in the bathroom. Later, they sat together at the table and enjoyed the delicious meal. Elliot talked about his work, but his father seemed absent. He looked more tired than usual, and he had the impression that something was bothering him. After dinner, his father noticed the photos on the table in the corner of the living room. Elliot stopped hesitating and looked at his father.

"I wanted to ask you something, but maybe it's not a good moment now?"

"Tell me. What do you want to ask?"

"Well, remember when I was sneaking around in your room a while ago?"

"Yes, I remember that."

"At the time, my eye had fallen on some photos. There were some really beautiful ones of mom in that pile and I was wondering if I could put some of them on the table in the living room for her commemoration this Saturday?"

His father looked again at the table in the corner.

"Sure, why not? Let me have a look."

He got up and disappeared into his bedroom. Elliot cleaned up the kitchen and prepared some tea. He picked his favorite green tea, which was mixed with bergamot and orange. It gave off a lovely smell. He put a cup on the table for his father and waited for him while he sipped his own. His father was staying away quite long and after finishing his cup, he stepped into the hallway. He heard him crying softly. It broke his heart to hear him like this.

"Are you all right, dad?"

It was silent for a moment, and the crying stopped.

"I'm okay. I'll be right out."

Elliot returned to the kitchen to pour himself another cup of tea. After a while, he heard the door open and his father joined him. He held a stack of photos in his hand.

"Here, you can choose the ones you like. I'm going to bed. I'm exhausted."

Elliot tapped his father on his shoulder. He appreciated it that he was so nice to him, even though he felt something was terribly wrong with him.

"Thanks, dad. Sleep tight and I hope you feel better tomorrow."

"Good night."

His father left the room quietly. He couldn't help worrying about him while he stared at the untouched cup of tea in front of him. He had a bad feeling, but he couldn't figure out why. At that moment, Elliot could not know that he had just seen his father for the last time.

13.

On Monday morning, Dylan woke up next to Elizabeth. He knew she could use all his support in the coming days. The evening before, they had discussed what arrangements to make for her late mother. They were planning a farewell ceremony on Wednesday, after which the resomation would take place. Because of environmental concerns, the government banned cremation decades ago. Burials had become less popular and there were fewer spaces available. Resomation used a process of alkaline hydrolysis that dissolved the body in a heated, pressurized solution of water and potassium hydroxide. Elizabeth's mother had indicated that she preferred resomation.

Elizabeth went next door to join her father and Matteo. Dylan told her he would join them for breakfast after his call with Sorenson. A moment later, his boss picked up the phone.

"Hi Dylan. How is your mother-in-law doing?"

"She passed away yesterday."

"Oh, I'm sorry to hear that. My condolences."

"Thanks. We're planning her resomation ceremony on Wednesday, so I was thinking of returning to Ikast on Thursday morning. I should be back in the office after lunch."

"Sure, take all the time you need."

"Thanks."

After hanging up, he joined the others next door. They were all sitting at the table in the kitchen and, to his surprise, they were having a lively discussion about politics. Matteo and Elizabeth were debating if Europe would not have been better off with a one-party system like in China. About five years ago, China had been the first large country in the world to reach a zero-emission economy. Europe had always aspired to be the first, but the old European Union structure slowed down progress. There were always individual countries that put their own interest first and neglected the zero-emission goal.

After the great reform, which was triggered by a massive debt crisis, Europe got rid of all country governments and centralized all institutions in one central European government. Switzerland even joined the European Union. From that point on, Europe finally started tackling its biggest problems at a much higher pace. They took drastic decisions to counter the disastrous consequences of climate change. Last year, Europe had finally become a zero-emission economy. Unfortunately, climate change had ravaged the planet for too long and the only way to get the carbon dioxide levels down in the atmosphere was through negative emissions. Europe started to invest in enormous carbon dioxide capture plants, causing companies like Enviro to flourish.

The discussion switched to comparing Europe to the United States. Matteo criticized Europe's government for being too large and spending more than the American government.

Elizabeth clearly disagreed and said, "At least in Europe all citizens get a respo from the government and the poor get some minimum support. Not like in the United States where the poor cannot afford them and the life expectance rates have tumbled much more than in Europe,"

"I don't think I would like to live in a society like in America, where many anarchic groups have taken over parts of the country. Even the rich only survive thanks to their private armies protecting them," Elizabeth's father added.

"Well, America is not doing that bad if you compare it with the anarchy in certain African or Latin-American countries. Especially Africa. I would really not like to be born there," Matteo said.

"I agree. The world is unsafe in lots of places. At least in that aspect, I think Europe is doing a good job," Dylan said as he joined the discussion.

"True, and that's why everybody wants to come and live here. Thank God they have limited immigration and installed this high-tech security border. Otherwise, the refugee stream would overwhelm us and our whole social security system would collapse," Matteo said.

"I guess this is the typical moment where mother would have told you to stop talking, Matteo. Remember how she hated this border and its inhumane treatment of refugees?"

Matteo looked at Elizabeth and nodded with a sad look on his face.

"Yeah, I'm going to miss her."

They all nodded, and a silence fell.

14.

Marco walked nervously back and forth in the room. With his square, muscular body, he looked like a rhinoceros turning around. From time to time, he stopped and looked at the computer screen. He knew these things took time, though patience had never been his strong suit. He tried very hard to refrain from asking Ricardo for the fourth time how long it was going to take. In front of the screen a nerdy-looking man wearing glasses typed computer code. His fingers flew and the clicking of the keyboard filled the silence in the room.

The day before, he interrogated Hakim for hours. It surprised him that a chubby guy like him could resist torture for so long. They started with simple beatings, but he wouldn't budge. His silence annoyed him the most. Besides moaning from time to time, he just did not speak at all. The ship was going to leave in less than two hours, and he had to find the memory stick before they could put him on board. He lost patience and kicked him faster and faster until one of his men pulled him away. Hakim just moaned on the floor.

Soon after, he thought back to what his boss had said and checked Hakim's arm. After searching for a while, he detected a hard bump in his right shoulder. He clearly felt the shape of the chip, like a little tube. His men tied Hakim to a chair, and Marco looked him in the eyes.

"I'm losing my patience with you. You'd better tell me where the memory stick is or I'll really have to hurt you."

Hakim looked at him exhausted, but did not say a word. Marco got angry and took a soldering iron from the toolbox. He heated the iron and in front of Hakim he melted a piece of soldering tin and dropped it on his leg. It burned a hole in his trouser and Hakim moaned, but he did not speak.

"You'd better start speaking or I'll burn this chip in your arm until it melts inside."

Hakim looked terrified. Still, he did not speak. He just shook his head, left and right.

"Where's the memory stick?"

Again, no answer, and he pushed the soldering iron into his shoulder. Hakim squirmed and squealed in agony.

"Please… please stop."

"Okay. Tell me where the memory stick is!"

"I don't know."

Irritated, Marco pushed the iron deep in his shoulder until he could see the chip. Blood ran down his arm. Hakim squirmed and moaned.

"Please… stop!"

"No problem, Hakim. Just tell me what you did with the memory stick?"

Hakim didn't answer, and Marco pushed the soldering iron another time deep into his shoulder. The smell of burned flesh filled the room. Hakim screamed in pain now. His legs flopped around in spastic movements. He dropped his head down the moment that Marco took the soldering iron out of his arm. The chip had completely burned and melted.

"Okay, Hakim, what did you do with the memory stick?"

"I lost it."

"What do you mean you lost it?"

"What did you do with it?"

"I don't know."

Marco had always been good at detecting a lie. He looked at the clock on the wall. He was running out of time and then suddenly it came to him.

"Okay, Hakim, you leave me no choice. I'm going to call my men now and tell them they can do whatever they want with your sister."

Hakim lifted his head and looked horrified at Marco. He started shaking his head left and right while Marco dialed a number and talked to another man on the phone loud enough for Hakim to hear it.

"He doesn't want to talk, so I suggest you go to his sister and you and your men rape her until he talks. Make sure to live stream it to me."

Hakim continued to shake his head while Marco was calling. A moment later, he showed the screen to Hakim, who looked disgusted at it. He saw Aisha sitting on a bed, and a dark man sat next to her. He could hear the man talking.

"She's really pretty, your sister."

The man started touching her and put his arm around her while touching her breasts with his other hand. Aisha cried and looked terrified. Tears dropped from Hakim's eyes.

"Please, stop it! Don't touch her!"

"Sure, just tell me what you did with the memory stick."

On the screen, he could see how the man moved his hand between her legs and his sister screamed. Another guy sat next to her on the other side, and she cried and screamed. Hakim cried and yelled, "Stop touching her! I gave it to someone from Enviro!"

"To whom?"

"I don't know his name, but he works at Enviro and he would bring the memory stick back to Enviro."

"I don't believe you."

"I'm telling you the truth. I gave it to this man from Enviro in the restaurant next to the hyper-loop station. Please leave her alone."

Marco looked at him for a few seconds and then spoke to his men on the phone.

"Okay, that's enough. Leave the girl alone."

Now a day later, Marco paced back and forth next to the desk where Ricardo was trying to hack into the camera system of the restaurant. He feared that the memory stick had been brought back to Enviro already, though he had to be sure. Soon his boss would call him and he feared his scorn. His attention drew back to the computer, where a video screen opened. Immediately, he looked over Ricardo's shoulder, who continued typing on the keyboard.

"I've entered the security system and searched for the video images from yesterday morning. Based on the timeframe you gave me, these should be the right images."

"All right. Maybe you can show them at an accelerated pace."

Ricardo sped up the video while Marco stared at the screen. He saw people entering the restaurant and walking around. He watched for more than ten minutes until suddenly he yelled.

"Stop the video! Go back a bit. Stop right here."

On the screen, he saw Hakim entering the restaurant.

"Okay, could you play from this point on in slow motion?"

"Sure."

They both looked at the video and could see how Hakim ran through the restaurant toward a dark man sitting in the back, next to the window.

"Could you zoom in on that part?"

Ricardo zoomed in and they saw how Hakim seemed to talk to this Indian-looking guy. Hakim grabbed the man's hand and a few seconds later, he ran out of the restaurant.

"Could you do a facial recognition search on this man?"

"Yep. Just a moment."

He scanned the face of the Indian-looking guy at the table, and the computer searched for several minutes. Then a screen popped up and Marco looked at it.

"Dylan Myers. Working in the Environmental Technology division at Enviro Technologies in Ikast. Great, now continue the video."

They both looked at the screen until they saw Dylan leaving the restaurant.

"Could you get me the footage from the outside of the restaurant?"

Ricardo searched for a moment and opened a map of the building.

"Outside, that would be the hall of the hyper-loop station. Their security cameras are probably better protected, but let me try."

Several hours later, Ricardo called his boss.

"It was more difficult to hack into their security system, but I've gained access to the camera footage. I searched all the different cameras for this Dylan Myers and look what I've found."

Ricardo opened the video screen and showed the footage to Marco. On the screen, they saw Hakim rushing out of the restaurant, and half an hour later, they saw Dylan leaving the restaurant. He switched to a different camera that showed him walking across the large hall of the hyper-loop station. He walked in the direction of one of the platforms. Again, they switched to another camera, and now they saw him entering a hyper-loop cabin. Fifteen minutes later, the door to the hyper-loop closed.

"Could you check where that hyper-loop went?"

"Sure, just a moment."

Ricardo typed on the keyboard and searched for a while until he found it.

"He boarded the hyper-loop which left at 10:55 for Bern in Switzerland."

Marco looked away from the screen and stretched out. He felt his nerves relaxing, his muscles loosening, and a moment of relief. At least he did not have to disappoint his boss.

15.

That morning, Elliot woke up and noticed that the door to his father's bedroom was ajar and peered inside. His father was not there. He continued to the kitchen to prepare himself some breakfast. His father would often wake up before him and leave for his work early in the morning. This morning felt no different.

After breakfast, he left for work. As usual, he took the route through the park. He climbed the stairs and walked out through the doors at ground level into the gardens of the dome. He loved the smell of herbs and flowers in the air as he walked toward his office. All the lush greenery around him gave him a peaceful feeling. On the other side of the garden, he took the stairs to descend to the nuclear fusion development center.

In the morning, he had a meeting with Elias and his project team to discuss the proposal to increase the energy output from the nuclear fusion reactor. Elias started the meeting with praise for Elliot and his team. He loved their proposal and believed they should move ahead with the implementation. After the meeting, Elliot thought of his father. He could not wait to tell him about the praise. He was sure it would make him proud.

Back at it his desk, he discussed the next steps with his teammates. The discussion got interrupted when he received a phone call from his father's assistant.

"Hi Mary."

"Hi Elliot. Sorry to disturb you, but do you know where I can find your father? I didn't see him in the office this morning. And now he didn't show up for a meeting with Conan."

"Strange. This morning he had already left the apartment before I woke up. I thought he had gone to the office early today. Did you try his mobile phone?"

"Yes, I tried all morning, but I get his voicemail every time."

"That's not like him. I'll go home to have a look. Maybe he went back home and fell asleep or something. He looked very tired lately."

"That would be great, Elliot. Tell him to call me as soon as you find him. I'll ask around here."

Elliot hung up the phone and had a bad feeling about all this. He apologized to his colleagues for leaving this suddenly and dashed out of the office. He wanted to go home as quickly as possible, so he took the underground route. He rushed through the maze of gray corridors. He did not really know why, but he was very concerned about his father. Something might have happened to him. He ran through the long hallway and at the end took the staircase to the floor to their apartment.

Anxiously, he opened the front door and rushed in.

"Dad? Dad, are you here?"

It remained completely silent inside. He took a quick look in the living room, in the kitchen, and then continued to his father's bedroom. The bed looked exactly the same as this morning. He looked behind the bed and then turned around. One of the cupboards behind the door was half open. On the floor, he noticed a black lid. He opened the cupboard further and then he saw the empty black box. He had seen this box before. It was a while ago, during his search in his father's bedroom. Suddenly, he felt adrenaline rushing through his body as he remembered what had been in the box.

16.

On the day of the resomation ceremony, it was pouring outside, and the sky was gray. Dylan put on an elegant black suit and Elizabeth a long black dress. He helped to close her dress and gave her a compliment. She looked beautiful with her long brown hair. They went next door to pick up her father and Matteo, who were having some tea together. Her father looked at her.

"You look stunning."

"Thanks. Are you ready to go?"

"Yes, we are. Shall I call a taxi?" Matteo answered.

"I already did. It should arrive in fifteen minutes."

"Enough time for another cup of tea?"

Matteo smiled at her and poured her a cup.

"Dylan, tea?"

"Yes, please."

While they were waiting, they discussed the last preparations for the ceremony. The moment the taxi arrived, they all took their respos and went downstairs. They got in the driverless taxi and as soon as the air filtering system inside had done its work, the green light went on and they took off their respos. Elizabeth's father coughed several times, and it took a while for him to breathe normally again. She put her arm on his shoulder to comfort him, but she looked worried.

Over the last decades, the air quality deteriorated gradually. About fifteen years ago, it became so poor that the first respos appeared on the market. Initially, people wore them only when the pollution levels were high. Soon after, when levels remained high for longer and longer during the year, they started wearing them on a daily basis. With the enormous rise in pollution related diseases, health organizations recommended wearing respos whenever someone ventured outside. Europe provided all of its citizens with respos, and the incidence of respiratory illness among younger persons went down. For older people, the damage had been done already and life expectancy dropped steadily in the last decades.

The taxi left the underground parking and as soon as they came out of the tunnel, the loud noise from the heavy rain made any normal conversation difficult. Dylan thought back to his frightening taxi ride from Bern to Lausanne and was happy not to be alone in the car this time. He looked outside. It was relatively calm on the road, with no cars in front of them and only a dark van behind them.

Fifteen minutes later, they arrived at the funeral center. They stopped in front of the main entrance and all went in. There was a chapel where the ceremony was going to be held. Together with the staff, they prepared everything and half an hour later, the first friends and family members started arriving.

After the ceremony, they went next door to attend the reception. Dylan spoke to some of Elizabeth's friends. At some point, Matteo tapped Dylan on his shoulder and joined the conversation. He complimented him on his touching words. His father had also spoken, and Elizabeth had dedicated a poem to her mother.

Slowly, the guests started leaving and when everybody had left, the four of them took a taxi back home. The rain was lighter now and they could see the clouds break open on the horizon. A faint rainbow appeared in the gray sky. On the way back, they talked about the ceremony and about the people they had spoken with. When they entered the tunnel to the compound, none of them had noticed the dark van that had followed them.

Back in the apartment, they prepared lunch while Elizabeth's father rested. Dylan had planned to meet up with one of his old professors from the Swiss Federal Institute of Technology that afternoon. After lunch Dylan grabbed his coat and respo to leave. Elizabeth walked with him to the door.

"Don't make it too late, huh? Since you're going back to Ikast tomorrow morning, it would be nice to spend some time together today."

"It shouldn't last too long. I guess I should be back somewhere around half past three, possibly a little later. Maybe we should dine in town together tonight?"

"Yes, I would like that. Shall I make a reservation at this new Japanese restaurant near the lake?"

"Perfect!"

They kissed, and he went downstairs. His driverless taxi was waiting for him in the underground hall. The doors opened automatically, and he stepped inside.

"Good afternoon, Dylan Myers."

He took a seat inside the four-seat vehicle. The sliding doors closed behind him and the air-filtering system hissed.

"Where would you like to go, Mr. Myers?"

"To the Swiss Federal Institute of Technology in Lausanne, please!"

"All right, your expected arrival time is five past two."

Outside, the sky was gray and there was still some light rain. Dylan stared at the horizon and thought back of his university time, completely unaware of the black van following his taxi.

17.

Elizabeth looked at the time; 17:34 already. She wondered why Dylan was late. Maybe the meeting with his professor had run late, or he had run into some other acquaintance at university. She had booked the restaurant for seven thirty, so they still had plenty of time. After preparing what clothes to wear for the evening, she went back to her father's apartment.

Her father was reading in the living room, and Matteo was preparing some snacks.

"Where are you going for dinner tonight?" Matteo asked.

"We're going to try this new Japanese restaurant on the lake."

"Ah, nice. Let me know if it's good."

"Why? Are you planning any dinner date soon?"

"Maybe."

Matteo grinned.

"Tell me! Tell me!"

"Well, I exchanged phone numbers with Elena the other night and I'm thinking of asking her out."

"What a great idea! If this Japanese place is no good, you could go to the Palais Gourmand further down on the lake. The views are magnificent and the food is good."

"I heard about that place. Someone in my Special Forces Command unit recommended it as well."

About half an hour later, she started to get really worried about Dylan. She called him on his phone, but he did not answer and she left him a message. This was not like him at all. He was always reliable and punctual. Matteo noticed his sister's distress.

"What's wrong, sis?"

"Dylan told me he would be home at three thirty, maybe a bit later."

"At three thirty? Strange, it's almost six thirty now. Did you call him?"

"Yes, but I got his voicemail."

"Where did he say he was going?"

"He was going to meet with Professor Briner from the Swiss Federal Institute of Technology. You remember this guy with the funny glasses and the long beard at his graduation ceremony?"

"Yeah, I remember. Maybe you should call him to see if he knows where Dylan is?"

"Good idea. I'll call the university right away."

She dialed the general number of the Swiss Federal Institute of Technology. A man answered the phone.

"Hi, this is Elisabeth Muller speaking. I would like to speak to Professor Briner from Environmental Sciences?"

"Hold on, please."

It was silent for a moment and then the man said, "I'm sorry, but he has left already."

"I really need to talk to him. Do you have his mobile number?"

"Sorry, but we are not allowed to give out private numbers to anyone."

"It's really important. My boyfriend had a meeting with him this afternoon and he didn't come back home after. Could you please call Professor Briner on his mobile phone and ask him to call me back?"

"Mmm, I see. Just a moment, please."

She waited for several minutes until suddenly she got connected.

"Hello, Miss Muller? This is Hans Jakob Briner speaking. I understand you're looking for Dylan?"

"Yes, he told me he was going to meet you at the university this afternoon, but he hasn't returned home yet and I'm starting to get worried."

"Well, we had a meeting planned at two o'clock, but he never showed up. I found it strange already, and not like Dylan at all. Around two thirty I called him and left him a message on his voicemail, but he didn't call back."

She thanked him, and he promised to call if he would hear from Dylan. She hung up and looked at Matteo.

"He never showed up at his meeting. Something is wrong, Matteo. Where could he be?"

18.

With his heart pounding in his chest, Elliot called back his father's assistant. After finding the empty box in the bedroom, he became extremely worried about his father. He had been behaving weird and absent lately, and Elliot had even heard him cry a couple of times. He had no idea where his father could be, but he could use all the help he could get in finding him.

"Hi, it's Elliot. I just arrived home. My father isn't in the apartment either. I have a bad feeling about all this. I think we need to start searching on the premises."

"I agree. This isn't like your father at all. Maybe something has happened to him. Okay, let me put you through to Liam. He reports to your father and is in charge of internal security."

"Thanks, Mary."

A moment later, he spoke to Liam, explaining everything.

"All right, Elliot. Thanks for informing me. I'll launch a search immediately. With all the cameras all over the dome, we should find him in no time."

"Great. Could you call me as soon as you find him?"

"Of course, Elliot."

He hung up and paced back and forth, wondering where his father could be. He was deeply concerned. What if he had a heart attack and was lying somewhere unconscious? Last year, his father received a heart transplant, and even though there were no complications, the thought crossed his mind. The empty box in his father's bedroom worried him much more, though. He tried to calm himself down. He glanced at the photos on the table in the corner of the room. On one of them, his father was hugging his mother in the gardens of the dome. They looked happy. In a flash, the picture triggered a memory from his childhood. Right after, he dashed out of the apartment.

It was a small chance, but he had to check. There was one spot in the gardens upstairs that had been his parents' favorite spot. His mother had told him about it when he was a young boy. He ran as fast as he could through the maze of apartments. He rushed up the stairs toward the gardens.

When he came out and entered the gardens, he looked up at the gigantic dome high above his head. The sky was clear, and the sun illuminated the gardens. He looked around to check if he could see his father somewhere. It was quiet. He rushed through the orchard. He remembered that his father and mother would often sit together next to the field of sunflowers. He could not be sure, of course, but he had to check. Deep down he had a terrible feeling, and worried about his father.

It was quite a walk to the field, as it was completely on the opposite side. He took the shortest route right through the middle. As he came closer, he noticed two security officers rushing in the same direction. They came from the right and must have been fifty meters ahead of him. The field of sunflowers was right in front of him now. A beautiful sight with the large, bright yellow flowers all facing the sun.

The security officers disappeared into the field. He paused for a moment next to the bench in front of the field. He heard voices further away from the direction where the security officers had gone. His heart started pounding in his chest again. The negative thoughts he had since seeing the empty box in the apartment suddenly overwhelmed him. He rushed into the field and a moment later sunflowers were surrounding him. He looked around him as he walked toward the voices.

In between the yellow flowers, he spotted several men. A security officer came his direction. Right after, he recognized Liam. He was giving instructions to one of the security officers.

"Liam?"

Liam turned his head, and the moment he spotted Elliot, he rushed to him.

"Elliot? You'd better go back."

He tried to push Elliot back, but he was in total panic now as he looked at the body lying on the ground.

"Is that my father? Is he okay?"

Liam grabbed him and tried to keep him away from the body. Elliot noticed the black high-tech handgun on the ground next to his father's hand. It felt as if someone swept the floor away from under him. This could not be true. A security officer came to stand in between the body and Liam, who was desperately trying to push Elliot back.

"Elliot, please go back. He's dead."

"No! No! No!"

Elliot screamed and cried, hanging helplessly in Liam's arms.

19.

Outside, the streets were quiet and Dylan thought back to his university time in Lausanne as the driverless taxi drove to the center of town. He looked forward to meeting with his professor. He could not wait to talk to him about the project he was working on at Enviro. His professor had been very proud of him when he joined Enviro, and it had been a long time since they last met. The rain was less intense, although the streets remained empty. A sun ray beamed down through a hole in the clouds.

A dark van suddenly blocked the light. He heard the engine growl as the speeding van passed by him. It continued straight and when it was about five hundred meters in front of Dylan, it swerved to the left into the oncoming lane and then abruptly turned with a sharp bend to the right. It stopped right there in front of him, blocking the road.

He sensed instantly something was wrong. As his taxi approached the van, he saw the sliding door on the side open. Three men wearing black ski masks stepped outside. They were carrying heavy firearms, and they did not look like they were from the police or the army. A muscular man with a heavy build raised his arm, signaling him to stop. Meanwhile, the driverless taxi slowed down. Dylan freaked out. This did not look good. What did they want from him? Why were they stopping him? He had no intention of finding out. His only plan was to get the hell out of there.

"Turn around and return to the compound immediately!"

"All right, sir. Your expected arrival time is two fifteen."

The taxi stopped fifty meters in front of the black van and started turning. Now he heard the men yelling.

"Stop the car or we'll have to shoot!"

They started walking toward him with their automatic rifles in their hands. Dylan thought the whole turning was taking way too much time. They programmed those driverless taxis to drive carefully, but he did not want to drive carefully; he wanted to get away from that van as fast as he could.

"Please drive as fast as possible to the compound! This is an emergency!"

"All right, sir, but I'm not allowed to go above the maximum speed limit of fifty kilometers per hour. Your expected arrival time is two fifteen."

Just my luck, he thought, stuck in a driverless taxi while some heavily armed thugs are after me. They completed the turn and started driving away from the armed men. The sound of an automatic rifle firing startled him. He dropped onto the floor, covering his head with his hands. At the same time, he heard the sound of bullets penetrating the windows. The taxi continued driving and reached the maximum speed of fifty kilometers per hour.

The air filtering system started hissing. The sound of the firing automatic rifle stopped. He climbed back up and peered over the backseat. The back window had several bullet holes in it.

"Please put on your respo. The air quality cannot be guaranteed."

Dylan put on his respo, although the air quality was not his biggest worry as he saw the men getting back into the van. They turned the van to continue their pursuit. The van quickly caught up with him. Where could he go? This driverless taxi was too slow to shake off the van. Frightened, he looked around. Fortunately, he knew this neighborhood well. In a flash, he spotted an opportunity to shake them off.

A few seconds later, the van passed by near the taxi and stayed next to him. Dylan looked ahead of him. On his left, he noticed that the sliding door of the van opened. The armed men were gesturing him to pull over. Now was the right moment, he thought, and yelled, "Immediately turn right in the next street!"

"All right, sir. Your expected arrival time is two seventeen."

The driverless taxi turned right into a narrow one-way street. He looked behind him. The van continued straight, and he felt relieved. He managed to shake them off for now. He drove through a narrow residential street with poles separating the road from the walkway. He realized he should call the police. Halfway down the street, he looked behind him again, and his heart skipped a beat when he saw the dark van approaching fast. He took his phone out of his pocket and dialed the emergency number. With the phone against his ear, he turned his head to look behind him. He became terrified as the van continued to come closer.

In a reflex, he attached the seat belt and put his head down. With a colossal blow, the van rammed into the rear of the taxi. Dylan was pushed forward, and the belt hurt on his shoulder. The phone dropped out of his hand onto the floor. The driverless car swung forward and then slowed back down to the maximum speed of fifty kilometers per hour. Further down the road, he noticed another side street. Just at that moment, the van crashed another time into the rear of the taxi, pushing him forward again. It was worth a try, he thought.

"Stop here, please!"

"All right, sir."

They braked and slowly came to a stop. He looked behind him and waited a few seconds. The van braked as well, and as soon as it stopped, two men with automatic rifles jumped out of the sliding door on the side. Just at that moment, he yelled, "Drive away as fast as you can! Now!"

"Right away, sir, although I'm not allowed to drive above the maximum speed limit of fifty kilometers per hour."

It drove him mad, even though he knew they programmed it to obey the rules and there was nothing he could do about it. He looked behind him and saw the men rushing back into the van. They drove after him and he looked in front now, at the narrow side street. It could work.

"Turn right, now!"

"All right, sir. Your expected arrival time is two nineteen."

The taxi turned right and, since the van was right behind and still speeding up, it crashed against the side of the car. They hit a pole on the corner of the side street. Dylan got pushed to the side from the impact and the belt hurt him on his side. Fortunately, the taxi continued driving into the side street. He looked behind him and saw his pursuers continuing straight. The diversion had worked.

As he turned his head to look back in front of him, he lost all hope. The taxi had driven into a cul-de-sac. At the end of the street, there was a large building and just in front of him, the street ended in a large circle, allowing cars to turn. Stressed out, he looked over his shoulder. The dark van was just turning into the street behind him. He searched on the floor for his phone. On his knees, he found it back under the backseat. As he got up, he noticed the van was approaching at high speed. He had no time to lose.

"Stop the car! I want to get out, now!"

The taxi stopped right at the end of the cul-de-sac and the door opened.

"Thank you for driving with us. We hope you've enjoyed your ride and wish you a pleasant day."

Dylan did not wait a second and rushed out. He heard the dark van approaching at high speed as he ran into a small pedestrian alley. The tires of the van screeched behind him. The men came running after him. Why were they pursuing him? He had no time to think and ran further. At the end, it turned to the right around a large building. Running as fast as he could, he continued around the corner.

It was another dead-end. At the end of the alley, about thirty meters away from him, there was a glass door. He could not turn back, so he was hoping the door would be open. He ran toward it and pulled the handle. It was locked. Damn it, just my luck, he thought. With both hands around his eyes, he looked through the glass and saw an older man walking down the hall. He tapped on the glass.

"Hey! Hello! Open the door, please! Help me, please!"

The older man looked warily at him. Even so, he approached the door. He was about to open when he suddenly backed away and looked frightened at something behind Dylan.

"Please, open the door!"

The terrified man pointed with his finger to the alley and then ran away. Dylan turned around and saw the four heavily armed and masked men were standing in front of him. Three of them were aiming their automatic rifle at him. In the middle, a muscled man was looking at him.

"Hello, Dylan Myers. I believe you've got something that belongs to us."

His heart pounded in his chest, and he stood with his back against the glass door. Petrified, he tried to figure out what the hell they were talking about.

"What d… d… do you me… mean?"

"Our mutual friend Hakim Sayed gave you something that belongs to us."

In a flash, he remembered his strange encounter with Hakim in the restaurant the week before. He put his hand in his pocket and felt the tiny memory stick that Hakim had given him. He remembered how terrified he had looked and how he said he was in trouble. All of a sudden, it all became clear to him.

"Where's Hakim? Is he all right?"

The muscular man grinned back.

"He's all right. Now give me the memory stick!"

In disbelief, he wondered if those men had killed Hakim; they looked pretty dangerous. Then he remembered how Hakim had insisted he should take the memory stick back to Enviro. He had emphasized nobody else should take it. Suddenly, he felt the weight of the responsibility. What if it contained important information? The muscular man in front of him seemed to lose his patience and aimed his automatic rifle at him.

"Give us the memory stick, or I'll shoot you!"

Dylan slowly took the memory stick out of his pocket and held it up in front of him.

"Why do you want it? What did you do to Hakim?"

"That's none of your business. Now hand it over!"

He couldn't just hand it over. Hakim had clearly told him not to let anybody else take it. He looked behind him one more time through the glass door. The old man had gone away. He was stuck and had nowhere to go. He had no choice. They might kill him anyway. He quickly moved his hand to his mouth and swallowed the tiny memory stick. He felt it going down his gullet. The muscular man in front of him looked flabbergasted. With an enraged look on his face, he came closer.

"You shouldn't have done that."

He turned his automatic rifle and hit Dylan with a powerful blow in the face with the back of the rifle. It knocked him out, and he fell unconscious on the floor.

20.

After trying his cell phone another time in vain, Elizabeth began to cry. Matteo tried to comfort her by saying Dylan might have lost his phone, even though he also had a bad feeling about it. This was not like Dylan at all. He would have called or sent a message even if he had lost his phone. He thought for a moment and then got a great idea.

"Okay, I agree something is off. Let's try to track him down. Do you remember that tracking app we installed on our smartphones in New York last year?"

"Yes. That's a great idea!"

She stopped sobbing and checked her smartphone. She launched the app when she found it. They both looked at the screen.

"Mmm, he seems to be offline. It just shows the last logged address, at twelve past two. Let me enlarge this map."

"That's in the Eclubens neighborhood. He was right next to the Route du Bois in some cul-de-sac."

"What was he doing there?"

"Are you sure this app is accurate?"

"I think so. Look, when I click this button, it shows me his route. That's strange. He seemed to have turned around when he was almost at the university. Then he turned right a few times to arrive in this cul-de-sac."

"Weird that the signal stopped there. Do you know what taxi company he has used?"

She closed the app and searched for a moment on her phone.

"Let me see. He always uses the same one. Here, I have it."

Matteo dialed the number and navigated through an automatic menu until he finally got to speak to an operator.

"Good evening. This is Matteo Muller speaking. Our friend Dylan Myers took one of your taxis at ten to two today, but he never arrived at his destination. We're worried something might have happened to him. Could you please check if the taxi reached the destination?"

Elizabeth stood close to Matteo to follow the conversation as he communicated all the details to the operator.

"Let me see… at ten to two, the taxi with number F635 picked up Mr. Myers with destination the Swiss Federal Institute of Technology. And then… ah… mmm… that's strange. Just a moment, please."

They looked puzzled at each other and waited for the woman to get back on the line.

"I'm sorry for the wait, sir. I had to check with my superior. A warning appeared when I was checking the details about the ride. Apparently, something happened and the police are investigating it at the moment. My superior recommends you contact the police directly. Let me give you the details."

Matteo noted down the phone number and the name of the police officer in charge. Elizabeth grabbed the phone out of Matteo's hands.

"What happened? Is Dylan all right?"

"I'm sorry, but I'm not allowed to give you any further details. Please contact the police officer in charge."

21.

The next morning, Elizabeth felt broken after a night full of stress and poor sleep. After speaking to the operator the night before, they tried to reach the police officer, Henri Favre. Unfortunately, they got his voicemail. They left him a message, but he did not call back that evening. Later, they called the general number of the police station in Lausanne, but they also could not reach him.

Elizabeth was restless, pacing back and forth in the living room. It drove Matteo crazy, and he convinced her to go to the police station that same evening. They filed a missing person report at the police station. The officer explained that they would enter the report into the European police system so they could use all connected cameras on the territory to search for him. The police officer filing the report tried to comfort them by saying that most people just showed up after a while. Still, Elizabeth had a bad feeling about it all.

After breakfast, they tried calling Dylan's mobile another time, but got his voicemail again. Later, while she was preparing an espresso, the phone rang. She rushed to answer. Henri Favre was finally returning their call.

"I received your message and I'm sorry I couldn't get back to you earlier."

"Do you know what happened to Dylan?"

"Well, I'm not sure yet, since we're still investigating at this very moment. Could you come to the police station at eleven thirty, then I can brief you about our findings so far?"

"Yes, we'll be there," Elizabeth answered immediately.

The rest of the morning, she and Matteo contacted several of Dylan's friends in Lausanne to check if they had seen him and ask them to call if they did. Unfortunately, nobody knew where he was and she became increasingly worried. Time seemed to pass slowly, and Elizabeth was getting on Matteo's nerves again with her pacing around in the living room. Her father tried to comfort her, although with little effect.

Ten minutes past eleven, Matteo and Elizabeth went downstairs together. They entered the taxi, which was waiting in the underground hall, and left for the police station. Elizabeth was biting her nails on the way, which she had not done for a long time. A bit before eleven thirty, they entered the police station and asked for Officer Favre at the reception. They told them to wait in the waiting room.

Twenty minutes later, a small, skinny, balding man with a dark mustache showed up at reception and immediately came their way.

"Are you Elizabeth Muller?"

"Yes."

"Hello, I'm Henri Favre," he said and shook her hand. Then he glanced at Matteo.

"This is Matteo, my brother," she said.

"Nice to meet you. Please follow me."

They followed the small man. On the way to his office, he explained how the taxi company had called them to report a shooting.

"A shooting?" Elizabeth asked.

"Apparently the taxi returned to the company because of a reported malfunctioning in the air filtering system, and when they inspected the car, it was full of bullet holes."

In his office, he gestured them to take a seat in front of his desk.

"We examined the taxi and inside we found seven-millimeter caliber bullets from an automatic rifle. Dylan Myers was the last passenger who used the taxi before it automatically returned to the company. We've requested all the GPS data and video footage from the taxi company and have analyzed everything this morning."

Henri Favre opened his laptop and typed for a moment, after which he turned the screen toward them.

"Before I continue, I'd like you to confirm the identity of the victim. This is an image taken with a camera inside the driverless taxi. Could you tell us who the man on the screen is?"

Elizabeth and Matteo looked on the screen and saw Dylan filmed in the taxi while he was looking anxiously at something behind him. The stress was visible on Elizabeth's face, and her hands were trembling.

"Yes, that's Dylan. Is he all right?"

Henri Favre paused for a moment and looked at Elizabeth and Matteo with piercing eyes.

"Was Dylan involved in any criminal activity?"

Elizabeth looked completely dumbfounded at the police officer and then at Matteo, who also looked flabbergasted.

"Dylan? No, definitely not."

"Are you sure? Sometimes people have deep secrets."

"No, I'm one hundred percent sure. I live with him in the same apartment in Denmark. No, I'm positive. What happened to him?"

"Well, we believe someone has kidnapped him."

"Kidnapped? By whom?"

"We don't know yet, but the video footage showed that a dark van tried to stop the taxi. Heavily armed men, wearing black ski masks, shot at it. The taxi turned around and tried to get away. A wild pursuit followed, but since these driverless taxis are programmed not to break the legal speed limit, the dark van caught up quickly. The pursuit stopped after Dylan had ordered the taxi to enter a dead-end street. On the video footage, we saw Dylan running away into a small alley, followed by four armed men. Eight minutes later, the four men returned, taking Dylan away with a black bag over his head."

Elizabeth did not know what to say anymore and stared in disbelief in front of her. Her hands were trembling. Matteo tried to comfort her and touched her hand. Then he looked back at Henri Favre.

"Were you able to identify the four men?"

"Unfortunately, they were wearing masks, but we have their license plate and have entered it into the European police system. It won't be long before they'll signal it somewhere."

"Did you try to trace Dylan's mobile phone?"

"I've just received his details from the taxi company, and I'll place a trace request right after we finish our meeting."

Still puzzled, Favre probed another time.

"What type of work is Dylan involved in? Could the kidnapping be related to that?"

Elizabeth gave him a blank stare as she tried to think if there could be a connection, but it made little sense.

"No, that would be really far-fetched. He works at Enviro Technologies in Denmark in the Environmental Technology division. Currently, he's working on improving a new climate plant that captures nitrous oxide from the atmosphere. I don't think he has made any enemies with that, and he's not senior enough to be an interesting target for kidnapping."

Favre frowned and then rubbed his chin.

"Mmm, I guess you're right. It doesn't make any sense."

At the end of the meeting, Henri Favre promised to call them when he had any news.

"You can call me anytime, day or night," Elizabeth said desperately. Then she left the police station with Matteo.

22.

It was dark by the time they arrived at the Marseille harbor after a long drive. They only stopped briefly in a parking lot after entering French territory, where they switched the license plates and got rid of all likely traces. Marco knew how to stay off the radar by constantly changing, like a chameleon. Now they were close to the harbor, driving in between several large driverless trucks toward their destination. On one side of the road, there were thousands of containers piled up in long rows and, on the other side, there were several warehouses. A man was waiting at one of them next to a large, open sliding door. The black van drove in and the man closed the large door immediately.

Inside, they parked next to the small office all the way to the back of the hall. There were several containers inside and a number of other vehicles. Marco jumped out and rushed to the office. The others got out, and one of them looked at Marco and yelled.

"What do we do with this guy?"

"Just keep him in the van for now and keep an eye on him, just in case he tries to escape."

In the office, he grabbed one of the scanners out of the cupboard and then rushed back. He had to be sure before calling his boss. His men looked puzzled at him.

"Open the back!"

They opened the back of the van. Inside, Dylan was lying on the floor with a black bag over his head, hands and feet tied up.

"Make him stand up."

Two men pulled Dylan up, and Marco stood in front of him. He moved the scanner over his body and it beeped right above his hips.

"Good. Put him back inside and watch him."

Marco returned to the office and closed the door. He prepared himself an espresso. Meanwhile, he contemplated the entire operation. With a satisfied feeling, he felt comfortable enough and believed he had thought of everything. This time, he was going to bring some good news to his boss. He dialed the number and waited until he answered.

"Yes?"

"Hi boss, I've got the memory stick."

"Great! Did you check if all the information is on it?"

"Well, not yet."

"What do you mean?"

"Hakim Sayed gave the memory stick to a colleague from Enviro Technologies, a guy called Dylan Myers. I tracked him down and detained him. Unfortunately, he swallowed it. I tried to make him throw up, but it didn't come out. We took him with us and scanned him with a metal detector. It seems to be somewhere in his intestines. I wanted to check with you, to see what to do with him. I mean, I could cut him open and take out the memory stick or I could wait until it comes out the natural way?"

"I'm not sure we can risk keeping him too long. The police might track him down, and I can't risk losing this memory stick. What work does he do at Enviro Technologies?"

"He works at the Environmental Technology division."

"Ah, I believe that's where they make the air filters. You know what? I think I could use him over here. Put him on the next shipment and I'll tell my men to take care of him when he arrives and to retrieve the memory stick."

"All right, I'll ship him the usual way then. Let's see. I think I could fit him on our next shipment on the boat at twenty past eleven tonight. I'll send you the details."

"Perfect. And Marco?"

"Yes, boss?"

"Good work!"

23.

The days following his shocking discovery in the sunflower field, went by in a haze for Elliot as he went through the motions of daily life. Every morning he woke up with the silence inside the apartment. He had difficulty accepting his father was no longer there, especially after losing his mother when he was ten years old. It felt surreal to him. He was the last one of his family on this godforsaken planet.

Elsa spent lots of time with him and had been very supportive, but he needed time alone as well, time to think. Why had both his parents taken their lives? What horrible secret lay hidden beneath all this? Elliot did not understand, but he had to find out otherwise he felt it would be difficult to get some closure on his loss.

Today the resomation ceremony was taking place in the little chapel in the middle of the gardens. Elliot put his best suit on while Elsa prepared some espresso for them. She looked beautiful in her black suit, and he felt grateful she was there for him. After drinking their espresso, they left together for the ceremony. The sun shone and illuminated the gardens. Nature's beauty magnified by the light.

After walking for a while, they heard the gentle hum of voices. The closer they got to the chapel, the louder the chatter became. Elias had warned him already that they were expecting lots of people at the ceremony. His father had been the head of defense for a long time, a high-profile and important function within the dome. His death had created a shock wave throughout the community. A large crowd stood in front of the small chapel. Elsa grabbed Elliot's arm as they walked through the crowd. Although most people tried to be discrete, he noticed them staring and whispering to their neighbors. Barely anyone had died in the dome, and that made his father's death even more exceptional. As the unfortunate son, he grabbed the attention and attracted pity, compassion, and curiosity. He tried to ignore it and continued walking to the chapel.

He saw many familiar faces inside, and he slowly moved forward through the crowd. His friends, colleagues from work, Elliot's boss, Elias, and even the full Council had come to the chapel to pay their respects to Amos. Abe, the head of the Council and founder of the dome, greeted him and came toward him. Elliot had met him one other time in the past, and Abe had left a deep impression on him. The fine man had so much charisma.

"Elliot, I'm truly sorry for your loss and wish you strength in this difficult time. Your father was a great man and dedicated his life to the dome. Let me know if there's anything I can do for you."

"Thank you, Abe. I appreciate your support and kind words."

After taking his seat all the way in front, the ceremony started. Elsa sat close next to him, holding his arm. He was happy she was there. Without her, it would have been so much harder. His father's coffin stood in front of them, next to the altar. Several people spoke briefly about his father and his achievements and, at some point, Abe gave a short speech as well. He emphasized his father's accomplishments within the community and explained how his obsession with defense had ensured the safety of the entire community.

"… Amos was a dedicated and loyal man and we'll miss him. Our community has lost a great gentleman. Elliot, words are lacking to describe your loss. Our thoughts are with you. We send you our love and support and we wish you strength in this troublesome time."

Elliot nodded to Abe as if to thank him for his kind words. The priest continued the ceremony. When he reached the end, he invited everyone to say farewell to Amos by passing his coffin at the front of the chapel. Elliot went first, together with Elsa, and they walked up to the closed coffin. They had placed a beautiful picture of his father on top of it. Elliot felt tears running down his face. Elsa put her arm around him. They both touched the coffin one last time, and then they left the chapel.

The next morning, Elliot woke up next to Elsa. He was happy she had stayed that night with him. He looked at her while she was still deep asleep. Her long, blond curly hair draped over the pillow. Quietly, he stepped out of bed and prepared breakfast. He had just finished when she entered the kitchen in her nightgown.

"Morning."

"Mmm, what a nice surprise," she murmured and kissed him softly on the lips.

It was strange not to have his father around. Despite the pleasant conversation with Elsa during breakfast, he remained distracted and questions continued to haunt him. Why did his father end his life? Was he so unhappy? What problems could he no longer handle? Was it because he had insisted too much about his mother? He had felt for so long that his father was hiding things from him. That there was some terrible secret he kept. He had to find out.

Right after Elsa had left, the doorbell rang. It was Liam, carrying a small box in his hands.

"Hi Elliot, sorry to disturb you. I've brought you your father's belongings. It's all we found on him in the sunflower field. I thought you might want to have it. The investigation is still ongoing, but these items have been cleared. How are you holding up?"

"I'm okay. I guess it'll need some time before I get used to the idea that he's no longer there."

"Yes, it's strange. At work we're all still in disbelief. I've worked closely with your father for a long time and we're going to miss him. You know, he was always so proud of you. Anyway, if there's anything else I can do for you, just let me know."

"Thanks, Liam. Thanks for dropping by."

He closed the door and looked at the box. He wondered if its content would provide him with some answers. He walked to the living room and put the box on the table. Now was the time to find out.

24.

Late in the afternoon, Elizabeth was pacing back and forth in the living room, worried sick about Dylan. She had tried to call him several times, but only got his voicemail. She even tried the tracking app one more time, though it kept showing the same thing. His phone was offline. Her father tried to calm her down, but it had the opposite effect. She almost exploded out of frustration.

"You tell me to trust the police and let them do their work, but those armed men have kidnapped Dylan. I can't just sit here and wait. They might hurt him or even kill him. We have to do something," she said with a desperate look on her face.

"I agree with you," Matteo said. "It feels like we should be out there looking for him, even though we've no clue where to look. It's crazy. I still can't believe they've kidnapped him in broad daylight right here in the middle of Lausanne. It all feels so surreal. Who would have thought that after last year?"

Abruptly he stopped talking and looked at Elizabeth as if he just had a revelation.

"Of course, that's it! I know how to find Dylan. Stupid, we didn't think of that in the first place."

Elizabeth looked puzzled.

"What do you mean?"

"Last year when you got kidnapped in New York, we got help from Enviro Technologies to track you down through this chip you have in your arm."

"That's a great idea. I'm going to call Dylan's boss immediately."

She picked up her phone. Matteo looked at her with a hopeful look on his face while she was dialing the number. She noticed and put the speakerphone on.

"Hello, Mr. Sorenson. It's Elizabeth Muller. Sorry to disturb you, but I really need your help."

"Hi Elizabeth, I was just thinking of calling you. Dylan didn't show up at the meeting this afternoon and I've tried his phone several times, but I got his voicemail. Do you know where I can find him?"

"Actually, that's why I'm calling. He didn't come home yesterday. This morning we went to the police in Lausanne. They've found evidence that several men abducted him yesterday."

"Abducted him!?"

"Yes, I still can't believe it myself. Dylan, of all people. He would never harm anyone. I really don't get it. The police are trying to find him and his abductors. We've tried to track him through his phone, but it didn't work. We're worried sick, and we just remembered how Enviro tracked me down last year when I got abducted in New York. I was wondering if you could track Dylan down?"

"That's a great idea. Let me talk to Steve Hawkins from security right away."

She hung up the phone. Matteo tried to comfort her.

"Perfect. Like this, it won't be long before they track him down. Don't worry. We'll find him."

Fifteen minutes later, Sorenson called back.

"Hi Elizabeth, I spoke to Mr. Hawkins. He's going to call you as soon as they've located him. Apparently, someone else in the company has been reported missing as well. Hakim Sayed hasn't shown up at a meeting last Friday. I thought Hakim and Dylan knew each other, isn't it?"

“Hakim? Yes, they’re friends. They often play VR games together. He disappeared? Strange. Do you think there is a connection?”

“Well, Mr. Hawkins couldn’t tell me if there’s a connection. He just said it was a strange coincidence. They’ve tried to locate Hakim, but they couldn’t connect with the chip. It’s like it has stopped working. Do you know when Dylan has spoken with Hakim for the last time?”

“I’m not sure. I think he played a VR game with him on Thursday morning. After that, I don’t know. He didn’t mention it to me.”

“Okay, thanks Elizabeth. Anyway, it’s probably just a coincidence. Mr. Hawkins told me he was going to work on it right away. He’ll contact you as soon as he has located Dylan. Don’t worry, Elizabeth. We’ll find him.”

“Thanks.”

25.

The sound of water droplets falling on the floor. A howling wind around him. A low humming noise below. Something like an engine running in the distance. Dylan woke up disoriented and with an enormous headache. His mouth was dry and his throat raspy. It was painful to swallow. He felt dizzy, weak, and had difficulty breathing. The air was warm and musty. What had they done to him? His right shoulder felt sore. Had he been sleeping on it? Or had they hit him the day before? He couldn't really remember. They had tied his wrists together with something sharp. It hurt him whenever he moved. He rubbed his neck, which felt stiff, the way it would after sleeping all night in a wrong position.

There was darkness all around him. He tried to stand up, but they had tied his ankles together as well, causing the same piercing pain as on his wrists. He could vaguely distinguish shapes in the darkness and when he finally crawled up, he noticed a faint light further away, shining through several small holes. He bent down and then he no longer saw the light. He deducted there was something in front of him obstructing his view. He distinguished several large boxes in the darkness in front of him. He was sweating and felt dizzy and nauseous. He looked at the floor and noticed something next to his feet. It was too dark to see what it was, so he reached out with his hand. It was a bottle. He lifted it and there was some liquid inside.

Carefully, he opened the bottle and smelled. He felt really thirsty, but was also afraid it would not be drinkable. First, he tried a small sip. It tasted like lukewarm water. He was too thirsty and couldn't resist anymore. Away with the cautious behavior. Thirst was stronger than fear. His mouth filled with water, and he started to feel better. Still, he felt sick and disoriented. Like the ground was moving, or maybe everything around him was moving. It reminded him of seasickness. He became convinced he might be on a boat and the way it moved gave him the impression it was a large one.

In the past, he had used a simple trick to get rid of his seasickness. He would stare at a fixed point on the horizon, and it always worked. But here in the darkness, it was not possible to do that. When he stood up, he could only see the holes in the back. A faint light came through. He tried to stare at the lit holes, but it did not help. He felt groggy and lightheaded, and then he lost his balance. He touched the wall. It was a metallic surface. He realized he must be inside some sort of container. His nausea became too strong, and he sat down. His head kept turning, and he lay down flat on his back.

After a while, the urge to throw up slowly diminished. He tried to remember what had happened. Gradually, it came back to him. The driverless taxi. The wild chase. The masked armed men firing their guns at him. The rest was blurrier. They had put a dark bag over his head and he remembered being taken away in the van. A long ride that seemed to last forever. Clearly, they were after the memory stick that Hakim gave him. He understood now why Hakim had been so stressed out. He wondered what happened to him after their encounter at the hyper-loop station.

He couldn't help thinking about what would have happened to him if he just would have given them the memory stick. Would they still have kidnapped him? Maybe they would have killed him? They looked ruthless. Hakim had been clear. He had emphasized that he should bring it back to Enviro and nobody else should get it. Now he wished he had done so, but at the time, he didn't feel like postponing his trip to Lausanne. All he had thought of was joining Elizabeth as soon as possible. Now it seemed like an unfortunate decision.

Gradually, he started feeling better and sat up on the floor. He leaned his back against what felt like wooden crates. He tried not to move too much, as it made him sweat more. He drank some more water. Apparently, it had not made him sick. The bottle felt lighter, and he wondered how long he would stay locked up in here. He tried to keep some for later. At least he no longer had a dry mouth and raspy throat. He felt around with his hands. He found his respo on the floor and put it on his face. Breathing became easier. He continued checking his surroundings. Except for the wooden boxes, there was the metal wall around him. No opening or door. He was locked up with nowhere to go.

After exploring his surroundings and realizing there was no way out, he relaxed and sat back on the floor. He felt tired and warm. The howling winds around him and the low humming vibration continued endlessly. He wondered what was awaiting him. The concept of time got lost in the darkness. He sat like that for a long time, becoming drowsy, and eventually fell asleep.

26.

Tuesday morning, Hawkins looked puzzled at his screen. Jack Rowling, the head of the Drone department, a large department within the Security division, had called him late in the afternoon the day before. Hakim Sayed had not shown up at a meeting on Friday afternoon. Apparently, he had never done that before. They had tried to call him on his mobile phone, but it went straight to his voice mail. Since he did not show up at work on Monday either, they went to check at his apartment, but he wasn't there. That same day, Rowling reported him missing.

Hawkins had asked one of his employees to trace Hakim and present him a full report on Tuesday morning. After seeing the report, Hawkins could not believe it and now he was double checking the findings himself. After trying for a second time, he still got the same result. The system showed that they had lost the signal of Hakim. It had simply stopped and they could not establish a connection with the chip anymore.

There were only two potential explanations. The first was that they had put Hakim in some sort of construction that worked like a Faraday cage, which is an enclosure used to block all electromagnetic fields. The second was that they had completely destroyed the chip, either by removing it from his armor by harming him. Hawkins didn't like any of these explanations.

Immediately after checking the system, he ordered his employees to check the backup. The chip worked by emitting a signal to the company's mainframe every fifteen minutes. The data, coming from the chips from all the Enviro Technologies employees, was stored on the mainframe system as a backup. Now it could give information about where Hakim had been until the chip had stopped emitting.

Later that day, he received the location report. It showed that on Friday morning, after traveling to Copenhagen, his location had changed southward all the way to the south of France. From the fifteen minutes intervals in the location data, they deducted he traveled by car from Copenhagen all the way to the suburbs of Marseille in the south of France. Down there, not too far from the harbor, Hakim's chip stopped emitting. Hawkins found it all very strange and feared for Hakim's life.

After checking all the data, he contacted the local police in Marseille. He sent them all the information, including a picture and description of Hakim. He explained that he had gone missing and might have been kidnapped. The police were going to send a patrol to check out the last coordinates they had picked up. In the meantime, Hawkins ordered his assistant to do some research on the area around the last coordinates. It was an industrial area, and he wanted to know which companies were nearby and who was owning them.

On Wednesday morning, he spoke again with the police of Marseille. They had searched the area, but found no trace of Hakim anywhere. Four companies were located around the last coordinate, two on each side of the road. Two had allowed the police to search their premises, but they had not found him there. The two other companies had insisted on seeing their search warrants. The police officer explained to Hawkins that they had left a police patrol nearby to monitor their activities while they filed a request for a search warrant.

Late in the afternoon, Hawkins received a call from the police officer in charge in Marseille. They had obtained the search warrant and had searched the two other premises. Unfortunately, they still found no trace of Hakim. After hanging up the phone, Hawkins realized that this search for Hakim was going to be more difficult than expected. He called Jack Rowling back and asked him to interrogate all of Hakim's close colleagues. Maybe they knew where he went on Friday.

The next afternoon, Hawkins received another call and couldn't believe his ears. This time it was from Olav Sorenson, the head of the Environmental Technology division, who explained to him that Dylan Myers, one of his employees, had been abducted yesterday in Lausanne. Flabbergasted, Hawkins listened to the entire story. He found it too much of a coincidence and asked Sorenson if he knew whether Dylan had any contact with Hakim. He was not sure and promised to ask Dylan's girlfriend about it.

After hanging up, Hawkins couldn't help thinking there had to be a link between the two cases. His curiosity had been triggered, and he immediately ordered one of his employees to trace Dylan Myers. This time, he stayed at his employee's desk and waited anxiously for the result. The employee was clearly not used to having his boss looking over his shoulder. He nervously worked like a demon while Hawkins paced back and forth behind him.

After a while, he turned his head toward Hawkins.

"I've traced Dylan Myers, sir."

Hawkins turned his head and rushed to the desk.

"Could you show me the coordinates on the screen, please?"

A large map opened on the screen, and a moment later, a dot appeared. Hawkins approached to have a closer look.

"Too much of a coincidence. At least his chip is still working. Could you show the last location we have from Hakim Sayed on the same map?"

"Of course, sir."

Almost on the same spot as the first dot, a second dot appeared on the screen, and Hawkins made a fist with his right hand.

"I knew it!"

He grabbed the phone and called Elizabeth Muller.

"Hi Miss Muller, this is Steve Hawkins. I've located Dylan for you. Let me send you his coordinates."

27.

The small box stood on the table in the living room while Elliot prepared himself some green tea. Then he sat down on one of the chairs at the table in the living room. He looked at the box with curiosity, and after taking a sip of his tea, moved it closer. He wondered whether it would give any answers to his questions. On one hand, he felt eager to find out what was inside. On the other, he feared what he might find out about his father. He sighed deeply, then opened the box and looked inside.

His eye first fell on his father's necklace. He used to wear it under his shirt and it was never visible. Still, he wore it day and night, as it was a gift from his wife. She gave it to him at their wedding. The long chain with small blood-red ruby stones and a pendant on the edge had a deeper meaning. The story goes that if you would wear it near the heart that it would control emotions and strengthen love. People believed that the chain with stones would bind its wearer to their eternal powers. Elliot did not think his father had believed much in those powers, but wore it mostly out of love for his wife. To him, it was a symbol of their love.

After taking the necklace out of the box, he looked at the other items inside. There was a cream-white envelope, a black pen, a rectangle-shaped key, and his phone. He took out the envelope and saw it had 'Elliot' written on it in his father's handwriting. He felt shivers going through his spine as he opened it. He unfolded the letter and read it.

Dear Elliot,

I apologize for my shameful and cowardly departure. It ripped away half of me when your mother stepped out of this world. Unfortunately, the half that remained was not the best part. I have tried to be a good father to you, though I realize I failed you a long time ago. I am ashamed of the choices I made in the past and of imposing them on your mother. The guilt and regret I carried with me all these years simply have become too much to bear. Recently, I realized I have not learned from the past and continued making the wrong choices. I have failed as a father. I am sorry to leave you behind all alone on this godforsaken planet, but I must have peace, and this is the only way. I hope you can let go of the past and make the best out of your future.

Your father.

Elliot's hand was shaking. He dropped the letter and cried. He had hoped it would bring him answers, but it left him confused and with more questions. So many thoughts rushed through his head. It dazzled him. Why had he left him like that? What choices had he imposed on his mother? Was it his fault she took her life? What guilt and regret had been such a burden for him to carry? Why had he taken his life now, more than a decade after her mother had done the same? What horrible secret lay beneath all this? It made no sense to him. He had to understand. He wiped his face dry with the sleeves of his shirt and looked back in the box.

Slowly, he took out the rest of the items one by one. He moved the pen to the side and tried to access the phone. Even though he knew he probably could not unlock it, since it used biometric recognition. The phone indicated his fingerprints did not match and denied access. He tried to access it by entering a code. After trying three times, it blocked. Only his father could open it. He put the phone aside. Maybe his father's assistant could help him with it.

Now he focused his attention on the gray rectangle-shaped key. He had never seen it before. During his search of his father's room, he had found several keys, although this one had not been among them. It looked like a modern key, probably made of some graphene alloy. On the side, they had engraved the number 387, followed by a letter D. With the key in his hand, he wondered what it was for. In their apartment, he knew all the keys and locks. Maybe at his work there was a locker or cupboard somewhere.

He finished the green tea, now cold, and got up. He grabbed the key and the phone from the table and barged out of the door. He was not going to wait any longer. He had to find out what secret his father had been carrying with him all these years. Why did he end his life? He rushed through one of the many underground corridors. He wanted answers.

28.

Elizabeth and Matteo rushed out of the driverless taxi the moment they arrived in front of the hyper-loop station in Geneva. She was excited since Hawkins had called her. He had located Dylan in a suburb of Marseille in France. Matteo booked the earliest possible hyper-loop from Geneva to Marseille. There was no station in Lausanne, so they had taken a taxi to Geneva. Elizabeth felt agitated and worried about Dylan the entire way. It had been driving Matteo nuts and had been a proper test for his skills in understanding and patience.

Now it felt good to rush toward the hyper-loop with her. In the taxi, they took a closer look at the location in Marseille. It was some industrial area near the harbor. Matteo had a bad feeling about it, but he did not share his thoughts with Elizabeth. She was stressed enough already. Their trip had been well planned, and they were lucky that the traffic was light on the way from Lausanne. They took their seats in the hyper-loop cabin and the doors closed five minutes later.

In less than half an hour, they arrived in Marseille. A police officer was waiting for them in front of a van at the exit of the hyper-loop station. They got in and quickly drove off. There were four police officers in the van. One of them explained they had just obtained a search warrant ten minutes earlier. Several other units were almost at the site, and they were going to join them right away.

They entered the industrial zone close to the harbor of Marseille. The number of driverless trucks was overwhelming, and the road was congested. After a while, they arrived at a shabby-looking warehouse. There were four other police cars parked in front of it and police officers were walking around the terrain and inside the building. Matteo checked the map on his phone where he had entered the coordinates of Dylan's location.

"It looks like Dylan should be right behind this warehouse."

They parked behind another police van, and everybody got out immediately. It was hot and humid outside. They entered the large warehouse. Inside, they saw how some police officers were interrogating three wicked-looking, muscled thugs. They walked all the way to the back and, after passing through another door, they arrived at an outside storage space. Several police officers were standing around the trash containers next to the building. There was someone standing in one of them.

As they came closer, the police officer who had escorted them spoke briefly with a colleague standing next to the container. Then he walked back toward Elizabeth and Matteo.

"Apparently, the coordinates are right on the spot of that trash container. They've searched it but didn't find Dylan in there. It could be that they've buried him underneath."

Elizabeth freaked out. She put her hands in front of her face and interrupted the man.

"What!? You think he might be dead?"

The police officer gestured to Elizabeth to calm down, and Matteo put his arm around his sister.

"I'm sorry. That's not what I meant to say. Actually, my colleague doesn't believe so, since there are no traces of digging. Yet it's strange he's not there. Could you maybe double-check with Hawkins, if the coordinates are correct? Maybe they've moved Dylan to another location in the meantime?"

"All right, just give us a moment," Matteo said.

Elizabeth calmed down and dialed Hawkins's phone number.

"Hello, it's Elizabeth Muller. We're with the police at the coordinates you gave us, but there's no sign of Dylan. Could you check if he has moved?"

"Let me check it right away and call you back."

She hung up and looked worried at Matteo and then at the trash container. The ground under it did not look like someone had been digging, although they would have to move it away to be sure. She waited anxiously while Matteo tried to comfort her.

Fifteen long minutes later, Hawkins called back. She put him on the speakerphone so everybody could listen in.

"Hello Miss Muller. We've traced his location again, and the coordinates haven't changed since last time. The chip is still transmitting, so he really has to be at that spot."

Elizabeth started trembling and looked pale.

"Okay. Thanks, Mr. Hawkins."

The police officer looked at one of his colleagues and said, "It has to be on this spot. Could you bring the electromagnetic scanner from the van?"

The police officer ran back to the van. Several minutes later, he rushed back with the scanner in his hand. He turned it on and first scanned at the exact coordinates right on the spot of the trash container. It beeped immediately. He climbed into the container and continued scanning as he went through the trash with his hands. He searched like that for a while. The lower he bent, the faster the scanner beeped. They were getting closer to the chip. At the bottom, the signal was the strongest. Elizabeth looked terrified at Matteo.

"Oh no, it looks like it might be under the container."

Matteo kept his arms around Elizabeth. They heard the scanner beeping faster and faster until it became one long, monotonous peep. The sound moved up and suddenly the police officer stuck his head out above the trash container. He held his hand up high and was holding something between his fingers.

"I've got it! I've found the chip!"

Elizabeth looked flabbergasted at Matteo, who looked puzzled and muttered, "They must have removed it from his arm."

Terrified, Elizabeth held her hands in shock in front of her face. The police officer had a good look at it and pointed at it.

"It has some blood on it."

29.

The low humming sound had stopped, and Dylan didn't know what to think of it. He just woke up and had no idea how long he had been sleeping. He was not seasick anymore, and he realized they were no longer moving. He tried to sit but felt weak, too weak. His water was gone and his throat felt dry and painful. His clothes were soaking with sweat and he felt dizzy with the heat. His arm still hurt. Suddenly, he remembered what had happened to him. They were holding him tight while someone cut in his arm with what looked like a surgical knife. At the same spot, it felt painful, a biting and itching feeling. He felt something dripping from his arm and wondered if it was blood or sweat. No way to tell in the dark.

He looked around him and had the impression he could distinguish more. Maybe his eyes had adapted to the darkness, or maybe it was lighter. Above him, there were several beams of light, probably coming from the holes he had seen earlier. He could clearly distinguish the shape of the crates next to him. He felt weak and had the impression it was much hotter inside than before. Desperately, he tried to sip another drop from the empty water bottle. He thought of Elizabeth. She must be so worried. Then he thought of that strange encounter with Hakim. If only he had brought the chip back to Enviro right away. What was so important about it to kidnap him?

His thoughts were interrupted by a strange sound outside. It was far away but seemed to approach. A whirring sound with a high buzzing noise and then followed by the sound of metal pieces hitting each other. It moved away and came back again. Every time he heard this metal clunking, it appeared closer and closer. He heard it again, and this time, the light inside the container increased slightly. He could now read the numbers on the wooden crates next to him. In the corner, he noticed a bucket. He crawled toward it and looked inside. It was empty. He felt dizzy again. It was hot, and the heat tired him even more. He tried to rest and lay flat on his back.

Suddenly, he became startled by a metal clunking noise louder than before. He had the impression that this time, something touched the container on the outside. Another time metal clunked, and a moment later, everything moved. It felt like something lifted him off the ground, like he floated through the air. He felt disoriented and tried not to move. He felt his stomach churn and he felt himself descending fast, like being in an elevator. As sudden as it went down, now it braked. Again he heard a louder metal clunking noise, and the container shook.

For a while, there was a silence. It had stopped moving. Not too long after, though, the silence was broken by a low buzzing sound. The container moved abruptly, and he felt pushed to the side. It accelerated and then continued moving at a constant speed. He felt some warm air circulating now, and it seemed to come from the holes where the light came from. The circulating air made the heat more bearable. He tried to sit up straight and felt less dizzy than before. Grabbing onto the wooden crates, he pulled himself up until he was standing. The light coming from the holes on the other side was bright, and he felt the warm air blowing. They were moving at high speed now.

The container turned, and Dylan was pushed to the side. He lost his balance, but prevented a fall by grabbing onto the crate in a reflex. He still felt weak so he sat down. Several times they turned. At some point, the turning stopped, and they seemed to drive even faster. He felt slightly better thanks to the air getting in. He wondered where he was and where they were taking him. He dozed off for a while until an abrupt move woke him up. He heard distant noises outside. The container seemed to move slowly now, and the air circulated less. It felt much hotter inside. The heat was hitting him. He felt dizzy and weak.

After a long drive that felt like eternity to his weakened body and soul, they came to a complete stop. He heard voices outside. They came closer and heard a language he did not understand. It resembled Arabic. A sharp metal clinking noise sounded through the container and from behind the wooden crates, a blinding light came in. He closed his eyes to adapt slowly to the bright light. He heard a mechanic noise and a humming sound. It sounded like they were unloading the wooden crates on the other side of the container. He slowly opened his eyes a little, and he put his hand above them to protect against the bright light. Was he finally going to get out of this grave-like oven?

The mechanic noise gradually came closer. He tried to peer outside, past the remaining wooden crates. He saw some sort of forklift truck unloading the crates. Further away, he noticed a group of men all dressed in dark clothes. Black scarves covered their faces. They looked fearsome with their automatic rifles. The sky outside looked bright yellow. The forklift lifted the wooden crates next to him and he backed away immediately to avoid getting hit. He sat with his back against the corner, all the way in the back. After the forklift removed the last crate, the shabby-looking men came closer.

Two dark men climbed into the container and they talked in what sounded Arabic to Dylan. He did not understand what they were saying to him. One of them walked straight to the bucket in the corner and looked inside. Then he looked around on the floor, searching for something. The biggest of the two approached him and said something. The man removed his scarf and Dylan noticed his scarred, black face. He grinned at him, exposing his white teeth. He was missing one tooth in front. Suddenly, he reached out with his hand and grabbed the respo from Dylan's face. He laughed and said something to the other guy. He put the respo on his own face. Then he spoke through it to Dylan, while holding one hand on the automatic rifle hanging over his shoulder.

"You, up!"

Dylan understood what he meant, but felt too weak. He tried to get up, but he was so dizzy that he fell back onto the floor. The man with his respo grabbed his arm and yelled something to the other guy, who then helped to lift him up. While lifting him, one of the automatic rifles bumped against Dylan's back. It was heavy, and the blow on his back made him squirm from the pain. They carried him outside. They both smelled horrible. Dried sweat. Like they had not washed themselves for a long time. While they were carrying him, his hand touched their dark clothes. They were all sticky and dirty.

Outside, he pinched his eyes as the bright sun was blinding him. He felt the sun burning on his skin and the sweltering heat hit him in the face. In the burning sun, he felt even weaker than before. As they carried him to an old yellow house, he noticed the dome-shaped roof with a half-moon on top of it. This clearly did not look like Europe anymore. Where had they taken him? A tall man with a beard came walking out of the yellow house. He was holding a metallic object in his hand. He came straight to Dylan and said something to the others. The two men lifted Dylan higher and held him in front of the bearded man. He raised the metallic object that looked like some sort of scanner. He waved it in front of Dylan and moved it all over his body. At the height of his hips, it beeped.

He nodded and said something to the other men before returning inside. They carried him next door to what looked like an entrance to an underground parking garage. They entered and carried him down the driveway. As soon as they walked in the shade, the temperature seemed to drop by a few degrees. They walked down another floor and it was darker here.

Dylan noticed several containers standing in the parking spots. It was cooler. The place was faintly lit by some lights on the ceiling. They carried him toward a container in the back. One of them opened the door, and the others carried him inside, where it was much darker. In the back, he noticed a matrass on the floor. Next to it, there was a small table with two bottles of water and what looked like a candy bar. They put him down on the matrass. The man with the respo brought a bucket from the corner and held it in front of Dylan.

"You. Shit here."

He put it next to Dylan and pointed at the table.

"Drink. Eat. Shit."

They left and closed the door behind them. He stayed there all alone in the darkness. Above his head, he noticed some holes in the container and a faint light came through. Slowly, his eyes adjusted. Next to him, he distinguished the two bottles of water. He opened one of them and drank for a moment. The lukewarm water lessened his thirst. He just sat for some time with his back against the container wall. Slowly, he started feeling less dizzy.

When he felt slightly better, he looked back at the small table next to him. He noticed the candy bar on the table and grabbed it. He tried to read the text on the packaging, but it was too dark. He opened it, smelled it, and then took a bite. It had a strange smell he did not recognize, and it did not taste like a normal candy bar. The moist, sticky texture had a weird taste. It had a slightly nutty flavor. He felt too hungry to care much, and he finished it quickly. After another sip of water, he lay down on the matrass. He wondered what was going to happen to him. Then he fell deep asleep.

30.

As he spoke on the phone in his large, dark, windowless office, Abdul stared at the expensive painting on the wall in front of him. He loved that painting. It touched him deeply. The hope of a rescue. The desperation. About survival in a cruel and unjust world. It also reminded him of all the people who had tried to cross. His brother in particular. He still remembered that dreadful day clearly. The day he lost his brother.

The moment he got off the phone, he heard someone knocking. He looked at the door, then checked the screen under his desk to see who it was. He pushed the button under his desk and the door buzzed. The electronic lock opened.

A tall man with a beard entered the room.

"Morning, boss. The boy arrived. He still has the chip inside, so we've locked him up. All we've got to do now is wait until it comes out."

"Very well, Ahmed. Let me know when you've recovered it. How are we doing with our fleet?"

"Yesterday, I arranged another five. Later this week, I'm hoping to get another seven. Everything is going according to plan, so far."

"Good. The way I like it."

"What do you want to do with the other guy?"

"We still need him, so keep him alive."

"Okay, boss."

Ahmed bowed his head and left the room.

Abdul glanced back at the painting and thought back to that dreadful day. He had argued with his brother just the day before and Maheer became pissed at him. They fought regularly when they were kids, but later they worked quite well together. Although their role division had been classical. He was the older one and clearly in charge. Everybody treated him as the boss and Maheer was always the younger brother. Until the day Maheer died, he never realized how much that must have frustrated his younger brother.

Their fight started after Maheer's announcement that he was planning to cross the Mediterranean Sea. Abdul reacted fiercely. He told his younger brother that he had to be patient and that it was way too early. Maheer disagreed and didn't seem to understand the grand plan of his older brother. Now he regretted his reaction that day. Maybe if he had talked longer with Maheer, things would have turned out differently. But he was quite busy and thought he was bluffing. He had simply forbidden him to go.

Unfortunately, Maheer was extremely stubborn and impatient. Not at all like his older brother, who had mastered the skill of patience to perfection. By the time he realized his brother had been serious after all, it was too late. The next day, Ahmed was the first to notice that he had left and immediately warned his boss. They rushed to the harbor and noticed several boats were missing.

They took his fastest yacht for the pursuit, but Maheer had left a long time ago. On the radar, they spotted the six boats on their way to Spain. At high speed, they went after them. He desperately tried to reach his brother on his phone, but the line was constantly busy. Then he noticed on the radar that the boats were already approaching the security border and he got nervous. He pushed his own yacht to the maximum speed. It bounced violently over the water. But by the time they spotted Maheer on the horizon, the drones were already flying above them. He witnessed, peering through his binoculars, his brother's obliteration.

Now, almost four years later, he still had nightmares about that dreadful day. The painting in front of him reminded him of his younger brother's failed attempt. He looked at the shipwrecked sailors on the raft in front of him. The rescue boat was visible on the horizon, but sailed away without seeing them. It depicted his brother's vain hope. He felt alone after losing his brother. He was the only one left from his family on this cursed planet.

He and Maheer were very close and had gone through highs and lows together. However, he always had taken the lead. Apparently, this had driven his brother to undertake this unfortunate attempt to cross the European sea border. He had underestimated the amount of frustration his brother built up over the years. Maheer no longer wanted to stand in the shadow of his older brother. He regretted he had not seen this coming.

During their childhood, he often guided and protected his younger brother. Deep in thought, he remembered an incident with another kid. Abdul must have been ten years old and Maheer almost eight. They had moved three years earlier from Khartoum in Sudan to Cairo in Egypt. It had not been easy for them to adapt, and they were poor, very poor. They lived in one of Cairo's slums, in a tiny apartment. They all shared the same room, and he shared a mattress on the floor with Maheer. They both attended the same school, where there was an older boy called Mido.

One day after school, he found his younger brother on the ground in the street next to school. He had a cut on his face that was bleeding heavily. Apparently, Mido had beaten him up in front of a group of friends. By the time he found Maheer, the group had dispersed already. Mido, who was probably thirteen years old at the time, had called his brother a poor dog. This enraged Maheer, and he attacked the much bigger boy. He felt humiliated after losing the fight. His older brother helped him back on his feet and carried him home. They lied to their parents about what had happened so their father would not be angry.

Their father always told them they should never accept any humiliation. If someone humiliated them, there was only one solution, and that was revenge. After the incident with Mido, they both swore to take revenge. Maheer wanted to go after Mido the next day already, but Abdul made it clear to him that patience was one of the most important virtues in life. He explained they would take revenge, but that it was better to wait. Revenge was a dish best served cold. They had to wait for the perfect moment, but he guaranteed him that when that moment would come, their revenge would be so much more satisfying.

Almost six months passed, and Mido had long forgotten about the incident. He always rode on a shiny blue bike through the neighborhood. His parents had more money than theirs, and he knew how to rub it in. His clothes were always new, a large contrast with their old and worn-out clothes. Often he passed by them on his bike, sometimes making fun of him and his younger brother. What Maheer didn't realize was that his older brother was planning his revenge. The day that perfect moment arrived, Mido did not see it coming. Even Maheer got shocked, as he had imagined revenge on a more modest scale.

On that unfortunate day, it was getting dark already. The streets were empty. When they passed through one of the small back alleys on their way home, they spotted Mido driving quite fast on his bike. Abdul looked around until he saw a thick wooden stick on the floor. This was his chance, he thought. He picked it up. He looked around him. The streets were empty. Maheer looked puzzled at him. Then Mido passed by them on his shiny bike and right at that moment, he stuck the stick in his front wheel. The bike flipped over and Mido fell off the bike. He bumped his head on the hard pavement as he fell flat on the floor. He tried to get up and turned his bleeding head. He looked at them.

"Help me, please."

Right at that moment, Abdul jumped on his back, and Mido's head banged back onto the pavement. He moaned in pain. He looked briefly at his younger brother.

"Time for our revenge, little brother."

Maheer looked astounded at him when Abdul pulled a plastic bag out of his pocket. Sitting with his knees on Mido's back, the poor boy had nowhere to go. He opened the bag with a swift movement. A second later, he pulled the plastic bag over Mido's head. Then he held the bag tightly closed around his neck, while his poor victim jerked around with his legs, attempting to scream, though only producing a muffled noise. He tried to breathe, and the bag moved in and out of his mouth. He held him like that for several minutes while Maheer yelled, "You're going to kill him like that."

"Yes. That's our sweet revenge. Nobody humiliates our family."

Mido turned pale and stopped moving. It was a new feeling to Abdul, to experience how the life went out of his victim. He still waited several minutes before removing the plastic bag. He had committed his first murder. Many more would follow, although it never felt like that first time. The first time was always special. It was unique. He felt invincible. Maheer wanted to steal his bike, but he told him to leave it. He had carefully planned his revenge. Stealing the bike was not part of it. He put the plastic bag back in his pocket. Then he ran away with his younger brother. Leaving the lifeless body behind in the street. He made Maheer swear never to talk about it to anyone. It was their secret.

In the days after, Maheer feared they would get caught by the police. But Abdul knew the police did not care much about the poor. He had been shrewd enough to make it look like an accident. He had not acted out of impulse, but had carefully planned and waited for the right opportunity. The police never came. Soon everybody was talking about this unfortunate accident. The entire school mourned the poor Mido.

He looked back up at the enormous painting. He missed his younger brother. His childhood seemed far away, but it had shaped him to the man he had become, a ruthless and feared leader. A man with a mission. He had come a long way since then. Step by step, he worked on his grand plan. Determined, he was about to take another big step in his life. That Indian-looking man inside that container was about to hand him the key to his next move. Another step closer to his ultimate revenge. Unfortunately, he would have to travel this path all alone, without any family.

31.

The smell of dried sweat and urine combined with the hot, humid air made him sick. Hakim lay flat on the dirty mattress on the floor. It had been several days since he arrived in this horrible place. The horrendous journey in the container and the painful wound on his shoulder had crippled him. The guards had carried him out of the container and put him in this dark underground prison. Locked up in a filthy room with half a dozen other people.

The first few days, he felt too weak to move and slept most of the time. His arm hurt constantly, and at night Hakim suffered from nightmares. He relived the torture he had endured over and over in his dreams. Most dreams finished with him waking up screaming loudly. Slowly, he regained some strength, although they got little to eat. Every day, two guards brought several bottles of water and something that looked like a candy bar for each one of them. One of his cellmates, who had been so kind to pass him some water and this bar, explained it was made of some kind of paste comprising insects. It didn't taste too bad. At least everybody seemed to be quite considerate, and nobody fought over the food or water.

Today he woke up still feeling extremely weak. He wondered if he had a fever. He worried about Aisha. Since his refusal to give them the memory stick, he wondered what they had done to his sister. He had shown her picture to all his cellmates, but no one had seen her. Yesterday, he asked one of the guards, but he had not seen her either. He got up from the bed and felt dizzy. He walked slowly to the table next to the door where the bottles of water were kept. A tall man finished drinking and passed him a bottle of water. He looked at him. He looked friendly and physically fit.

"How do you feel today?"

"A bit feverish."

"You should ask the guard for some aspirin."

"Do you think they would give it?"

"Yes, of course. If they wanted you dead, you would have been dead already. They locked you up in here because you're still of some value to them."

"I guess you're right. What is your name?"

"I'm Omar, and you?"

"I'm Hakim. Why did they put you in here?" he asked as he took another sip from the bottle.

"They kidnapped me a few weeks ago in Cairo. My parents are wealthy and they're trying to get a ransom."

"That's horrible. Your parents must be extremely worried."

"Yes, I guess they are. And you? Why are you in here?"

"Well, they've kidnapped my sister, and they wanted me to give them certain information. I refused, and then they brought me here."

"Strange, they didn't take you for questioning yet."

"Yes, I guess. Well, I'm more worried about my sister. Do you know if they keep more prisoners somewhere else?"

"I really don't know. I haven't seen any other cells like this around, but I've only been outside a few times."

"I really have to find her."

"Well, first you should get some aspirin, you're all shaking."

Omar banged on the door and yelled for the guards. About five minutes later, they showed up. He explained about the dire state of

Hakim, who lay on the mattrass now, and insisted on getting some aspirin.

The next day, Hakim woke up quite late. He had slept much better, thanks to the aspirin. Still, his arm hurt, and he had the impression the wound on his shoulder was stinking. He tried not to pick at the festering wound, although the constant itching made it hard to resist. He tried to get up, but got dizzy immediately. He sat back on the edge of the mattrass. He felt weak, and the heat in the room made it worse. Slowly he tried to lift himself up, and then he walked to get himself a fresh bottle of water.

After drinking, he felt better and made his way to the one mirror in the room. He took off his shirt to look at the wound. It looked still swollen and around the gaping hole in his shoulder there were red circles of different shades of red. He saw some yellow and white spots inside the hole. Some puss came out of one of the spots. He tried moving his injured arm, but it was still extremely painful. Maybe it got infected, since it did not look very healthy. He leaned over to smell the wound, which stank horribly.

A moment later, he heard the door behind him open. He turned and his mouth fell open when he saw whom the guards brought inside.

"D… D… Dylan!?"

Dylan looked flabbergasted at Hakim standing in the room in his bare chest, then he glanced quickly at the other people in the room before stammering.

"Th… th… they abducted you as well!?"

Hakim shook his head and put his hand on his mouth.

"No, no, this can't be true. I feel so bad now. This is my fault."

"Don't blame yourself, my friend. You didn't kidnap me. I should probably just have handed over the memory stick instead of swallowing it."

"You swallowed it?"

"Yes, stupid idea."

"I should never have given it to you. It's my fault you're here now."

"Don't worry about it. We've got other things to worry about. What happened to your shoulder? That looks really bad."

Dylan approached Hakim and looked closer at his gaping wound.

"They burned the chip with a soldering iron."

"Ai, that must hurt."

"Yes, it does. They wanted to force me to tell them what I had done with the memory stick. I resisted quite long."

"It looks infected. A doctor should look at it."

"I guess you're right, but I don't think they care much about us in here. I'm happy they gave me some aspirin, because I was feeling terrible."

"Do you have any idea where we are?"

"Well, Omar, over there, told me he believes we're somewhere in North Africa."

Dylan turned his head to Omar and walked over to introduce himself. They shook hands.

"So, I understood from Hakim that you think we're in North Africa?"

"Yes. They kidnapped me in Cairo, and I've quite a good sense of direction."

He looked at his watch and smiled.

"They forgot to take my watch, so I kept track of the driving time. We drove westward for over forty hours. That would get us to

Algeria. Although a lot depends on the average speed, so it could be West-Libya or Tunisia as well. Morocco would surprise me, as it's too far."

"Well, all those countries would fit with the boat trip I was on from Marseille. Omar, since you've been here longer than us, has anybody escaped from here already?"

"Huh, not that I know of. I don't think it's so easy. I mean, the guards are heavily armed and trigger-happy. The few times they took me out of here, I didn't see any opportunity to run away. On top of it, even if you would escape, I wonder how far you would get. I mean, you must have noticed the heat outside. We are close to the Mediterranean Sea, but also close to the Sahara Desert, one of the hottest and driest spots in the world."

"Yes, I noticed. I nearly fainted when I arrived here. Even down here, it's hot. Hakim, you look so pale."

Hakim was sweating and wiped his forehead. He sat back down on his mattress and looked up at Dylan.

"You don't think someone will come and look for us? Can't they trace us with those chips in our arms?"

"Well, they can actually, but looking at your arm, I doubt your chip still works, and they've removed mine from my arm," Dylan said while rolling up his sleeve and showing the stitches on his shoulder.

"Shit, then it doesn't look good for us. How the hell are we going to get out of here?"

"No idea, Hakim. But I really think we need to get you a doctor. You don't look good. Try to rest a bit."

32.

After their disappointing trip to Marseille, Elizabeth and Matteo returned to their father's apartment in Lausanne. She felt desperate the whole evening. She tried to reach Hawkins, but with no luck. She left him a message. Matteo tried to calm her down. He thought that finding the chip meant Dylan was still alive and someone did not want him to be traceable.

After a sleepless night, Elizabeth called the police station in Lausanne and asked for Henri Favre. She got connected through and Favre gave her an update. He just received a call from the police in Marseille. The DNA from the blood on the chip matched Dylan's. Unfortunately, they had not found any other trace of him. They were still checking the video footage from all the cameras in the area for any clues to the whereabouts of Dylan.

The bad news was that the tracing of the license plate from the dark van had hit a dead end. It matched another car that had been reported stolen. They spotted the license plate for the last time with a camera at the French border. The next cameras along the highway had not spotted it anymore. Favre concluded they must have switched the license plate. He explained they were still analyzing all the data. They were focusing on the trajectory between the camera that had last spotted the license plate, and the closest camera that had not spotted it anymore. He believed that in the footage from the latter camera, the van should appear with a new license plate that was not spotted by the first one. He promised to call her as soon as they had results from this analysis.

Later in the afternoon, she spoke with her father and Matteo. They were discussing what else they could do to find Dylan when her phone rang. It was Hawkins, and Elizabeth explained why she had called him earlier on.

"I've tried to reach you after our visit to Marseille yesterday, just to keep you up to date. I don't know if you've heard from the police in Marseille already, but they found the chip yesterday. Unfortunately, no trace of Dylan. We're so worried about him."

"Yes, I heard from the police of Marseille that the kidnappers had removed the chip. They seem to have insider information from Enviro, and we're taking this matter very seriously. Last night, I've discussed it with our CEO, Jeff Tusk. We've reason to believe that some criminal organization is targeting Enviro. We believe there's a connection between the abductions of Hakim and Dylan, and that they're linked to our company. Today we've set up a special task force to investigate the matter."

"That's great. I'm really happy to hear that."

"Well, that's not all. This morning I've spoken to Europol and they're forming an international police task force to investigate the two abductions. I understood that Henri Favre will be on the team, together with members from the Danish police force and from the Marseille police district. We'll be working closely together with them."

"Great! I had the impression the police were running into a dead end and were giving up, but this sounds good. I'm so worried about him. I can barely sleep at night."

"I promise you that we'll do whatever we can to find him. There're still plenty of leads to work on, so hold on."

33.

Steve Hawkins hung up and checked his email. He couldn't help thinking back about his conversation with Elizabeth, and he sincerely hoped he wouldn't have to disappoint her. They had so few leads to work with. His gut feeling told him something big was brewing. Something that could damage Enviro Technologies, but he did not have enough facts yet to back up this feeling. Luckily, the two abductions had been serious enough to convince his boss to set up a special task force.

After reading an email from Martin Nielsen, one of the task force members, he walked over to his desk. Martin looked up from his computer and greeted him enthusiastically. Hawkins looked at him with curiosity.

"So, what good news do you have for me?"

"Remember the signal trail of Hakim's chip?"

"Yes, from Denmark to Marseille."

"Well, I matched it with the one from Dylan's chip. The trails actually came together on the same Friday in a restaurant next to the hyper-loop station in Copenhagen. They also came together in Marseille, although in this case on different days. This morning I received the video footage I had requested."

Enthusiastically, Martin showed the trails on a map, and then he switched to another screen where he had the video footage.

"Look, first I'll show you the footage from the camera in the restaurant where Hakim and Dylan met. Here you see Dylan arriving at the restaurant at nine twenty-five. Most likely he went there to wait for the departure of his hyper-loop to Bern at ten fifty-five."

He fast forwarded the images and added.

"Here at twelve past ten, Hakim comes rushing in. He runs to Dylan's table and hands him something. Then he leaves."

Martin zoomed in on the images, and Hawkins could clearly see how Hakim was putting something in Dylan's hand.

"Hakim looks terrified in these images."

"Yes, I believe some people were chasing him. Dylan leaves about twenty minutes later, goes to the station, and then catches his hyper-loop to Bern. From the signal trail, I can see that Hakim went to some other restaurant in Copenhagen before coming to meet Dylan in this one. I've tried to get video footage from as many cameras on his route, starting from his arrival at the air-taxi platform until his departure from Copenhagen."

He opened some other videos and started playing them, while Hawkins looked over his shoulder.

"Look here. He arrives at the air taxi platform from Ikast. He takes a taxi to a restaurant in the center. Here you can see him entering the restaurant and walking to a table. Ten minutes later, at nine fifty, this guy with all the muscles comes to sit at his table and they talk for a while."

He zoomed in on the face of the muscled man with the shaved head.

"I scanned his face and entered it in our face-recognition system. He's Marco Rossi, an Italian with a criminal record for assault and possession of unregistered weapons. He served five years in prison in Italy. At some point, Hakim walks to the back of the restaurant and doesn't return. A couple of minutes later, Marco follows him. I tried to get video footage along his route from this restaurant to the one next to the hyper-loop station. I only found this street camera, where you see Hakim running and later you see Marco going after him. Then there was the meeting with Dylan, and I found Hakim back on the images of a camera on the square next to the hyper-loop station. Look here. The images are not ideal, though here in the back you see Hakim coming out of the hyper-loop station and running toward that street. Here you see a broad-shouldered man, whom I think must be Marco Rossi, running after Hakim. Then a van stops in front of Hakim. I'll zoom in further. Here you see how several men push him in the van and drive away."

Fascinated, Hawkins looked at all the images.

"Good work, Martin. Do we have the license plate of the van?"

"Yes, it's the same number the police of Lausanne had found, but unfortunately they switched the license plates in France. I understood that Henri Favre is still analyzing the highway camera footage to try and identify the new license plate."

"Very good, Martin. Send me the file on Marco Rossi, then I'll contact the Europol team to transfer all the details to them. They should be able to track down this guy and maybe after apprehending him we'll find more about the whereabouts of Dylan and Hakim."

34.

While Elliot rushed through the underground maze of corridors, he continued thinking about his father's letter. He felt there was a lot he did not know about his parents and had to find out more to understand it all. He believed it would be the only way for him to get some closure and acceptance of his father's death. In a haze, he continued walking toward his father's office. It had been a long time since his last visit to the Defense department.

When he was younger, his mother often brought him along to his father's office. They would all three have lunch together in the gardens upstairs. He still remembered how his mother would smile at him before lunch.

"Let's surprise your father with a visit."

As a child, his father's work fascinated him. He still remembered how he would show him the latest drone or the latest weapon. He would explain passionately every little detail to him, feeding Elliot's fascination. However he never took him outside and created this image that the outside world was dangerous, and it was better to stay away from it. Elliot always thought his father was overprotective, and his visit to the outside reactor last year confirmed that feeling. He thought his father had been a bit too alarmist. Although he understood why he had done that. He simply followed the general policy guidelines formulated by the Council. People inside the community could never leave the dome, and therefore, they glorified life inside. The dome was the last paradise on Earth, and its habitants were the lucky ones.

After rushing through the network of corridors, he finally arrived at the entrance door to the Defense department. Next to a thick metal door, there was the familiar reception screen. Elliot stood in front of it and looked at the beautiful Asian woman. She was wearing the official uniform of the Defense department. He remembered how the door would open automatically when his father took him to his office. Not this time.

"Hello, Elliot. How can I help you?"

"I'm here to visit my father's assistant, Mary."

"Let me check for you, just a moment, please."

The woman seemed to be checking something on her computer. He always found it a bit odd talking to a meta human, a computer-generated person. It looked like the real thing. Still, he always felt there was something missing. Like he could not really feel the person like he would with an actual human. He knew from his work very well how this system worked. The camera on the screen had just recorded him on video now, and Mary would receive this on her phone. After watching the video, she would have the choice to approve his visit.

"Okay, Elliot. You can proceed to room C 534. The red lights on the floor will indicate the direction. Have a nice day."

The screen turned dark and the heavy door in front of him slid open sideways with a hiss. He followed the blinking red lights on the floor, passing several offices before he arrived at the elevator. A man looked up from his desk when Elliot passed through the corridor. The doors opened automatically, and he stepped inside. The elevator descended automatically to the floor where his father had his office. He got out downstairs and continued to follow the red lights on the floor until he arrived at his father's office. Mary came walking toward him. She gave him a hug and looked concerned.

"How are you holding up, Elliot?"

"Okay, I guess. It's silent in the apartment without him. I still can't believe he's no longer there."

"Yes, it was all so sudden. It's hard to accept this new reality. We all miss him. He was a good man."

"It all still feels so surreal. I miss him. I hope it'll get less painful with time."

"Time heals all wounds. I've worked for so many years for your father. The office is not the same without him."

A silence fell, and Mary looked sad. Elliot looked around in the office. She quickly snapped out of her thoughts.

"Anyway, what can I do for you, Elliot?"

"I was hoping you could help me out," he said, while pulling the key and the phone out of his pocket and putting them on the table in front of Mary.

"I'd like to access my father's phone, but I don't have the code. Do you have it?"

She checked the phone for a moment and then looked back at Elliot.

"I don't have his access code, but I could give the phone to our technical department. I'm sure they know how to solve this."

"That would be great. I also found this key in his belongings. Would you have any idea what it's for?"

She picked it up and looked closely at it before answering.

"Mmm, I've never seen this key before. Just give me a moment."

She left the room, and while waiting, Elliot peered into his father's office. On his desk there was a picture of Elliot with his arm around his father. It was taken in the lavender field in the dome's gardens a couple of years ago, during one of their weekly walks. It made him realize that last year they had made no walks together at all. His father had often been in a grim mood, so he went walking alone or with Elsa.

Mary returned to her office with a pleased look on her face.

"Elliot, I know what this key might be for. I just spoke to Liam. He thinks it might be for a locker. Apparently on floor minus seven in the West section there is a large space full of private lockers."

"Great, I'll have a look. Thanks for your help."

"Anytime, Elliot."

"Ah, I'd also like to take his belongings from his office. Could I have a look?"

She hesitated for a moment and looked concerned.

"Well, no, actually. This guy called Conan, from Internal Affairs, has instructed me not to clean up his office yet until he finishes his investigation."

"Investigation?"

"Yes, but I'm not allowed to talk about it."

Elliot noticed she looked uncomfortable.

"It has something to do with this intrusion a while ago."

"You mean this intruder who managed to reach the dome?"

"Yes, but hey, you didn't hear that from me, huh?"

"Okay, thanks, Mary."

"Take care, Elliot."

35.

It was hot in his office. Abdul walked over to the air conditioner in the corner and held his hand in front of it. The air was blowing, but not really cold, more lukewarm. He tried to change the settings, but nothing helped. Then he heard someone knocking on his door and rushed back to his desk. He sat behind his large wooden desk on a heavy leather office chair. He checked the screen under his desk to see who was standing in front of his office. It was Ahmed. Abdul unlocked the electronic lock. He had been working for him for almost ten years now, gradually moving up in his organization to become his righthand. He trusted him with his life.

Ahmed entered his office, clearly excited. He was as tall as Abdul, but slender, which gave him the look of a lean marathon runner.

"Boss, we've got the memory stick. It's still intact."

"Did you give it to our tech guys to examine?"

"I did, but there is a password, which they are trying to crack."

"Why don't you bring this Hakim guy to our tech department and I'll join you in fifteen minutes. I'm sure we can convince him to tell us the password."

"All right, boss. See you there."

The silence in his office returned. He glanced at the enormous painting on the wall. After saving Ahmed's life more than ten years ago, he became his most loyal worker. He knew he could trust him completely. Together, they prepared their plan meticulously. Step by step, his international empire had grown. Over the years, he moved increasingly to the background. With many loyal people working for him, he managed to run his empire while staying in the shadows. Expanding his wealth and power, he slowly reached toward his ultimate goal. Ahmed was one of the few people who knew his entire plan. With this memory stick finally in his possession, they were getting closer to the next big step in this grand plan.

It all triggered a long time ago. Staring at the dark wall of his office, he thought back to his troubled youth. He still remembered how one day his father had come home all upset. At the time, he was thirteen years old. It had taken him years to understand what had actually happened during that unfortunate winter in the year 2026. His mother tried to calm his father down, but he was furious. They sent him and Maheer outside so they could talk. Yet they were quite curious to find out what all the commotion was about. They stayed in the corridor in front of their small apartment and listened at the door. He heard his father yell that it was not fair. Then something about not planning to budge because of some rich man's building plans.

"What have our neighbors done?" his mother asked.

"They told me they've all agreed to sell. I spoke to Youssef, next door. He signed yesterday. I asked him why, but he didn't want to tell me at first. I insisted, and apparently his boss had told him that if he wouldn't sell, he could no longer employ him."

"But that's blackmail."

"Exactly. Criminal. But that's not going to happen to us. Nobody threatens the Jabbar family!"

He heard his mother trying to calm him down, and his father lowered his voice. Abdul had difficulty following the conversation, so he put his ear on the door. He heard his father clearer now.

"Today, the police stopped me in the street while I was trying to sell my goods."

His father worked independently. He sold all kinds of merchandise on the street. The products he sold changed frequently. At that time, he sold second-hand phones.

"They asked if I had a permit. I got a fine, and they confiscated my phones. Then I received a call from the real estate agent of this rich jerk. He told me I'd better sign the contract, otherwise he was certain the police would show up more often. What a bastard!"

"That's horrible. This is getting out of hand, maybe we should just sign?"

"Never! I'm not letting this guy humiliate me!"

The discussion stopped there, and for months he did not hear his parents talk about the issue anymore. Until one day his mother came home crying. She did not want to say much to him and Maheer, but apparently, two men had harassed her in the street. Later that evening, when his dad came home and heard what had happened, he exploded. He called the real estate agent and accused him of harassing his wife. He said he was going to go to the police, but the real estate agent convinced him to first drop by his office. His father demanded an apology and shouted he would never sell the apartment.

That evening, they left for their appointment with the real estate agent. He and Maheer stayed at the apartment. His father emphasized that he should take care of his brother and make sure he went to sleep on time. When his brother was asleep, he stayed up worrying about his parents. They did not come home that night.

The next morning, the police showed up at their door. Apparently, his parents had been killed in a traffic accident. Later, he understood that a large truck had hit them while they were crossing the street. They were killed instantly. They had to move out and were forced to live with their uncle, his mother's brother. He already had four children and treated him and Maheer as second-rate children. His own children always got new clothes, while they had to wear their old clothes. They would always eat separately from the family and ate the leftovers. Whenever he would protest, his uncle would beat the shit out of him. His brother preferred to keep a low profile, but Abdul was not like that and suffered regular beatings.

Together with Maheer, they always passed their old apartment on their way to school. One day, the surrounding streets were all closed, and the building was demolished along with the other buildings around it. Shortly after, they put a large wall around the enormous construction site, and they could no longer see what was going on. A few years later, he figured out what had happened. He was furious when he found out what his uncle had done. After the death of their parents, the judge had appointed their uncle as their legal guardian. Abdul and Maheer inherited the apartment from their late parents, but their uncle never told them about it. As their legal guardian, he was free to sell it using the argument that he needed the money to raise his late sister's children. In no time, he sold the apartment to the rich man to whom his father had sworn never to sell to. As soon as he found out, Abdul swore to take a revenge on his uncle.

At the age of sixteen, he saw his chance. His aunt had gone with all the children to the dentist. He stayed home claiming a fever. Later that afternoon, his uncle came home. His aunt had called him during the day because the air-conditioner had broken down. It often broke down, and his uncle always fixed it himself. Abdul was lying on a mattress in the bedroom while his uncle unplugged the air-conditioner in the living room and started opening it. He was unscrewing a part and did not see that Abdul was approaching him quietly from behind.

Just at the moment that he had both his hands deep inside the air-conditioner, Abdul took the power cord and plugged it back into the socket. He looked at his uncle, who screamed and trembled. A stressed look in his eyes. His hair stood up straight before he collapsed to the ground. He lay motionless on the floor with his hands all burned. He checked his pulse and his heart had stopped beating. Relieved, he waited for another hour before calling the hospital and explaining to them what had happened. They showed up fifteen minutes later but failed to reanimate him. That night, he felt good about what he had done and fell asleep without a problem.

At the age of eighteen, he had become extremely resourceful and built up a small business. Initially, he was only dealing marihuana together with his younger brother. Soon after, they expanded to other drugs. His aunt thought he had a trading business and had no clue what they were selling. He convinced her it was all innocent and legal. At some point, he made enough money to buy his own apartment. On the day he moved out of his aunt's apartment, she gave him a box with his late parents' belongings. Maheer moved in with him and one evening they went together through the box. It was full of photos, but there were also several documents. He found a letter with an offer for their old apartment. It was signed by the real estate agent, and his name and address were on it. The mystery surrounding his parents' death had always puzzled him, and he could never let it go. This box unleashed a whole chain of events in his life.

A prickling feeling in his lungs brought him back to the present. He had difficulty breathing. He tried to resist it, but then a gasp drew air deep into his lungs. He felt them contract, and he coughed loudly. He felt a pain stinging in his chest. He tried to clear his throat and spit up some slime. He held his hand in front of his mouth while he continued coughing. After recovering his breath, he looked at his hand. With a tissue, he wiped the blood away. He looked at the clock on the wall and left the room.

He walked through the concrete corridors toward the computer room. As his empire grew, the global network of technology experts working for him grew as well. They all looked at him when he entered the dark room full of computer equipment. As their fierce and ruthless leader, he inspired and impressed his people. With his tall and muscular proportions and the piercing look in his eyes, you could not miss him. Ahmed had not arrived yet. He looked around in the room.

"Who has the memory stick?"

At the back of the room, a Chinese man, with an anxious look in his eyes, raised his hand.

"Over here boss, I'm working on it."

He walked over to him and looked at his screen.

"I understood from Ahmed that the password is difficult to crack."

"Yes, I've tried different ways already, but it uses sophisticated encryption techniques. I'm still trying, although it's starting to look hopeless."

Right at that moment, Ahmed entered the room with several other men. Everybody turned to look at them. They carried the chubby Hakim inside. He looked sick and pale. He barely looked up when they brought him in front of their great leader.

"Hello, Hakim. We finally meet. I'm Abdul."

Hakim raised his head and gazed at the enormous man in front of him. There was the person who had blackmailed and threatened him for so long. He didn't like the look in the man's eyes. It scared the hell out of him, but he felt too faint to react much. Despite his sickness, he could only think of her. He muttered, "Wh… where's my sister?"

"You sister is safe, Hakim."

"You promised to let her go, if I gave you the data."

"Yes, I did. But you didn't give it to me. You gave it to your colleague, and we had to bring him over here as well. We took the memory stick from him, but you've protected it with a password. What is it?"

"I want to see my sister first. Bring her to me."

One of the guards twisted Hakim's arm for the impolite way he addressed his boss.

"That's going to be difficult, Hakim. She isn't here. She never left her home country. Let me get her on the phone for you."

Abdul called someone and said something in Arabic. It was Hakim's mother tongue, so he understood what was being said. Still, he was dumbfounded by what Abdul had just told him. He had assumed she would be at the same location as he, but apparently, she had never left Syria. Abdul stopped speaking and typed something into his phone. A moment later, he put the screen in front of Hakim's face. The moment he saw his sister, he seemed to regain some strength. She looked absolutely terrified. He could see she had been crying.

"Are you all right, Aisha? Did they hurt you?"

"I'm okay. But who are these people? What did you do?"

"Nothing. They want information from me."

Abruptly, Abdul pulled back the phone.

"Enough, chit chat. Now give me the password."

"First let her go."

He seemed to hesitate for a moment, but then Hakim heard him talk in Arabic.

"You can let her go. Leave her in a street close to the center. Call me when you release her and film it for me. Do it now, right away!"

He hung up the phone and looked back at Hakim, who was sweating and pale looking. He still needed Hakim, and it surprised him to see that he was in such a terrible shape. Abdul looked him in the eyes, and Hakim felt terrified. He feared this man could hurt him at any moment. He turned his head and looked at the screen in front of the Chinese man. He could see a message: 'File is password protected'. Below there was a bar with a blinking cursor.

Ten minutes later, Abdul's phone rang. He answered and then showed the screen to Hakim. He saw his sister standing blindfolded in a small alley. In the back, he noticed a large street and recognized the Salah Al Din statue. She was in Damascus in Syria. Suddenly, they told her to take off the blindfold and go. She did not hesitate for a second and rushed into the large, busy street. Hakim felt a wave a relief as he saw her disappear in the crowd in the background. At last, she was safe and unharmed. Then a voice said in Arabic.

"All right boss. We let her go."

Abdul took back the phone.

"Good, now get the hell out of there before the police show up." His piercing eyes turned back to Hakim.

"I kept my part of the bargain. Now tell us the password."

"Can I have a pen and paper?"

Cheng immediately handed them to him. Hakim wrote slowly with a trembling hand and handed the paper back. Cheng entered the password and a directory with files opened. Hakim was sweating more and more, as his fever increased. Abdul noticed.

"Ahmed, didn't I ask you to keep him alive?"

"Yes, he is alive. Isn't he?"

"Barely. Bring him back to his cell and send a doctor to take care of him!"

36.

That Sunday, early in the evening, Elizabeth arrived at the hyper-loop station in Bern. She looked at the screens above her head to check which platform she needed. She couldn't just sit and wait in Lausanne for a breakthrough. It was too stressful. It was better for her to return to work, provide a distraction from her worries. Her father agreed and encouraged her to go. Matteo promised he would follow up with the police in Lausanne. He moved in temporarily with his father. He could use the company. It would help him through this difficult period. This also made Elizabeth feel more comfortable returning to Ikast.

Ten minutes later, she was sitting in the cabin and waited for the departure to Copenhagen. The doors closed with a hiss, and she listened to the safety instructions. On the screen in front of her, she followed the countdown to departure.

"...three, two, one, ignition...pfffoom!"

She sank into her soft chair for several minutes, after which the pressure slowly decreased. Unfortunately, her concerns about Dylan came back right away. She tried to distract herself by selecting a program to watch. She picked a documentary about one of the biggest climate mistakes in the world's history. In the year 2035, everyone realized the global warming problem had completely spun out of control. In the heat of the moment, several billionaires in the United States convinced the desperate government to allow them to create a shield of small sulfate aerosol particles in the stratosphere. It became a historic display of human arrogance and ignorance to geo-engineer the planet. A big gamble gone wrong.

In the run-up to this unfortunate decision, temperatures rose faster than expected, and the amount of climate related disasters increased dramatically. The number of green initiatives skyrocketed as well, but it would take decades before they would have a significant impact. In a global climate of panic, scientists, financed by rich billionaires, proposed a daring project to the American government. They wanted to create a reflective shield in the sky to block sunlight and cool the planet. The government yielded and agreed with the rapid implementation despite enormous international protests and objections.

The year after this decision, planes and rockets injected a vast quantity of sulfate aerosols in the stratosphere. The skies turned white and cloudy around the globe. People had difficulty adapting to the disappearance of blue skies. The only positive note was the appearance of brilliant red colored sunsets. The government launched a marketing campaign in an effort to explain its actions to the rest of the world. Scientists explained on television how this shield was comparable to volcanic eruptions that injected enormous amounts of sulfur dioxide gas into the stratosphere. Carefully presented analogies with the eruption of the Pinatubo in 1991 in the Philippines were used to convince people. They made it sound like a harmless measure, but critics argued that volcanic eruptions probably had triggered the previous five mass extinction events on Earth. Scientists pretended to understand the complex climate interactions and thought they could predict the reflective shield's impact.

The controversy unleashed a heated global debate, and global political tensions surged dramatically. An imminent new world war was averted at the eleventh hour, since that same year temperatures dropped, and the climate cooled down. As a result, some countries even postponed clean energy initiatives. They continued relying longer on carbon-based energy. The lower temperatures were cheered upon, even though the reduction in solar radiation caused by the shield reduced the power generated by solar panels. Initially, it appeared they had successfully bought more time to take adequate measures against global warming.

Sadly, the effect did not last long. Less than two years after the creation of the artificial solar shield, it started dissolving. Global temperatures rose again, and the pace of global warming accelerated. The negative impact was the largest in the regions around the equator. Temperatures rose fast and horrendous droughts plagued those regions. In other areas, the weather became more stagnant. Leading to longer heat waves, longer periods of heavy rainfall or longer dry spells, causing more and larger disasters than ever before. Acid rains increased around the globe. The particles also reacted with the ozone in the stratosphere, creating new holes in the ozone layer. The acidification of the oceans accelerated, disturbing the entire biological chain, from coral reefs right up to humans. Unexpectedly, ground-level ozone and harmful air pollutants increased dramatically. The latter effect triggered a dramatic surge in respiratory illness and hospitalizations.

At the end of the documentary, Elizabeth glanced in front of her, contemplating what she had just seen. In the past, she had already heard about this solar shield. Nevertheless, seeing it all condensed in a program clarified many things. She thought about how Enviro had been one of the first companies to capitalize on this dreadful human failure. They launched their respo business and educated people to protect themselves from the unhealthy air. Life on earth had changed for the worse, although the documentary also clarified that the largest victims were in the regions around the equator. Unfortunately, they were already the poorest regions in the world. The planet was an unfair place where your birthplace determined your future.

The announcement of their imminent arrival shook her out of her thoughts. She strained against her seat belt until they came to a complete stop. She left the cabin and rushed toward her taxi. The journey back to Ikast passed in a haze for her. It felt surreal returning to the apartment without Dylan. When she finally arrived home, the silence inside fell over her like a depressing veil. She called her father to let him know she had arrived, safe and sound. Immediately after, she went to bed, hoping her depression would ease during the night.

The next morning, she woke up feeling tired after another restless night. Every little noise had woken her up, giving her the idle hope that Dylan would just show up at the apartment. After breakfast, she went back to work. The kidnapping of both Hakim and Dylan was the big story. Her colleagues asked her if she knew what had happened to Dylan. While explaining, she realized how horrible the whole situation was. She could barely concentrate on her work. She felt like she had to do something to find Dylan. The only sensible thing she could think of was calling Hawkins to check whether he had made any progress with his task force.

"Hi Miss Muller, how are you?"

"Well, not too well. I'm worried sick about Dylan."

"Yes, I can imagine it must be difficult. I guess you want an update."

"Please."

"Can you drop by after lunch, let's say, around two o'clock. I've got a conference call in half an hour with Henri Favre, so I'll be able to bring you up to date with their latest findings as well."

"Perfect, see you at two."

The rest of the morning, she could finally concentrate on her work. Before she knew it, it was time to go for lunch. Her colleagues picked her up, and they went together to the restaurant. After lunch, she said goodbye and rushed to the other wing of the Enviro complex. She approached her shoulder to the scanner at the door to the security department. The scanner automatically granted her access, since Hawkins had entered her details in the system. Normally she only had access to her own department, Energy Development. She always had found the security measures in the company a bit too extreme, but she knew it was all part of working in a leading technological company.

Elizabeth knocked at the open door of his office to announce her arrival. In front of the window, the slender Hawkins turned his head. He signaled he was about to finish his conversation on the phone. It was only the second time she met in person with Hawkins. The previous time was the year before when she went to thank him in person for his help during her abduction in New York.

After he hung up, he shook her hand and briefly his sleek, serious face showed a friendly smile. They sat down, and Hawkins explained what they had been doing so far. It comforted her that Enviro had set up this task force to investigate the abductions. He explained about how Hakim and Dylan met in Copenhagen, about the prime suspect, Marco Rossi and the involvement of Europol.

"They've issued an international arrest warrant for Marco Rossi, and they've entered his details in the European police system. If he shows up on any camera in European territory, the system will inform Europol immediately."

"And you believe this Marco Rossi is also responsible for kidnapping Dylan?"

"Well, he's involved, that's for sure. We've seen him entering the same black van that was used to abduct both Hakim and Dylan."

"Have the police made any progress with their search for this van?"

"They're still working on it. But there's news. I spoke to Henri Favre earlier today. They had a breakthrough with their analysis of the video footage. They were able to find the black van and identify the new license plate that was used after it crossed the border. They're working closely with the French team now to trace this van using the European police system. Later today or maybe tomorrow he's expecting to tell us more about it."

"And what about the investigation on the site where they found Dylan's chip?"

"The police of Marseille analyzed all the video material from the streets around the warehouse where they found the chip. They've got several clues about where to look for Dylan and Hakim. They sent me their analysis this morning. I can show it to you."

He gestured to indicate she should come and have a look at his screen.

"This is a camera from the street in front of the warehouse. It's dark already but you can still clearly see the black van arriving. We've compared the timing with the location data from the chip in Dylan's arm and they coincide. We believe Dylan was most likely inside this van. More than an hour later, a truck with a large container left the warehouse, followed by the black van. After that, there was no more activity. We didn't see any other cars or people in front of it until the police of Marseille arrived at the site."

"So, Dylan was either transported away from the warehouse in the dark van or in the truck."

"Exactly. At the entrance of the harbor of Marseille, another camera picked up the same truck, but without the van this time. Here we have a clear image from the driver of the truck. They ran his photo through the police database. It's Farid Ben-Chaib, a French citizen who served a ten-year sentence in prison for armed robbery. Next to him we have James Rook, an Irishman without a criminal record. Europol has issued international arrest warrants for both men. About half an hour later, they were seen leaving the harbor in the same truck, but without the container."

"Do they think Dylan was inside the container?"

"It's one of the possibilities."

"Ah, what are the other possibilities, then?"

"It's possible that they've transported him out of the warehouse in the black van. There's even a third possibility, although it's the least likely one. They could have moved him out by climbing over the fence in the back. Unfortunately, there's no way of checking this since there are no cameras there."

"Okay, and do they know where this black van went?"

"Yes, they do. They've traced the license plate of the truck. It was rented by this James Rook from a company located in one of the industrial zones around Marseille. From the video footage of the rental company, we found that after dropping off the containers at the harbor, they went there to return the truck. James Rook entered the rental office and then returned outside. There he entered the same black van together with Farid Ben-Chaib. The van later popped up several times on cameras along the road all the way into Spain, where they were last spotted close to Figueres several days after shipping the container. Unfortunately, here we've lost track of them. The police believe either they switched the license plates again or they took the smaller roads into the mountains avoiding all cameras."

"So, if I understand well, Dylan is most likely either inside a container in the harbor in Marseille or somewhere in Spain in this black van. What if they dropped him off somewhere else on the way?"

"Yes, that's also possible. I hope not, though. Since then, it'll be extremely hard to find him," Hawkins replied, and caught a glimpse of her despairing face.

"We have to stay positive. The police are actually convinced that Dylan was most likely transported away inside that container."

"But why do they believe that?"

"Well, because we believe there is a link between the abductions of Hakim and Dylan and they have something to do with Enviro. A day after Hakim's abduction in Copenhagen, the police found images of this black van entering the same warehouse in Marseille. Again, a while after, they saw the dark van leaving, followed by a truck with a container. At the entrance of the harbor, they've spotted the truck, and it left the harbor afterwards without the container. Exactly like with Dylan."

"Yes, that's quite a coincidence. Were they able to trace the containers?"

"They were able to identify the numbers on both containers. They loaded them onto different ships on different days, but both had the same destination."

"The same destination? Where did they ship them to?"

"Both to the harbor of Algiers in Africa."

"Africa!? Oh my god!"

37.

Elliot left the Defense department slightly puzzled. While he walked to the West section, he thought about the investigation Mary had mentioned. Why was his father being investigated? He had worked faithfully and hard for the Defense department for as long as he could remember, and his record had been nothing short of exemplary. What had he done wrong? It did not fit his father, who had always followed the rules of the community. Was that the reason he ended his life?

A moment later, he arrived at the elevator, and the doors automatically opened. He stepped inside and addressed the control panel.

"To minus seven."

The doors closed, and he felt his stomach as the elevator descended fast. He took the key out of his pocket and looked at it, wondering if it would help him answer his questions. The doors opened, and he peered into a dark corridor. He tucked the key back in his pocket, stepped into the darkness and looked around as the lights went on automatically. It was chilly, colder than at the Defense department. He walked to the end where there was a T-junction. He went right, and twenty meters later, the corridor ended. There was a metal door, but no control panel nor any indications. He noticed a sensor, and he waved his hand in front of it. Nothing happened. He put his face in front of the sensor. Still nothing. He took the key out of his pocket, but there was no keyhole. He held it in front of the sensor. Nothing happened.

Puzzled, he decided to try the other direction and walked back to the T-junction. It was completely silent. He only heard his own footsteps. The eerie atmosphere stressed him out. The cold air did not help either. In the other corridor, he continued all the way to the end, where there was another metal door. There was some sort of control panel next to it this time, much smaller than the one at the Defense department. The panel had a small dark screen and below it a gray metal button with a question mark on it. He moved his face in front of the screen, but nothing happened. Slightly annoyed, he pushed the button. A few seconds after, he heard a voice.

"How can I help you?"

"I'd like to enter the locker room."

"Access is only possible with a key."

"I have a key."

"To open the door, hold your key in front of the screen."

Elliot took the key out of his pocket and followed the instruction. He heard a click and the metal door slid sideways open with a hiss. There was a long corridor behind it with dozens of doors on either side. The deserted place gave him a creepy feeling. He walked further until he heard a hiss behind him. He turned his head and saw the door had closed. He wondered for a moment what would happen if he got stuck down here. Then he looked back at the rows of doors. Each one was marked with a letter, and here there were keyholes. He continued until arriving at the door marked with a D. He pushed the key in the keyhole. A clicking sound and the door slid open sideways.

Another long corridor. Here there were two rows of lockers on each side. They were all numbered, and each had a keyhole below the number. It was as chilly here as on the rest of this floor. Elliot checked the number on the key, then started advancing through the hallway. He heard the entry door close behind him. About thirty meters further, he arrived at number 387. His heart started pounding as he stuck the key in the keyhole and heard a beep. The door clicked open. He opened it further and peered curiously inside.

A large gray box filled more than half the dark locker's interior. He carried it out and put it on the ground carefully. It was heavy. He checked the locker to make sure he had missed nothing, but there was nothing else inside. He opened the box and there were several smaller boxes inside. He took them out, one by one, and placed them on the ground. Under the boxes he saw a thick pile of documents. There were no tables or chairs anywhere in the corridor. He hesitated for a moment, but then he crouched next to the large box and opened one of the small boxes. It was full of photos. He took one out and looked at it. His father and mother were standing in front of a beautiful palace. Thanks to his history classes at secondary school, he recognized the palace immediately. It was the Taj Mahal. His parents looked young, and his mother looked stunning. They looked in love.

Quickly, he checked the other boxes. They all contained photos. This was going to take some time. He started shivering in the cold. After hesitating for a moment, he put everything back in the large box. He closed the empty locker and lifted the heavy box using both arms. He walked back through the long corridor. When he approached the door at the end it did not open. He put the box down and put the key in the keyhole. It opened with a hiss. He continued further and repeated the same ritual at the next door.

Happy to leave the chilling corridors behind, he made his way back as quickly as he could to the elevator with the heavy box. He went back to his apartment. Out of breath with cramps in his arms and a terrible thirst, he opened the front door and put everything on the large table in the living room. He grabbed a glass of cold water.

Then he opened the box and took out all the smaller boxes and the thick pile of documents. The empty box he put on the floor to make more space on the table. He sat down and opened one of the smaller boxes marked 'Susan'. He took all the photos out and looked at them one by one. There were pictures of his mother when she was young. In the first picture his mother was posing together with a dozen of other nurses, all in light-green uniform. He turned the picture over and looked at the back. In pencil was written 'New Delhi, October 2021'. His mother was then twenty-two years old. She looked beautiful, and Elliot understood why his father had fallen in love with her.

As he continued going through the pile of photos, he felt a strong feeling of love and affection for her. It touched him deeply to see his mother when she was young. She was an adorable little girl. There was even a picture from the year 1999 of her as a newborn. Her parents looked so proud and happy next to her. In between the photos, he found a birth announcement card. He looked at the name on the card: Tanvi. It was the first time he saw his mother's name from before she moved into the dome. His parents had never spoken about their original names. He had only known her by the name of Susan. All those years, they had kept this a secret. It felt so strange to learn the truth now they were both no longer there.

Slowly, he went through the pile of photos and looked at them in detail. Not only did he learn about his mother's youth and family, but also about the outside world from the year 1999 till the year 2029. The cars, the houses, nature, all the background details fascinated him. His mother had been quite poor, especially when she was young. He wished he would have spoken more about it with his parents.

He put the photos back in their box and opened the box labeled 'Amos'. In one of the more recent pictures, his father posed with a bottle of sanitizer in his hand in front of a large machine inside a factory. He stood proudly in between other staff members. On the back side, it was written 'Management team, SaniCorp, Bangkok, 2020'. There were many more pictures with his father at different companies. His father had told him in the past that he had owned many companies and made a fortune investing. Still, it fascinated him to see his father in all those pictures.

He sifted through the pile and there were more and more pictures of his father's childhood. Amos also came from a poor family. It left a deep impression on Elliot as the photos showed how his father had started poor and slowly grew richer, building his wealth step by step. It felt unreal to see how much he resembled his father when he was young. Eventually, he arrived at the baby pictures and found his father's birth announcement card as well. His birth name was 'Vikram', born in the year 1979. He was a cute baby and his parents looked so happy with him.

After going through this pile, he put them back in the box and got up. He finished his water and was still thirsty. He prepared himself some green tea and then returned to the living room. He opened the next box, but there was nothing written on the lid this time. It was full of pictures of his parents together. Beautiful pictures of them on holidays on tropical islands. Pictures of them dressed up for parties. There were so many pictures that he did not realize how the time was flying by.

He moved to the next small box, and he got even more exhilarated by what he saw. His mother was pregnant now and showed a large belly. Both his parents looked so happy in the photos and his mother looked radiant. Fascinated, he went through the pile until he suddenly saw his mother in the hospital. He could not believe his eyes and he looked at the mind-blowing picture that overwhelmed him. How was this possible? They had never told him anything.

38.

After picking up James and Farid, they left the Marseille region and drove westward through the darkness toward their hideout. They had ample time to reach their ultimate destination in order to assist their boss in the next step of his grand plan. A couple of hours later, they left the highway and drove toward the small house on the outskirts of Perpignan in the south of France.

Ten minutes later, James got out of the van to open the old metal gate. They parked the van inside the small courtyard. Marco felt more at ease now that they had arrived here. Nobody could see the van with the walls all around them. He opened the wooden front door of the neglected house. Inside, all the furniture was covered with white sheets against the dust. He immediately climbed the squeaky wooden stairs.

"I'm exhausted. See you all tomorrow morning."

"Yeah, I'm going to bed as well," replied Romano, his loyal righthand.

"Good night, boss. I'm first going to open one of those wine bottles. I could use a drink. You want a glass of wine, Farid?" James asked as he grabbed the bottle of red wine on the table.

"Yes, I'm bloody thirsty," Farid answered while he took a white sheet off the couch in the living room.

Marco continued to one of the bedrooms on the first floor. He locked the door behind him and looked around in the bare room. He removed the protective cover from the bed and dusted off the nightstand next to it. He hung his jacket in the corner and took the holster of his gun off and put it on his nightstand. The nights before, he had not slept much. Finally, he was going to sleep in a normal bed. Still, he could not help thinking back to the last few days. He had an uncomfortable feeling. They had taken too many risks. However, it was not like he had much choice. Disappointing his boss was not an option.

While lying on the soft bed, he touched the cross hanging on his necklace. It had been his father's and was the only physical memory he had of him. He died when Marco was sixteen years old and despite his mother's efforts to keep him on the right path; he still followed in his footsteps. His mother warned him over and over about the downsides of a life like his father's. He knew well that his father had paid with his life for his illegal activities. Despite it all, he had rolled into this life, which seemed to fit him like a glove.

After his mother's death, he ramped up his illegal activities. She had died young, like most people nowadays. A mere consequence of climate change and another reason he felt he should not worry too much. If his life was going to be short anyway, he preferred to live it on the edge. He thought back to how he had started out trading stolen goods in his childhood and extorting other kids in the slums of Naples, where he was born. He and Romano were already working together, but he always was the more ambitious one. He later expanded his activities to arms trade, human trafficking, drugs trade and extortion, just to name a few. His network grew and relatively quickly he became one of the most important criminal leaders in Italy.

He first got in contact with his current boss, Abdul, through his human trafficking activities. Abdul was already one of the major global players in that field, and he started working increasingly with him. They made quite a bit of money together, and slowly he became part of Abdul's inner circle. Abdul involved him in most of his European activities and Marco was raking in the money. His current activities for Abdul were different somehow. He understood they were really important to him and acted accordingly. He didn't know the entire plan, though he knew Abdul was planning something big. So far, he had done well, but he had to be careful not to make any mistakes.

The following days, they stayed in the house, maintaining a low profile. They took turns buying groceries and went into town as little as possible. Whoever went into town wore one of the older respo models, which had the advantage of covering part of the face. After a few days, they began to act on one another's nerves. Marco was glad to hear his boss had successfully recovered the chip so they could proceed further south into Spain for the next part of their plan.

Just after sunset, they left their hideout and continued south on the highway. After less than an hour of driving, they crossed the Spanish border. No border controls. Marco slowly started to feel he might have worried too much. Still, he preferred to be too careful, as it had brought him this far in his career. They ran out of cigarettes and left the highway at Figueres. They pulled over at the first shop they found open. He looked at the others in the van.

"I'll get cigarettes for everyone. Anything else you need?"

"Maybe a bottle of Coke."

"Okay. Make sure you all stay in the van and out of sight of the cameras."

"All right, chief!"

Marco stepped outside and entered the shop. Except for the shop owner, it was completely empty. He grabbed a large bottle of Coke and ordered a large box of cigarettes at the counter. Just behind it, a television screen was showing a news broadcast. While paying at the counter, he suddenly froze. His heart started pounding in his chest as he saw a picture of himself on the screen next to the pictures of Farid and James. Then he saw a video of their black van leaving the warehouse in Marseille. The heat in the shop bothered him more, and he started sweating. At least he had put the old respo on his face. The shop owner did not seem to recognize him. He paid and left.

Outside, he rushed to the van and took the seat next to the driver. He yelled at James.

"Drive! Let's get the hell out of here. We've got a major problem."

James started the van and drove away. They all looked at Marco, waiting for him to explain himself. Marco focused on the road, though.

"Turn right here."

He guided them out of Figueres heading west toward the mountains. After leaving town, he turned to them.

"They're searching for us. In the shop, the television showed pictures of me, Farid, and James on the news. They also know about our van."

"What about me?" Romano asked.

"Nothing about you. I think we should get rid of this van as quick as possible and we should be really careful from now on. There're cameras everywhere nowadays."

They continued along a deserted mountain road away from the city lights behind them. They switched their route constantly until Marco peered at a faint light in the distance.

"James, why don't you drive to those lights over there? It looks like a farm. Let's have a look."

They left the main road and entered a small dirt road. James turned off the lights, and they drove slowly through the darkness. About a kilometer farther, they could clearly see the lit farmyard.

There were three barns and a main house. The lights inside were all out. As they approached the first barn, a dog came running to their van, barking loudly. Romano got up.

"Let me take care of the dog."

He took something that looked like cookies from a cupboard in the back, and he opened the side-door just enough to throw the cookies. The dog immediately started sniffing and swallowed them. Then it continued searching for more, but at some point, it slowly rolled over on the floor. They all looked at the dog passing out, and Romano opened the side-door again.

"It should be safe now."

They got out and started walking toward the barns. Marco opened the first one and looked inside.

"Perfect," he whispered to Farid, who was standing next to him.

There were two tractors, several agricultural machines, and next to the tractors, a white van. They walked up to it and tried to open the door.

"It's not locked, perfect. Let's try to find the keys somewhere."

Farid searched in the van while Marco looked in the barn. James, who was keeping watch outside, whistled. Marco went outside, and James pointed in the direction of the house next to the barn. On the first floor, the lights were now on. Marco whistled at Romano and gestured to follow him.

"Stay here and keep watch. We'll take care of this," he whispered to James. Then he walked toward the house, with Romano right behind him.

Meanwhile, Farid had found a key locker in the small office in the barn's corner. He broke it open and found several keys. He tried them all until he found the right one. He started the engine and drove outside, then parked next to their old van. Together with James, they moved all their equipment to their new vehicle. At some point, Romano and Marco came back. James looked at them and then at the house. All the lights were out now.

"No problem, they won't disturb us."

They continued transferring all their belongings. When they finished, James drove the black van into the barn all the way to the back. While James and Farid cleaned and disinfected the inside of the black van, Marco discussed the route with Romano. An hour later, they left the farmyard. They drove further west using minor roads only. After a couple of hours, they turned south. Marco stared out into the night, contemplating all the recent events. They had to be careful now.

They drove all night long, stopping as little as possible. They took turns driving while the others slept. By the time the sun rose, they were passing through the deserts in the south of Spain. Most of the small towns were deserted because life had become too difficult in this region. People had moved to the larger cities. Eventually, they arrived in Granada and stopped at a large shopping center.

"All right, let's make this as short as possible. Romano, you're the only one whose face hasn't been on the news. So, you go buy us a couple of wigs, hats, sunglasses and some products to dye our hair. I mean their hair, since I've nothing to dye. And anything else to change our appearance. Clear?"

"Yep, no problem."

Three quarters of an hour later, he returned with two large bags. Romano wiped the sweat off his forehead when he entered the driver's seat.

"Jesus, it is early in the morning and already bloody hot here."

Quickly, he started the engine and drove away. Now they continued through the back roads until they arrived at their next hideout, a small white house on the outskirts of Granada. Romano stepped outside to open the gate, and then they parked within the white walls of the property.

Inside, they took the white sheets off the furniture and James immediately turned the air conditioner on at maximum power. After lunch, they changed their clothes and looks. Farid shaved off his beard and mustache and dyed his dark brown hair light blonde. He put some fake glasses on and returned to the living room. He walked straight to Marco, showing his light blond hair.

"How do I look?"

"Perfect, Farid. Like a different person."

Marco tried out a wig with medium length black hair. It felt warm on his head, and he was not used to the heat. He looked in the mirror and smiled. He smiled even more when James entered the room. He had completely shaved off his shoulder length red hair. He had even shaved off his red mustache, and he looked like a totally different person. Romano stood laughing behind James with the razor he used to shave James's hair still in his hand. Romano was happy he did not have to change anything, as he was quite proud of his long, dark brown hair, which he always wore in a tail. They laughed until at some point Farid asked,

"All right, boss. What's next for us?"

Marco took off the wig, which was already making his head sweat. He hung it over the empty vase on the coffee table in the living room. He dropped himself into the comfortable leather armchair in front of the television. Then he looked briefly at Farid while he turned it on.

"We just wait and maintain a low profile until Abdul calls us with our next assignment."

39.

When the guards carried Hakim back to the prison cell, he looked pale and was sweating heavily. They put him on his mattress and walked back toward the door. Hakim started shaking all over and clearly had a high fever. Dylan looked worried at his friend and then at the armed guards who were about to close the door behind them.

"Wait!"

The guards looked annoyed at him, wondering what he wanted.

"Could we get some aspirin for him, or maybe a doctor? He looks really sick."

"We will be back soon," one of the guards said.

They left and locked the heavy door. Dylan looked at Omar, who also looked worried.

"Let's get his temperature down. Could you pass me one of those towels?"

Omar handed it to him, and Dylan poured water on it from the tap in the bathroom. The water was brown and smelled bad. Still, it was colder than the bottled drinking water. He wiped Hakim's face with the wet towel and then put it on his forehead. Hakim opened his eyes for a moment. A faint smile appeared on his face before he passed out. Dylan checked his pulse and breathing. Then he looked at Omar.

"He's sleeping. I guess it's better like this, but I'm really worried about him. Without medication he could die in here."

Hakim did not hear his friend anymore. He was running in a field with high grass. His sister was running next to him, smiling in the sunlight under the blue sky. He grabbed her hand and felt lighter and lighter. Her long, dark hair waved in the wind. They both floated above the green field now, higher and higher. On his right, he noticed his parents sitting on a garden swing. They both waved to them as they flew over the trees. The light became brighter and brighter. It blinded him.

The doctor was shining a flashlight in his eye, and he couldn't help blinking. His dark face was close to his as he examined him. Dylan and Omar were standing behind the doctor and looking at him with concern. The doctor asked them for help to take off his shirt. He examined the swollen and gaping wound on his shoulder. A deep hole in the middle surrounded by swollen, half-burned skin. Yellow puss came out of the side, and the doctor started cleaning it. With a scalpel, he took out several remaining pieces of the burned chip. Blood mixed with the puss on his shoulder while the doctor cleaned the wound.

Meanwhile, Dylan explained to Omar about the chip. He explained that all employees had those chips. He showed him the cut on his shoulder when he told him that his abductors had removed his chip as well. It surprised Omar that employees accepted to be tagged like this. Dylan tried to defend it, explaining the advantages to him. Their conversation was interrupted by the doctor, who asked Omar to pass him the roll of bandage. While Omar helped the doctor dress the wound, Dylan stared at the doctor's neck. On the back of it, there was a neatly cut scar, and he had the impression there was a slight bump under it.

"What is that strange bump in your neck, doctor?" Dylan asked him.

The doctor glanced at him and seemed embarrassed. He moved the collar of his white coat higher over his neck to cover the bump.

"Ah, nothing special."

Dylan looked puzzled at the doctor. He did not insist further though, since he was happy someone was finally trying to heal his friend. After taking care of the wound, the doctor set up a drip and cannulated Hakim. Next to the mattrass he posed a metal stand, and he hung a bag of liquid on the hook. Apparently, the infection and fever had dehydrated Hakim severely. A few days longer and he would have died for sure.

The next day Dylan woke up sweaty. It was warm and there was a horrible smell. A damp mixture of sweat and urine. The result of too many men packed together in this small, hot space. He got up from his dirty mattress and checked on Hakim. He was still sleeping, but looked slightly better. He took a bottle of water from the table next to the door and drank deeply. When he turned around, he noticed Hakim was waking up.

"Morning, buddy. How are you feeling?"

"Morning. I still feel weak, but my shoulder hurts less."

"Good to hear. You looked so sick I thought you were going to die. Where did they take you yesterday?"

"They took me to their boss, a guy called Abdul."

"Abdul? Is he the one behind our abductions?"

"Yes, he's some kind of gang boss. Mean-looking fellow."

Omar, who overheard them talking, approached them.

"He's called Abdul Jabbar. Sudanese born, but raised in Egypt. He's a ruthless killer and a crime lord. They suspect him of heading a global organization involved in all kinds of crimes like human trafficking, prostitution, weapons trade, extortion, smuggling and fraud."

"Wow, a big shot. I guess the police are after him?"

"Well, he has been suspected of many things, but up till now no one was able to prove his involvement."

"Amazing, you would think that in this time of surveillance with our modern police force a criminal like that should be caught quickly."

"Yes, but Abdul is not a normal criminal. Apparently, he's extremely smart and they say he has a powerful grip on the police force in North Africa. I guess he must pay them well. They also say that all his men are extremely loyal and nobody rats on him. The few who did are dead."

The click of the lock interrupted their conversation. Two guards entered and looked around until they pointed at Dylan.

"You! Come with us!"

Dylan gave Hakim and Omar an anxious look and then left with the heavily armed guards. They tied his hands behind his back with tie-wraps. He looked back at the prison cell and he figured it had probably been a storage room before. It was located in an old, run-down underground parking garage. The rest of this floor was full of parked vans and trucks, and he saw several armed people walking around. It was as hot here as inside, but without the foul smells. The guards guided him to the stairwell and down the stairs. The temperature decreased the lower they went. The guard in front of him had a scar on his neck and a slight bump under it, just like the doctor. The buzzing noise he heard outside his prison cell was getting louder.

Two levels lower, they left the staircase, and he heard a mix of chatter and background noises. An overwhelming noise came his way as they entered the next level. Down here, the garage was packed with people. It shocked him to see this massive crowd. Makeshift partitions split the old parking spaces into compartments. The self-made rooms were full of people. In the corridors, there were groups of men and woman talking and trading together. It was vibrating with life. It was still warm, but much less than on the higher levels. Hundreds and hundreds of people gathered together.

The guards guided him through the crowd, and several people stared at him as he passed. He saw women and men of all skin colors and ages. Inside one of the compartments, he noticed several children. All of a sudden, he lost his balance as he tripped over a metal threshold. With his hands tied behind his back, he turned his head and shoulder sideways in a reflex to avoid a frontal impact on the floor. Just when he was about to hit the pavement, he felt two firm hands under his shoulders. He looked up. A friendly, dark brown man with a vigorous look had caught him and was helping him to get up.

"Watch your steps, you could have hurt yourself."

"Thanks, sir. I'm Dylan."

"You're welcome, Dylan. I'm Ebo."

The guards yelled in Arabic at the man and he backed away, frightened. The guard pushed Dylan hard to continue walking. He turned his head one more time to look at the kind man, but he was already walking away. Again, he noticed a scar with a bump on his neck. The guard shouted in his ear and pushed Dylan's head hard in front of him.

"Walk! No talking!"

They continued all the way to the back of the garage. At the end, there was a heavy metal door with two armed guards standing next to it. The guards escorting him spoke in Arabic to them and they opened the door. They entered and Dylan wondered where the hell they were taking him. One guard walked in front of him and one behind. They walked through the maze of corridors and Dylan looked around while they were passing several doors. Most doors were closed, but when he passed an open one, he peeked inside.

Several men were sitting behind computer screens in a faintly lit room. He wondered what they were doing, but the guard behind him pushed him forward. He pushed hard, and Dylan almost tripped again. They turned several times into different corridors until they arrived at a large black door with two armed men standing guard next to it. Again, they spoke in Arabic and then they opened the black door.

The office behind it looked different from what he had seen in the previous rooms. It was relatively dark. Walls painted burgundy red. In the middle there was a large wenge desk with wooden ornaments. An enormous man with dark brown hair in a tail in the back was sitting behind it. He glimpsed briefly at Dylan and then turned his chair and looked the other way, continuing his conversation on the phone in Arabic.

Not being able to understand much, Dylan looked around in the office while waiting next to the two guards. As he turned his head to the right, he could not believe his eyes. No, that just could not be possible, he thought as he looked at the large, dark painting on the wall. He checked all the details and, to his surprise, it looked really authentic. Abdul noticed him staring at the painting while he was talking on the phone. When he finally hung up, he looked at Dylan, who was gawking, fascinated.

"Hello Dylan, welcome to my humble office. I'm Abdul," he said in a loud voice, pulling him out of his thoughts.

Dylan abruptly turned his head back to look at him, still with an astonished look on his face.

"Is that the real one?"

Abdul smiled now, clearly enjoying this.

"Yes, it is. Nice, huh?"

"But that's worth a fortune. I thought it was hanging in the Louvre in Paris?"

"I can see you haven't followed the art news the past few years."

Dylan remembered that there had been something on the news several years ago. During the great flood of Paris, some thieves stole several famous art works from the Louvre. The Seine had burst its banks after a heavy month of rain, and a large part of Paris went under water.

"Ah, yeah, I remember there was a burglary at the Louvre."

Abdul nodded.

"Exactly, the poor thieves didn't realize how difficult it is to sell stolen masterpieces like this on the market. They had no one to sell it to, so I had a great deal. It's not every day you can buy 'The Raft of Medusa'."

"Amazing," Dylan replied, still staring in disbelief at the impressive painting.

"It's a masterpiece. I guess you know the story behind it?"

"Something about a shipwreck of some French naval frigate?"

"Yes, the frigate 'Méduse', which ran aground off the coast of Mauritania in 1816. It set adrift hundred fifty people on a hastily constructed raft. They floated for thirteen days on the open seas and endured starvation and dehydration. In their struggle for survival, the crazed and parched sailors slaughtered mutineers and then ate their dead companions. A dramatic struggle, beautifully depicted by the French painter, Théodore Géricault. Magnificent to see how he painted men rendered as broken and in utter despair. It reminds me of the desperate attempts of refugees trying to reach the richer countries."

“I see what you mean.”

“I guess you know why I had to take you out of your easy and luxurious life. You refused to hand over something that was meant for me. A stupid and regrettable move. Anyway, now that you’re here, we’d better make the best of it. I understand you’re an engineer with an expert knowledge of environmental technology. I want you to fix my air conditioning system and improve the air filtration. I want to breathe clean and cool air. Do you think you can do that?”

Dylan looked at the air conditioner unit on the ceiling and nodded to the large man in front of him. The look in his eyes, a mixture of determination, evil, and ruthlessness, gave Dylan a bad feeling.

“I guess with the proper tools that should be possible.”

Abdul looked at the guard next to Dylan and tapped his hand on the desk.

“Great. Alex, you can detach his hands. If he tries to escape, you just shoot him. You stay with Dylan at all times. If he needs any tools or parts, make sure he gets them. Understood?”

“Yes, sir,” Alex replied, and cut the tie-wraps around Dylan’s wrists with a large knife from his back pocket.

“Okay, get to work then.”

The guards escorted him out of the room. Outside, the guard called Alex gestured him to follow him, while the other one stayed behind. They walked through the maze of corridors until they arrived in front of another room. It looked like a large storage room, long rows of racks filled with boxes. Out of a cupboard in the corner, the guard took a metal toolbox and gave it to Dylan. It was heavy, and he had to carry it with two hands. The guard picked up a stepladder, and then they returned to the office.

When they entered, Abdul was talking on the phone again. Dylan tried to listen. He didn’t understand Arabic, but managed to understand the occasional word. While the guard posed the stepladder under the air conditioner unit, Dylan put the toolbox on the floor. He thought he overheard him say 'Omar'. Then a moment later, he heard the word 'deal'. Abdul almost seemed enthusiastic. This was one of those moments he wished he had learned Arabic. Then Abdul hung up, and with his imposing figure, he got up from his chair.

"Okay, Alex. I've got to go for a moment, keep an eye on our prisoner."

"I will, boss."

He rushed out. Dylan looked at the air conditioner and then looked around in the office. The moment he spotted it, he walked to the large desk and reached out his hand toward the laptop on the desk. The guard reacted immediately and kicked his hand away from it. It hurt his hand, and Dylan looked shocked at him.

"I just wanted to grab the remote control of the air conditioner unit. I need to check what's wrong with it."

"Next time, you ask me first. Okay?" the guard said in an aggressive tone and handed him the remote control.

Dylan climbed the stepladder and started testing the air conditioner while wondering what Abdul had been so excited about. What deal had he just made?

40.

Stunned, Elliot held the picture of his mother in his hands. He could not believe it. On the back of the picture, he saw the name of the hospital in New Delhi, with a date next to it. It was his date of birth. She was lying in a hospital bed. There were two babies in her arms. She smiled with a happy but exhausted look on her face. His father sat next to her on a white stool. How could this be? He sifted through the stack of photos, and they all confirmed it. He had a twin brother. Why had they never told him about it? What had happened to his brother after birth? So many questions ran through his head. It dazzled him.

Confused, he got up and walked to the kitchen to prepare another cup of tea. The thoughts kept flowing through his head. The only logical explanation was that his brother had died after birth. In that case, he could imagine his parents did not find it necessary to tell him about it. He sat back down at the table in the living room with a cup of green tea and picked up the next photo from the pile. More baby photos of him and his brother. After putting the last photo back on the table, he opened the last box of photos.

The first picture he took out showed his mother holding a baby on a terrace overlooking a city. He immediately recognized the skyline. It was New York City. Another picture showed his father with the baby. He searched through the stack, but this time, there was only one baby in the pictures. He checked the dates, and most photos were from a couple of months after his birth in New Delhi. He also found photos of them in front of the dome, next to the outer wall on a bus. Every time there was only one baby, so maybe he was right that his brother died right after birth.

It was getting late, and he felt hungry. He looked at the thick pile of documents, wondering if it would provide any answers to his questions. The doorbell rang. It was Elsa.

"My parents ask if you want to join us for dinner?"

"I'd love to. I'm starving," he responded, and gave her a kiss.

She looked over his shoulder and noticed the full table in the living room.

"Busy day?"

"Yeah, quite a day. Apparently, my father had a locker. That box was inside."

They walked toward the table in the living room, and Elliot explained what he had found out so far. He started by showing her just a few photos, but she was so fascinated that they ended up going through most of them. An hour later, she got startled when her phone rang. She looked anxiously at the time before answering.

"Hi Mom, yeah I'm sorry. We completely lost track of time. Elliot found photos of his parents. I'll tell you at dinner. Yes, we're coming right away."

She hung up and got up.

"Let's go, Elliot. They're waiting for us. These photos are amazing."

She glanced at the pile of documents.

"Anything interesting in there?"

"I didn't get to it yet. Maybe after dinner."

They rushed out to her apartment. Elliot had lost track of time going through the photos, but now he felt hungry. The dinner was a welcome distraction. Elsa's parents had been very supportive and kind after his father's death. They were both scientists in the medical science field. Her father had specialized in genetic engineering, and her mother was a research expert in bio-gerontology, or the study of the biological basis of aging and age-related diseases. Elliot's father used to joke that thanks to Elsa's mother, they all looked younger.

After dinner, he thanked her parents and returned to his apartment with Elsa. Since his father's death, they were practically living together. Her company helped him tremendously during this troubled time. He slept much better next to her than when he was alone. She went to prepare some green tea for both of them, while Elliot moved the pile of documents to the front of the table. Maybe he was going to find an answer to all his questions surrounding his mother's and father's death.

He read slowly through the pages. Elsa had offered to help, but he preferred to go through the documents by himself. She sat on the couch behind him, reading a book. He learned more and more about his late parents' life. His parents had owned a large and diverse portfolio of investments, but they sold almost everything in the year 2029, the year he was born. Reading through a deed of transfer, he found out that they used to own a large estate in New Delhi, which they also sold that same year. Skimming through the documents, his eye suddenly fell on a document.

"That's interesting. Come and look! Birth certificates."

Elsa got up and walked toward him, and looked over his shoulder.

"It looks like they're from me and my twin brother. Look at the dates."

Elsa moved closer and sat next to Elliot now, who showed her the certificates.

"Look at the names. Yagnesh and Ikbal. Both born in New Delhi on seven of April in the year 2029. I wonder which name was mine."

"Your father never told you your birth name?"

"No, my father was always so strict about the rules. I've asked him several times, but he insisted that all that mattered to me was the name I got when I entered the dome."

"And your mother, she didn't tell you anything?"

"Well, she probably would have, if I had asked her. But I was too young at the time and never did. I didn't even know at the time that people who were born outside got a different name when entering the dome."

He looked further into the pile until suddenly he looked astounded at one of the documents.

"I guess I was wrong."

Elsa looked puzzled at him.

"Well, I assumed my twin brother had died just after birth, but I was wrong. They gave him up for adoption."

He showed her the adoption papers. She looked dumbfounded.

"Yagnesh. So that means your original name was Ikbal."

"Yes. But I don't understand why they gave him up for adoption. It looks like they were extremely wealthy, so why give away your child?"

"Strange, yeah."

Elliot continued searching through the remaining documents and reading everything as fast as he could. Meanwhile, Elsa looked at the documents he had already read. At some point, Elliot said,

"Jesus, that can't be."

He read the letter with intense focus until he raised his head and looked at her.

"Look at this. It's an official reaction from the Council to a request from my parents to join the dome together with their twins. Here it says: The fee you have paid for your entry into the dome is only for three people. We understand you do not have sufficient funds for a fourth person. Unfortunately, we cannot simply waive this additional fee, as it would be unfair to all other future habitants of the dome. Unless you pay the additional fee before the stated deadline, we can only grant access to three persons."

Elsa looked shocked now as she understood the implications.

"What a horrible dilemma."

"You can say that. Well, it explains why they gave one of us up for adoption."

He continued going through the remaining documents until he found one that made him gasp.

"What?" Elsa asked.

"Look. The story gets even more shocking."

He pointed at a line in the adoption papers.

"Udayan Ghar orphanage? That's where they gave Yagnesh up for adoption to."

"Yes, now look at this press clipping."

He gave her a printed-out article with a photo of the Delhi police in front of a building next to what looked like a pile of body bags.

"Oh no," she exclaimed while reading the article.

"Yes, what horrible news. I can understand now why my mother got so depressed. Look at the dates. It all starts to make sense."

"Eleventh of August 2039," Elsa read out loud.

"My mother committed suicide in the winter of that same year. That can't be a coincidence."

"How horrible. Because of a power failure, the air conditioning stopped working. Apparently, all the children in the orphanage died during this heatwave that they called the deadliest one ever. During this heatwave wet-bulb temperatures rose above the limit of thirty-five degrees Celsius. At this temperature, humans can no longer cool themselves off by sweating and then the body overheats, leading to organ failure and death within several hours."

"My poor brother," Elliot mumbled with watery eyes.

Elsa put her arms around him to console him. She also got tears in her eyes. She was tired and proposed to go to bed. They put everything back in the large box.

Half an hour later, Elliot lay in bed. Elsa held him while resting her head against his chest. She fell asleep quickly. The warm body against him comforted him, yet his head remained filled with too many thoughts. He contemplated all the things he had learned that day. He now understood why his mother had taken her own life, but why had his father never explained all this to him? Many other questions raced through his head. Why had his father killed himself now? The horrible loss of their child had been so long ago. It made little sense to him. And why was Internal Affairs investigating him?

41.

Elizabeth was stirring in a pan with her homemade vegetable soup in the kitchen. Her thoughts wandered the whole time. Every night when she returned from work to their apartment, feelings of hopelessness and despair overwhelmed her. She worried about Dylan constantly, especially since learned that they may have taken him to North-Africa. She had never been to Africa, but what she knew about it was not good. The continent had been one of the biggest victims of climate change.

Over the years, multiple droughts struck the continent. Average temperatures in most African countries increased dramatically faster than the global average, making them inhospitable places to live. Central-Africa suffered from the deadly combination of high humidity and heat, like in India. The rest of Africa was much drier. The Sahara-Sahel desert zone expanded north- and southward, rendering vast swatches of farmland useless. Famine and war struck the continent. Anarchy prevailed in most countries, and governments and the army only controlled small parts. All this triggered flood waves of refugees.

Initially, Europe had tried to accommodate the increasing streams of refugees, but soon they became overwhelmed. Their societies and social security systems could not handle the endless flow. The logical consequence was to close all borders. But European frontiers were like a leaking colander. Refugees were seeping through, although with their numbers slightly decreasing. After much hesitation and debates, Europe finally installed the current high-tech security system. With this superior border control, the refugee stream dried up fast. But the ruthlessness of the border control system also shocked and outraged many people.

The ringing of her phone pulled her out of her thoughts. She rushed to the living room, where she had left it on the table. It was Hawkins, and her heart skipped a beat.

"Sorry to disturb you this late, but I've just received a call from a Danish police officer who's on the Europol task force."

"And?"

"They've found back the black van in Spain."

"In Spain!? And any trace of Dylan?"

"No. But it does help in narrowing down the possibilities."

"In what way?"

"Well, yesterday in a farm west of Figueres, a young man found his parents dead in their bedroom. They were both brutally murdered. Later, they also found the missing black van parked in a barn next door. A white van is missing and the police are searching for it now. There was a camera in front of the barn that filmed everything. The footage shows the three men we had identified earlier on, but also a fourth man with long dark hair in a tail, called Romano De Luca, who served eight years in an Italian prison for human trafficking. The Spanish police are actively looking for the white van and the four men. No one else was seen in the farmyard. The four men transferred all their belongings to the new van. So, either Dylan had been dropped off somewhere earlier on, or he was shipped out with that container to Algiers. I still believe the last option is the most likely."

"Did they make any progress tracing the containers?"

"They've transferred all the information to the Algerian police. With a bit of luck, they should get back to us tomorrow or the day after."

"The sooner the better. I'm so worried about Dylan."

"I understand, and we're really on top of it. I'll call you as soon as I hear something new."

She hung up and returned to the kitchen to have dinner. She could not help but worry. If those people had murdered that farmer's couple so ruthlessly, they would not hesitate to kill Dylan. She called Matteo to update him. He agreed with Hawkins that he was most likely transported to Algiers in that container.

The next day Elizabeth arrived exhausted at work. She had suffered another restless night and was getting more desperate every day. She knew the statistics about abductions. The more time that passed, the higher the chance would be that he was dead. Still, her work distracted her, although she had a hard time concentrating. Half way into the morning her worries came back to her, so she went for another coffee break. She had just taken a first sip from her espresso when her phone rang. It was Hawkins again.

"Morning. I just got off the phone with the Europol task force. The Algerian police have gotten back to them."

"And? Did they find the containers?"

"They did, but unfortunately, no trace of Dylan or Hakim. With the numbers on the containers that we gave them, they have traced both of them. They transported them from the boat to a storage and handling company in the harbor of Algiers. The police have checked the records of that company. A truck from a transportation company in Oran, a city in the west of Algeria, picked the first container up. Several days later another truck from the same transportation company picked up the second container, the one we presume contained Dylan. The problem is that they don't know where the trucks delivered the goods."

"What do you mean they don't know? Can't they get that information from the transportation company?"

"Well, normally they could. But on the shipping bill from the truck, there was only the address of the transportation company in Oran."

"Still, they should be able to check the records of that company in Oran, isn't it?"

"Well, no, they can't. Oran is located in the west of Algeria, which is controlled by a rebellious militia group, called MFF, which stands for Maghreb Freedom Fighters. The Algerian government has no control over this region. They've fought several battles over it, but for now, the militia group is in control. The police have no jurisdiction in that region. They've called the transportation company in Oran who said they're not allowed to give out any details about their customers."

"That doesn't sound good."

"I know, but wait, there's more. Both containers have returned empty to the same storage and handling company in the harbor of Algiers. The police inspected them and in one of them they've found traces of blood in the back. We've asked them to sequence the DNA from that blood sample and it's a perfect match with Hakim."

"Wow, so Hakim was actually in the container as we suspected."

"Exactly, and I bet you that Dylan was in the other one."

"But we've got no proof of that?"

"No, we don't, though it's probable, and it seems they were both moved to Oran."

"So, they're most likely in some rebellious region in Algeria. There must be some way to go and look for them there, right?"

“I fear there is not much we can do.”

“But they kidnapped two European citizens! We must be able to send a European police team to investigate over there? Or maybe the army can set up a search and rescue mission?”

“I don’t know. Europe can’t just send troops into other sovereign nations. It could be seen as an act of war, and I don’t think Europe wants to get dragged into a regional conflict like that.”

“But we can’t just leave them there? There must be something we can do?”

“I’m sorry. I will address it again with the Europol task force, but I don’t think they can do much. I’ll keep you posted.”

“Okay, thanks.”

After the call, she tried to work, but the whole day she had difficulty concentrating. Now that she knew Dylan was most likely somewhere in this city called Oran, she felt that they should take action. It frustrated her that Hawkins didn’t believe the police or military could take any action. Dylan was over there between those rebels. They had to do something to liberate him.

She left her work early to return to her apartment. She called Matteo and explained everything to him.

“It’s so frustrating knowing Dylan is probably out there and they can’t do anything to rescue him.”

“Yeah, it’s frustrating. But I understand. I mean, we have no hard evidence he’s actually in that region and we don’t know an exact location either. Besides the political and military risk Hawkins referred to, it’s quite difficult if not impossible to find someone in a large region like that.”

“I guess you’re right. God, I feel so helpless.”

"Come on, Elizabeth. We are not going to give up. I'm sure the police are going to find more leads. Maybe they'll catch his abductors in Spain and they might be able to tell where Dylan is."

"I know, but every day that passes I worry more that something might happen to him."

"You can't lose hope like that, Elizabeth. Hope is all we have for now. We'll find a way, I'm sure. You know what? Give me some time. I will talk to my friends from my Special Forces Command unit and I'll see what I can find about this MFF group. Don't worry, Elizabeth. We'll find him."

"Thanks, Matteo. I feel better already. Let's talk tomorrow."

42.

After reviewing the images repeatedly, Hawkins stared at the gray ceiling in his office. Something about these abductions gave him a bad feeling. Over the years, he had learned to trust his instinct. An immediate conclusion he unconsciously made, without being able to put the facts together about why he felt this.

He pressed the replay button once again of the video footage from the restaurant next to the hyper-loop station in Copenhagen, where Hakim met Dylan before he got kidnapped. The video played at maximum zoom and slow motion. He believed the reason that both men got abducted lay hidden in the quick exchange of an object. The video showed that Hakim put something Hawkins could not make out in Dylan's hand. He continued watching the video and observed the astonished face of Dylan after Hakim left in a rush. He slowed down the footage again a moment later. Dylan looked at his own hand under the table. Hawkins increased the zoom further. The images became less sharp. He noticed a tiny black object inside Dylan's hand. It could be a memory stick.

His gut feeling told him this had something to do with Enviro. Whatever it was, it was worth so much to somebody that they spared no means to get their hands on it. He had to find out and rushed out. Five minutes later, he barged into the office of Jack Rowling, Hakim's boss, within the Security division. Jack, who was sitting behind his computer, looked startled at the unannounced visitor.

"Morning, Jack. How far are you with the internal investigation?"

"Morning, Steve. We've checked almost everything. Hakim has logged on to only two different workstations in the last three months. We've checked the logs. He accessed hundreds of different files from the server, but made no copies. This is in line with our standard procedure. So, it looks like he didn't steal any data."

"Strange. I've just checked the footage of Hakim's meeting with Dylan, and it looks like he's handing him a memory stick. Are you sure about your conclusions?"

"Hundred percent sure. Every time someone opens a file, the system logs the person and the time of accessing the file. If he made a copy, it would have been logged instantly. The system logged no copies.

"Maybe he found a way around it?"

"Impossible. To do that, he would have to hack into the system on the server. Our security is top notch. Any attempt to hack would immediately have raised an alert, and there were none."

"Could you show me the two workstations he used?"

"Sure, follow me."

Several people looked up on the work floor when Jack passed. He was a tall, broad-shouldered man. He walked at a high pace, making his appearance even more impressive. Quite the contrast with the slender Hawkins. They stopped in front of a desk in the back.

"He sat here and sometimes over there in the other corner."

Both desks had a wall behind them and were in a corner. Difficult for someone to look over his shoulder to check what he was doing, Hawkins thought as he peered around. He glanced up at the ceiling.

"Do they record?" he asked as he pointed at the camera on the ceiling behind the workstation.

"Twenty-four, seven."

"Great. Could you send me all footage from the past three months from those two cameras?"

"Three months!? That is quite some data. When do you need it?"

"Yesterday!"

"I'll have someone send it to you right away."

"Thanks. And also send me the complete log of all files he accessed the last three months."

"No problem. You seem convinced he stole something from the company," Jack said as they walked back through the corridor.

"Yes, something is off about these abductions, and I think it could spell trouble for Enviro," Hawkins answered with a stern look on his face.

They shook hands, and Jack returned to his office. Behind him, he heard Hawkins say,

"And right away, Jack. I really need them fast."

Hawkins walked back to his office. He picked up an espresso from the coffee corner and briefly talked to a colleague. Back at his desk, he checked his email and grinned, pleased. Jack had already sent him all the data he had requested. He picked up the phone right after.

"Hi Martin, could you come to my office right away?"

He hung up and forwarded the data to Martin, who quickly showed up at his desk.

"Martin, I've just sent you several large files. They contain three months of video footage from the cameras behind the workstations Hakim Sayed has used. There's also the log from the server, with all the files he accessed the last three months. It's just a hunch, but I suspect Hakim has copied confidential data from our company. I want to know if this is the case and what he copied."

"Three months of footage and data? Phew… sure, boss. I'll start on it right away."

"Good, this has top priority! Keep me posted if you find anything, all right?"

"I will," Martin replied as he left the room.

43.

Dylan checked the air conditioner and prepared a list of parts he needed to repair it and improve the filtering system. The guard watched him closely while he took notes on a piece of paper. Abdul returned to his office, and Dylan gave him the list.

"If someone could order these parts, then I should be able to fix the air conditioner and improve the air filtration system as well."

Abdul glanced at him with contempt, and a grin appeared on his face.

"Ha, ha, order? That will take much too long. We've got a place where we dump all our broken equipment. Alex here will take you there. You can see if you can find the parts there. I don't care how you do it, as long as you fix it as fast as you can."

The guard pushed Dylan in the direction of the door. He looked annoyed at the guard and turned back toward the toolbox on the floor.

"Let me take some tools with me, to unscrew the parts later on."

The guard waited while Dylan grabbed a few screwdrivers and some pliers. Abdul sat behind his laptop and did not look up anymore. They went outside and the other guard joined to escort Dylan. They walked through the corridors eventually arriving back in the parking garage. The buzz of the crowd in the underground space was quite a contrast with the silence in the maze of corridors. The guards pushed him through the mass of people. At some point, Dylan recognized Ebo, the friendly man who had helped him earlier on. Their eyes briefly met, and he nodded at him. At the end of the garage, they entered the stairwell and climbed several stairs to access the parking garage at level one underground. It was much hotter up here. The guard pushed him toward the left of the parking lot, which sloped downward. Dylan looked at the right where the driveway in the parking lot was sloping up. At the end, he could see how the road turned upward, probably toward the exit. One of the guards pushed him hard with his assault rifle against his shoulder, and he stopped looking. The parking lot was filled with containers and wooden crates. At the end, before the driveway turned down, there was an area filled with discarded equipment like air conditioners, cooking equipment, and old washing machines. The guards waited in front, while Dylan looked for the parts.

Several hours later, he had found most of the items he needed. Soaked with sweat, he told the guards he had finished, and they escorted him back to Abdul's office. There was no one in the office anymore. One guard waited in front of the door while the other one came inside with him. Dylan climbed the stepladder and started unscrewing a part of the air conditioning. The guard monitored him the whole time, holding his assault rifle to the side of his body.

After a while, the guard seemed to get bored and took his phone out of his pocket. Dylan worked on the air conditioner and from the corner of his eye he saw the guard was busy with his phone. He looked around in the room and next to the laptop he noticed a phone. Abdul must have forgotten to take it with him. If only he could send a message to Elizabeth. It was probably the only way out of this mess. He was well aware that they had no way of tracing him without the chip or his mobile phone. He had to find a way to get a message to her.

"What are you staring at?" the guard suddenly yelled at him.

"Don't even think of getting close to that phone!"

Spooked, Dylan turned back and continued working. An hour later, he descended from the ladder and took the remote control out of his pocket. He tested the air conditioner and tried out different settings. Cool air filled the room. Even the guard next to the door showed a faint smile on his face. The air filtering system worked slightly better, but he really needed some newer parts to improve it further. He wrote down a list of parts he still needed. Just at that moment, Abdul returned to the office.

"Wow! It's fucking cold in here. You fixed it. Bravo!"

"Yes, just the air filtration isn't working properly yet. We're still missing some parts to fix it," Dylan said as he showed Abdul his list.

Abdul took the list and dropped it on his desk without looking at it. He picked up his phone from the desk and looked at the guard.

"We'll look at that later. I've to make some urgent calls now. Alex, take him back to his cell."

The two guards brought him all the way back to the floor to the prison cell. In front of the prison's door, he noticed a small office with a guard inside. They nodded to the guard, who waved back. Then they pushed him into the prison cell. Another guard came and added water and food bars and locked the door behind him. He wanted to talk to Hakim, but to his surprise, he was not there. The cell looked emptier than usual and there were only two men left who sat on the bed on the other side. Omar was also not there, and he was missing another man. His throat was dry and hurt him. He took one of the bottles of water next to the door and drank deeply.

The two men rushed to the door and grabbed a bottle of water, and took their food bars. Dylan quickly grabbed two food bars. He was afraid that the men would take them. He waved with the bars.

"One for Hakim, one for me," he said as he felt obliged to explain. He ate one of the bars, since he had eaten nothing all morning. He slowly felt better and walked over to the two men. One of them had black skin and Dylan guessed he was from some central African country. The other had a much lighter skin and looked more like someone from North-Africa.

"Do you know where Hakim and Omar are?"

The two men gave him a blank stare. Then they looked at each other and spoke in Arabic. Another of those moments Dylan regretted he did not speak more languages. The darker one looked back at him and raised his hands in the air and shook his head.

"No, speke Inles."

But Dylan was not going to give up so easily. He pointed at Omar's bed and then at Hakim's bed and gestured with his hands.

"Omar, Hakim, where?"

The North-African man seemed to understand. With his hands, he made a grabbing gesture and then waved at the door. Dylan noticed he wore a watch.

"Hakim?" he asked and pointed at the man's watch with an asking gesture.

He understood it and pointed at his watch. Dylan looked at it. It was six o'clock. The man pointed at the one.

Then Dylan asked, "Omar?" and pointed another time at the watch. Now the man pointed at the two.

At least it was clear to Dylan that Omar had left around two and Hakim around one almost five hours ago. He wondered what had happened to the third man, but since he did not know his name, he found it too complicated to ask. He took some more water and offered his bottle to the two men. They accepted and smiled at him. He lay down on his mattress. He tried to rest a bit, but couldn't help thinking about Elizabeth. He wondered how she was coping. He had to get a message to her. He had to find some way.

The noise of the door unlocking pulled him out of his light sleep. He had dozed off on his mattress. He looked up to see who was entering the room. A guard pushed Hakim inside and locked the door behind him. He looked exhausted and pale. Dylan got up and walked to Hakim.

"Are you okay?"

"Yes, I'm all right. Just tired and still a bit feverish."

"Here. Have some water."

"Thanks."

After sipping from the bottle, Hakim waddled to his mattress and lay down. Dylan sat down on his own mattress next to him. Hakim looked at him.

"Where did they take you this morning?"

"They forced me to fix the air conditioner in the office of Abdul."

"Did you meet him?"

"Yes, scary guy."

"Exactly. I hate that guy."

"Why? What happened to you today?"

"They took me to this computer room to help them with the information they took from that memory stick I gave you."

"What was on there, anyway?"

"Well, that's a long story," Hakim replied and sighed deeply.

He explained how they had approached him, and that initially he had refused to give them the confidential information they wanted. He talked about how they had kidnapped his sister, and Dylan looked shocked. Hakim did not care that they could hurt him physically. But Aisha was his weak point, and Abdul had understood that quickly. He didn't feel good about his theft and refused to help them today.

But when Abdul joined in the computer room, he threatened to abduct his sister again. He even showed Aisha walking in the streets. He simply had no other choice. Dylan nodded in agreement. Then he explained more about the information on the memory stick, and Dylan looked puzzled.

"What does he want to do with that?"

"Well, whatever his plan is, it can't be good."

"Absolutely. I've a bad feeling about this guy. The only reason we're still alive is because we're still useful to him. I'm afraid about what will happen to us when he no longer needs us. We really have to get out of here or send out a message before it's too late."

"I agree, but I don't see how. They're constantly watching us and pointing guns at us. We should check with Omar. He has been in here longer. Maybe he has some idea about how to escape. But where is he anyway?"

"The guards took him away. The strange thing is that I overheard Abdul mentioning his name on the phone. I couldn't understand what he was saying as he was speaking Arabic. The only thing I understood besides his name was 'deal'."

"Deal? Maybe, they have reached an agreement on the ransom. I hope he's all right."

44.

Today felt different. The guards passed by so often that Ebo knew something was happening. Most people ignored the guards, but he immediately noticed something was off. Maybe that important moment was almost here. He had left behind his country and most of his family for it. They stopped asking the guards when it would happen, because they could get aggressive. But he longed for it every day more. A new start. Who were those prisoners that they moved back and forth toward the office of the great Jabbar?

Ebo had traveled a long distance to get here together with his wife and son. He recalled how he had decided to embark on his trip. He was relatively well off in his home country and rented a nice apartment in Accra, the capital of Ghana. He was born and raised in Tema, east of Accra. At school, he had always done well and eventually ended up with a good job in the capital. But climate change hit his country hard in multiple ways.

The average temperature increased gradually in his home country, like in the rest of the world. In addition, rainfall decreased, but the variability of it increased, making agriculture more difficult. The periods without rainfall became longer and during the scarcer periods when it would rain, it would be much heavier. So much rain fell that the rivers overflew their banks, flooding homes and surrounding land, wiping out food crops and killing people. In the north, the Sahel expanded increasingly southward. Deforestation exacerbated the whole situation. Droughts hit the country regularly, causing bushfires and destroying food crops. Predicting extreme weather events was almost impossible. Drinking water became scarce and food prices rocketed. More people starved and died of hunger, dehydration or disease.

Meanwhile, he moved from a poor suburb to a slightly better neighborhood in Accra. Unfortunately, the sea level rose, and parts of the city were flooded regularly. Many people lost their homes. They lost a large part of the capital to the sea, and the remaining part of the city became overpopulated. This situation worsened as large parts of the population migrated south toward the urban areas. Heatwaves happened more often and the combination with the poor state of the power-grid proved to be a deadly mix. The heat hit especially the poor individuals living in slums. Every heatwave competed with the previous one for the title of the deadliest heatwave ever.

Ebo and his wife had saved enough money to buy an air conditioner, but most people could not afford this luxury. Although during most heatwaves his air conditioner did not work because of power failures. The accumulation of problems and disasters in the country reached an unbearable level. Anarchy broke out in the poorest parts of the country. The government lost control of more and more cities and villages. Militant groups took over in several regions. When a part of Accra fell under control of a ruthless militia, Ebo decided that enough was enough. It was time to pack their bags and leave, hoping to find a better life elsewhere.

They sold all their belongings and embarked on a long and dangerous journey northbound. It started with a long trip overland westward through neighboring countries until they bought a spot aboard a cargo ship in the harbor of Monrovia in Liberia. The living conditions aboard the ship were poor and unpleasant, still it was the best way to avoid traveling through the immense and deadly Sahara

Desert. They endured the horrible heat onboard and had to pay a fortune for food and water. Ebo had to defend his family several times against drunken or aggressive travelers and sailors. He had learned how to handle a butterfly knife as a child, and that scared off most attackers. The ship took them all the way up north to Rabat in Morocco.

Even though the trip had been difficult, long, and perilous up to this point, the most challenging part was yet to come. After investigating and asking around, it looked like their only hope was a man called the great Jabbar. People told him they could find him in neighboring Algeria. In the dangerous western part of the country, ruled by militias and warlords. They met a shabby-looking man, who told them he could bring them to the compound of the great Jabbar. The man claimed to work for him. Initially, Ebo didn't trust him, but he didn't have much choice and they paid the high fee he asked for the trip.

It was another long and dangerous journey in a van packed with people, but they reached the city of Oran in the end. Ebo felt relieved when he realized the man had spoken the truth and they arrived at the compound. Although he was slightly disappointed to find out that the compound was just an old underground parking garage. Lots of people were already living there, all waiting like them for that last part of their trip. It confirmed his feeling that this man, Abdul Jabbar, was the one who could really help them reach their goal. Ebo paid the last of his savings for the promise to be transported further and to be allowed to live in the underground parking in the meantime. Food and drinks were all supplied, and the man told them that the last part of their long voyage would start soon.

45.

Abdul looked over Cheng's shoulder at the computer screen and realized they had just come another step closer to the realization of his goal. Cheng explained all he had learned from the recovered information on the memory stick. They decrypted most of the information with Hakim's help. Now Cheng and his team used it to build their program. Abdul complemented him on his progress. He took his boss through all the next steps to complete everything and had never seen Abdul so happy.

"Sounds like a brilliant plan, Cheng. Make sure to have it up and running as quick as possible."

"We will! Nobody will leave this room until it's finished."

"All right, get to work then and let me know when you've got the instructions for Marco."

"I will, boss."

Abdul rushed out of the computer room into the corridor. As he walked toward his office, he felt a wave of euphoria. They had finally succeeded in getting access to the critical information from Enviro that he had been trying to get their hands on for years. At last, they could proceed and execute the next phase of his plan. It felt great after all these years. His thoughts wandered back to that moment in his youth when he had vowed to avenge the death of his parents. At the age of nineteen, he finally understood what had happened to them.

The letter from the real estate agent that they had found in his parents' belongings proved to be a crucial lead to the truth. Abdul still remembered vividly paying a visit to the real estate agent in Cairo. It was a hot and stuffy day in September, when he proposed to Maheer to go to Tony Gamal, the real estate agent. They walked together at the end of the afternoon toward the Christian neighborhood where the real estate agent's office was located. Egypt was predominantly a Sunni Muslim country, but about ten percent of its population was Coptic Orthodox Christian. First, they passed in front of the window and looked inside to check it out. They counted four people. Abdul had checked Tony Gamal out on their website and recognized his chubby face immediately. They waited further down the street.

An hour later, three employees left the office, but Tony Gamal was still inside. The sun was setting already, and the streets were getting darker. Abdul gave Maheer a poke in his side.

"Let's go in."

Maheer followed his brother. They peered inside through the large windows of the office. All lights were out in the front, but in the back, they saw a strip of light under a closed door. Abdul tried the doorknob of the front door. It was open. He glanced at Maheer, who looked nervous, then he went in and a ringing bell broke the silence. From the back, a voice yelled in Arabic.

"We're closed! Please come back tomorrow. We open at nine in the morning."

Abdul locked the front door behind them, and they tiptoed toward the office in the back. He opened the door, and they both looked into Tony's surprised eyes.

"I told you we're closed!?"

Abdul and Maheer ignored him and entered the small office. The two tall and sturdy brothers filled the room and towered above the chubby Tony, who sat at his desk. Abdul looked him deep in the eyes.

"We need to talk."

Tony looked anxiously at the two men and dropped his pen on the table.

"Who are you?"

"You knew our parents, Ali and Tahirah Jabbar."

"Jabbar? That doesn't ring a bell. I meet new people every day for the last twenty years that I've been a real estate agent."

Abdul walked around the desk and stood next to Tony with his intimidating body towering above him. He looked down at the chubby man.

"I think you know very well who they are. You bought their apartment for some rich guy from our uncle, just after my parents died tragically."

Tony started moving nervously in his chair and touched the cross hanging on the chain around his neck.

"I don't know what you're talking about. I can't possibly remember all the transactions that I've been involved in. You should both leave now. We're closed."

Abdul pushed the office chair and turned it so that Tony faced him.

"You're lying. I think you know very well what I mean. You bought an apartment from my uncle on Kholosi street. Some rich prick has demolished it to construct a large compound. You remember now?"

"On Kholosi, I… I… I believe it starts to come back to me."

"Good!" Abdul said, while he slapped his hand flat with a bang on the desk.

"Now we're getting somewhere. Your client tried to buy the apartment from my parents first. They visited your real estate office to discuss it, but when they refused, they died on their way back home. Apparently, a large truck drove over them in the street. It looked like an accident, but you and I know better, right?"

Abdul stared him deep in the eyes. Tony was perspiring now and sat back in his chair in an attempt to move as far away from the enormous man in front of him.

"I… I… I don't know what you're talking about."

Abdul nodded at Maheer, who stood behind the chair. Maheer grabbed his neck from behind and started strangling him.

"Tony, Tony, Tony. Stop lying. What was the name of your client?"

Maheer let go of his neck and Tony gasped for air with a terrified look on his face.

"W… w… we don't give out client's names. Leave now or I'll call the police!"

In a desperate attempt, he reached out for his phone on the desk. Abdul reacted in a reflex and with two hands he grabbed the stretched-out arm and pushed it hard on the desk. The weight on his arm pushed Tony down on the desk.

"I'll ask you one more time. What's the name of your client?"

Tony, with his arm still stretched flat on the desk, looked desperately at Abdul and shook his head left and right.

"I can't tell you."

Abdul kept pushing Tony's arm on the table with one hand as he lifted his other hand to grab a pair of scissors from the table. He looked one more time at Tony, who tried to move away from the table now. Maheer grabbed him by the shoulders and pushed him back.

"Tell us his name!"

"I can't. His people will have me killed."

With a furious look on his face, Abdul raised the scissors high before lashing them with all his force into the chubby hand. A loud scream erupted through the office. Tony moaned from the pain. With tears rolling down his face and his eyes wide-open, Tony muttered,

"J... Ja... Jabari... Jabari Saad is his name."

Abdul looked astounded at his brother. They had heard that name before. Jabari Saad was one of the most successful billionaires in Egypt. He had been on the cover of many magazines and newspapers. Abdul let go of his arm, and Tony looked horrified at the scissors sticking out of his hand. His moaning changed into sobbing and tears ran down his face.

"I... I... I didn't know. I swear I didn't know."

Maheer looked puzzled at Tony.

"What do you mean?"

"I didn't know he would have them killed. He had threatened your parents saying that they'd better agree to sell, before things turn ugly. He told them that Cairo was a dangerous city. But your father insulted Jabari and said he would never sell to him. The next day, I heard your parents died in a tragic accident. A couple of months later, Mr. Saad told me to make an offer to your uncle. All this because he wanted to construct a climate change resistant compound on this large piece of ground."

Abdul looked with contempt at Tony.

"Where does he live?"

With his free arm, Tony opened a drawer in his desk and took out a box with business cards. Shaking and still sobbing, he searched for a while until he found a card and lifted it up toward Abdul.

"Here's his business card. That's all I have."

Abdul grabbed it out of his hand and took a good look at it. He seemed to relax now and read out the name on the card.

"Jabari Saad. The bastard."

Maheer let go of him and walked toward the door.

"Let's go, Abdul."

Abdul looked bewildered at him.

"We can't leave him like this. He'll go to the police and rat us out or warn Mr. Saad."

"What do you want to do with him, then?" Maheer asked him.

"We've got to make it look like an accident."

Tony shook left and right with his head now and tried to take the scissors out of his hand.

"No! No! You don't have to do that. Just let me go. I won't tell anyone. I swear!"

Abdul did not hesitate for a second and reached for the cable plugged into the laptop on the desk. He unplugged it and while Tony was trying to get up, he wrapped the power cord around his fat neck. With his one free hand, Tony tried to move the cord away from his neck. But the strong Abdul pulled it tightly with both hands. Tony squirmed and desperately kicked with his legs against the desk. His head turned all red. He was snorting and choking as he desperately tried to pull the cord away. Maheer looked away while Abdul waited until slowly the life went out of the chubby Tony.

After he had stopped moving, Abdul removed the power cord from his neck. Then he grabbed the scissors and removed them with a jerk from Tony's hand. The poor man slid backwards into his chair and remained motionless. Abdul opened the filing cabinet next to the desk. He took out a pile of papers and set them on fire with his lighter. He used them to set fire to the other papers in the filing cabinet. The flames grew higher and higher. Together with Maheer, they spread the fire all over the office. Soon after, it spread to the thin wooden walls. All around them, the room looked like an inferno now, with flames moving upward toward the ceiling. The fire expanded quickly, and the heat hit them in the face. They both rushed out of the door. Abdul glanced one more time back in the office at the lifeless Tony surrounded by flames slowly consuming him.

The guard greeting him politely in front of his office took Abdul out of his deep thoughts. He went inside and dropped himself into the desk chair. He just sat there quietly for a moment. Realizing the progress his tech guys had made. He knew he was closing in. Looking at the massive painting with the remaining survivors in utter despair on the raft of the Medusa, he thought to himself; I will get you, bastard. My vengeance will be my salvation.

46.

Days after Elliot found out that he had a twin brother, he was still perturbed and puzzled by his father's death. He was sitting at the kitchen table with the farewell letter in his hands. Elsa had gone to work already, and he should leave soon, not to be late. He now understood better why his father had felt depressed after his mother's death. Unfortunately, the suicide note did not give him a complete answer. He read the letter another time and wondered what his father meant when he said:

I am ashamed of the choices I made in the past and of imposing them on your mother. The guilt and regret I carried with me all these years simply have become too much to bear.

He must have felt guilty about their decision to give Yagnesh up for adoption and entering the dome without him. But had he forced his mother to do this? Or had she done it out of her own freewill? Was it because Yagnesh had died in that heatwave that he felt guilty? He read further:

Recently, I realized I have not learned from the past and continued making the wrong choices. I have failed as a father.

What did he mean by that? What had happened? What wrong choice did he make lately? The questions running through his head gave him a headache.

A look at the time took him out of his thoughts. He rushed out of his apartment and went to work. Elias, his boss, had been quite understanding and insisted he take all the time he needed to process the loss of his father. Unfortunately, his work was piling up. He did not want to fall too much behind, as he feared his boss might hand his project to someone else. He worked hard and did not think of the family secrets for the rest of the morning.

At the end of the afternoon, Elliot walked back to his desk after a coffee break with his colleagues. He concentrated on his work all day and it felt good. It was the first day since his father's death that he actually stayed the entire day at work. He realized all this thinking about his parents was not good for him. Still, too many questions remained to just let the whole thing go. The moment he sat down behind his desk, he suddenly thought of something that Mary, his father's assistant, had told him. What if that was the reason his father had taken his life? He picked up the phone and called her. Maybe she was still in the office.

"Hi Mary. It's Elliot."

"How are you doing, Elliot?"

"I'm okay."

"What can I do for you?"

"You mentioned that my father was being investigated by Internal Affairs. Could you tell me who's in charge of the investigation?"

"Yes, Conan is in charge."

"Do you know where I can find him?"

"Well, he's actually sitting in your father's office at the moment."

"Can I talk to him?"

"Just a moment, let me ask."

Elliot waited for a couple of minutes before he heard Mary's voice.

"He can meet you in an hour."

"Perfect! Thanks."

An hour later, Elliot showed up at Mary's desk. She was already packing her stuff to return home, but when she noticed him, she came over to give him a hug.

"You can go right in."

"Thanks. Have a nice evening!"

"You too!"

He passed Mary's desk toward the door of his late father's office. It was ajar, and he stuck his head in the opening to look inside. Behind the desk, he saw a man with short red hair looking at a computer screen. Just then, he lifted his head and looked at Elliot through his square glasses. He stared quite long at him, as if something surprised him. Just when Elliot was starting to feel uncomfortable, he stood up.

"Oh, hi. You must be Elliot. Come on in!"

Elliot pushed the door. They shook hands, and he noticed Conan was checking him out. He told him to sit down, glanced at the computer screen, and then back at Elliot.

"Remarkable. Uh, sorry. What can I do for you, Elliot?"

"I understand from Mary that you're investigating my father. Since his death, I've so many questions running through my head that I was hoping you could provide me with some answers."

"It's good you came to see me. I also wanted to contact you."

"Really, what for?"

"I'll show you in a second, but let me first explain why I'm investigating your father. Last year, we had an intruder outside of the dome, and your father deviated from our protocol. That's basically what triggered the investigation."

"I remember how he got called away because of an intruder. He acted strangely in the days after."

"Strangely? In what way?"

"His behavior was weird. He seemed disturbed by something. He was moody and avoided talking to me. But in what way did my father deviate from protocol?"

"Well, the rules are that whenever there is an intruder, they must execute them. They did not apply this before, since all previous intruders died during their attempts. This was the first time an intruder actually reached the dome alive. Your father ordered his men to escort the intruder off the premises alive rather than apply the rule."

"That doesn't sound like my father. He always followed the rules by the letter."

"Exactly, but I think I know now why he did it."

"And why did he?"

"I think it's best if I show you the picture of the intruder."

Conan gestured to his computer screen. Elliot walked around the desk. His heart skipped a beat, and he couldn't believe his eyes. He approached further to have a better look before stammering,

"H… how… how is this possible? He looks exactly like me!?"

Elliot put his hands on the side of his face now as he continued.

"But… but… that would mean he didn't die. How can that be possible?"

Conan looked at him the whole time. Fascinated, as if he had been hoping for a reaction like this one.

"When I saw the video footage, I couldn't believe it myself. For a moment, I thought it was you, although that made little sense. I checked the dome's internal security system, and it showed you were in your apartment at this moment. This young man was wearing a special suit, and I took a sample from the blood on the suit. I had his DNA sequenced, and compared it to your DNA that we've registered in the dome's database. It was a match. Then I ran a more extensive test and found out that there were minor mutations telling the DNA apart from yours. The only logical explanation is that you have a twin brother. Did you know that?"

"Well, I didn't, until recently. I just found out going through my father's belongings. Apparently, I have a twin brother called Yagnesh, but I also found an article implying that he died during a heat wave in the orphanage where my parents had placed him. So, I actually thought he was dead and I think my parents believed the same."

"Yagnesh, you said? Strange, this man called himself Dylan Myers."

"Dylan Myers? Maybe he got adopted then?"

"He did actually. I've checked our global system. An American man called Lawrence Myers and his Swiss wife Eva Myers-Schneider adopted him in the year 2029."

"Amazing. They gave him up for adoption in the orphanage in the same year as we entered the dome."

"Correct. His father died in the year 2039 and…"

"What!? That's the same year my mother ended her life! Can you believe the coincidence?"

"Ah, I didn't realize that. His mother Eva died last year, before he came to the dome. He knew your parents' original names from their pre-dome period."

"I guess he must have found the names by tracing back his adoption records. How did he succeed in reaching the dome? I mean, that's nearly impossible, isn't it?"

"He's the first man ever to make it alive to the dome. He was wearing a special high-tech dark suit that made him invisible to our security system. Your father immediately implemented several changes to render this type of intrusion impossible."

"I still wonder why my father sent him away, though. I mean, it's his son. He could have allowed him to enter the dome."

"Your father knew the rules. No one enters the dome. The procedure was to execute any intruder. I can only guess for which reason he deviated from it."

"How can you send your own flesh and blood away?"

"You make it sound horrible indeed, and I can only guess what went through his head."

47.

In the morning, Marco was the first one awake, or at least he did not hear any other sounds inside the small house. He peered outside through the blinds. The brightness of the sun blinded him and he quickly checked if everything still looked in order. The white van barely fit into the interior place in front of the house. The street, as far as he could see, appeared completely deserted. He walked to the bathroom and washed his face. Then he went downstairs and entered the kitchen.

The empty wine bottles stood next to the dirty glasses on the kitchen table. Nobody seemed to clean up, which irritated Marco. He opened the fridge and took out a milk carton. The day before, Romano had gone out to buy some groceries. They should have enough food and drinks now for the rest of the week. Marco wanted to keep a low profile and limit the outside trips to an absolute minimum. Every time they risked being recognized or running into the police.

After preparing a large pot of coffee, Marco sat down at the kitchen table. He prepared himself some toast with strawberry jam. Just when he was taking a first bite, James entered the kitchen in his white boxer shorts.

"Morning, boss."

"Mm… morning," Marco answered with his mouth full.

James opened the fridge and scratched his crotch right next to Marco, who was taking another bite of his toast.

"Could you do that somewhere else, please? I'm eating, for goodness' sake."

"Do what somewhere else?" James asked while bringing the milk carton to his mouth.

"Scratching your fucking balls next to my face."

"Oh, I'm sorry, boss," James responded while milk dripped from his mouth. Then he wiped his mouth with his hairy naked arm and burped.

"Jesus, drink from a glass like normal people! Did your mother forget to teach you manners?"

"She overdosed when I was four years old. My education comes from my six brothers, since my dad was never there."

"Well, that explains it then."

"Buongiorno," Romano addressed the two bickering men.

He passed the shapeless milk-white body of James with a disapproving look and opened the fridge. He took out some cheese and sat next to Marco to prepare his own sandwich.

"So, what's the plan for today? Another boring day inside?"

"Not sure yet. I've got a call planned with the boss later in the morning. He sounded quite excited about the progress they've made yesterday."

After breakfast, they moved to the living room to watch the news. James went upstairs to get dressed. A moment later, Farid stuck his head around the corner on his way to the kitchen.

"Morning."

"Morning, Goldilocks," Marco replied.

Romano grinned at his boss. The night before, they had drunk a lot of wine, and they had made fun of Farid's light blond hair. They had burst out in laughter when James renamed the four of them Goldilocks and the three bears. Farid smiled and continued to the kitchen. Romano read a book and Marco watched the television. Later on, Farid and James joined them. They were playing a game of poker when Marco's phone rang.

"Hi boss. Yeah. We're still in our hideout in the South. I think we've shaken off the police for now."

They all looked at Marco as he spoke. They had been waiting for days now, and they were ready for some action.

"That's good news. All right, I'll check my email immediately. No problem, I'll make sure that everything will be ready in time. Don't worry, consider it done. Bye, boss."

He hung up, and everybody looked at him curiously. Farid was the first one to break the silence.

"And, any news?"

"Just a second," Marco replied while checking his email on his laptop. He stared at the screen for a moment before addressing them.

"Time to get to work. He sent us a list of materials and an elaborate instruction. Let's check which materials we've got in stock already and make a shopping list for everything we're missing. Farid and Romano, you take care of that. I'll send you the list right away."

"All right, boss. We'll start on it immediately," Farid answered and opened his laptop.

"James, you can help me with the instructions. They're here. We're only missing the software that we've got to upload."

"When do we get it?"

"They're still working on it, but they're expecting to send it to us in the coming days. We've got to get everything ready as soon as possible."

They all got to work, happy to break out of the boredom of waiting. At the end of the afternoon, Farid and Romano finished checking the list of materials against their inventory inside the van.

Luckily, they had most of it with them and they were missing only a few items. They prepared a shopping list for the missing parts and checked online where they could buy everything. There was a large shop not too far from their hideout. When they were about to leave, Marco was still worrying about the police. He got up and blocked the way to Farid and Romano.

"Farid, stay in the van at all times and try to park out of sight of any cameras. Romano, you enter the shop alone, since the police don't know your face. Try to come back as quickly as possible and don't take any risk."

"Don't worry, boss," Romano said while tapping Marco on his shoulder.

Outside, Romano opened the front gate, and Farid drove the van out of the small parking lot in front of the house. After closing the gate, Romano hopped onto the seat next to the driver, and they drove off.

Fifteen minutes later, they arrived at the shop. There was a large parking lot in front. It was relatively empty. After peering at the entrance and checking the surroundings, Farid parked the car at the edge of the parking lot, in between a high hedge and a large truck. Romano looked baffled at him.

"You want to make me walk as far as possible!? Why don't you park closer to the entrance? It's bloody hot outside. There're plenty of vacant spots over there."

"Look, Romano, there are two cameras close to the entrance. I prefer to keep the van out of sight and be extra careful like we promised Marco."

"Okay, okay," Romano sighed while stepping out.

He crossed the large parking lot through the blistering heat. By the time he entered the store, he was sweating heavily. He took a shopping cart, took out his shopping list, and passed the young, dark-haired cashier at the entrance. The cashier greeted him politely, and Romano nodded back. He continued further and looked at the indications on the long rows of shelves inside. The cashier immediately checked his phone, as if he was watching a program or something.

About twenty minutes later, he had collected almost all the items he needed. At some point, he noticed the cashier again. The man looked anxiously at him and walked away as soon as Romano glanced in his direction. Romano walked toward the rack with the connectors all the way in the back of the shop and looked for a certain model. He had a bad feeling about this cashier and rushed to collect everything he needed. When he had found everything on the list, he rushed in the entrance's direction with his shopping cart when his phone rang. It was Farid.

"Romano, the police have just entered the shop. Get the hell out of there!"

He peered carefully around the corner of a rack of shelves toward the cashier at the entrance. He was talking to two police officers and pointed in his direction. Romano did not hesitate a second. He turned back and hid behind the rack.

"Farid, meet me behind the store. I'll try to leave through the service entrance in the back."

He tucked his phone in his pocket and pulled his gun out of his trousers. He rushed through the aisle toward the back. At the corner, he glanced left and right and spotted what looked like a service entrance on his right. He continued right and passed several aisles. He glanced into every aisle before crossing cautiously on his guard for any police officers popping up. About ten meters away from the service entrance, he peered into the next aisle. A police officer was coming his way with a gun in his hand. The man spotted him instantly and yelled.

"Freeze! Put your hands up in the air!!"

Romano did not hesitate a second and aimed his gun at the police officer. He shot a bullet right in his chest and he collapsed on the floor, firing his gun in the air. He heard someone yelling from an aisle parallel to this one. Romano pushed the shopping cart fast toward the service entrance, while he heard the police officers yelling behind him. He rammed the shopping cart with brute force through the two-way swing doors of the service entrance. There was a small storage room behind it, and Romano grabbed a large bag from a table. He put everything into the bag and raced to the back.

Just before opening the back door, he heard a noise behind him. He turned and saw a police officer aiming his gun at him. He ducked in a reflex behind a pallet with air conditioners and heard the gun firing. The bullet missed him by an inch. He fired back, and the cop took cover immediately. Then he rushed through the back door and got blinded for a few seconds by the bright sun outside. He was about to panic as he did not see the white van anywhere, when he heard it coming through the street at high speed. Farid stopped with screeching tires right next to Romano.

Romano opened the sliding door as a police officer came out of the building. He threw the bag into the van, and was climbing inside when he heard the gunfire behind him. He felt a sharp pain as a bullet grazed his right leg. He turned and dropped on the floor inside the van. He fired his gun back at the shooter and hit him on his neck. The man fell immediately to the ground, while another police officer came through the back door.

"Go! Go! Go!" Romano yelled at Farid.

The van pulled out with squealing tires and smoke came from under. The police officer shot several times at the white van, but it disappeared quickly out of sight. Romano looked at his bleeding leg. Blood was gushing out. He took off his belt and strapped it around the upper part of his right leg. He pulled the belt extremely tight to stop the bleeding. He took off his shirt and wrapped it around the wound, while the wild turns of the van were pushing him from left to right. Farid drove at high speed through the small back streets of Granada. As soon as he noticed the police were not coming after them, he yelled, "Are you okay?"

"I got shot in my leg, but I think the bullet went through. Are they following us?"

"No, I don't see them anywhere. We've almost arrived at our hideout."

"Let me call Marco," Romano replied as he took out his phone.

"Marco, open the gate! We're almost there, but the cops are after us."

Farid turned into the street where the hideout was and looked one more time in his back mirror. Still no police behind them. The gate was open and Farid drove directly inside. Marco and James closed immediately behind them.

48.

Dylan woke up the next morning with the sound of the two Arabic men talking together. He looked around in the dimly lit room. Omar and the other man had not returned to the cell. Hakim was snoring next to him. He felt quite awake and stood up. He smiled in a friendly way at the two men on the other side. They returned the gesture and continued talking. Dylan walked to the table next to the door and opened one of the bottles.

A moment later, the snoring stopped, and he heard something moving behind him. Hakim was waking up. He looked less pale this morning.

"Morning. How do you feel?"

"Better. I even think the fever is gone."

"Thank God they sent in that doctor. I really thought you could have died otherwise."

"Yes. The pain in my arm is gone as well."

"Good. You want some water?"

Hakim nodded, and Dylan passed him a bottle. Then he pointed to the empty mattresses.

"Looks like our friend Omar and the other guy aren't coming back anymore."

"Yes. I hope they're still alive. We really have to find a way to get out of this place."

"Yeah, but how?"

They continued talking until they heard the lock on the door click. It opened, and an armed guard pointed at Hakim.

"You! Come with us!"

Hakim got up and looked at Dylan.

"See you later! Let's hope we get some opportunity today to do what we've discussed."

"Yeah, let's see."

The guards locked the door behind Hakim. Left behind with the two other men, Dylan felt bored. At some point, he did some push-ups just to kill the time. After a first set, he felt energized and continued with sit-ups. He could not help thinking back on what Elizabeth had told him last year. During her abduction, she had distracted herself by doing exercise. Who would have thought that so shortly after he would get into similar trouble? He wondered if they were making any progress in their search for him. It looked impossible to escape from here and he had his hopes pinned on a potential rescue mission from the outside.

An hour later, the guards returned. This time, they came for him. He followed them outside and looked around in the underground garage. On his right side, he saw the upward sloping ramp that turned upward at the end to the floor above. He figured it must be where he had looked for the old parts for the air conditioners. He wondered how many levels there were before he would be outside. The guard in the small guardhouse in front of him stared at him while holding an automatic gun in his hand. He did not look very smart and looked like he would not be someone to reason with. Dylan looked away to avoid his intense stare.

The guard behind him pushed him hard to the left.

"Walk!"

They took him to the stairwell, and they descended the stairs two levels lower. Down there, they walked through the underground parking garage floor. There were still lots of people in the makeshift houses, but he had the impression it was less crowded than the other day. He was happy they did not tie him up like they had the first days. At least he could walk a bit comfortably. With or without being tied up, it did not make much difference, since he still did not dare to make an attempt to escape. With the armed men in front and behind him, he felt he would have little chance of making it out alive. He figured they would shoot him down without hesitation. Also, on each corner, there were guards with heavy arms. It was too risky.

They arrived at the heavy metal door all the way in the back. There were guards on both sides of the door again and they opened for them. They walked through the maze of corridors until they entered a faintly lit room with rows of tables with computers on them. On the sides, there were shelves and cupboards. The tables were filled with people working on the computers.

While they pushed him toward the back of the large room, he suddenly noticed Hakim sitting next to an Asian man. They were both concentrating on the computer screen. Dylan noticed the armed guard standing behind Hakim. The room was very warm and damp and smelled like sweat. As he continued further, Hakim noticed him and blinked at him. All the way in the back, the guard stopped and pointed at the air conditioner on the ceiling.

"You! Fix!"

Dylan looked around and then replied, "I need the tools and the stepladder."

The man pointed behind him, and Dylan turned around. The other guard entered the room carrying the toolbox and the stepladder. Dylan climbed on it and held his hand in front of the air conditioner. Warm air was blowing out. He turned it off and opened it up. A dark-skinned man sitting in front of a computer right next to the air conditioner looked annoyed at him with his sweaty face.

Apparently, he preferred the warm, blowing air over no movement at all.

After a while, he had identified all the parts to replace and prepared a list. He looked for the guard. He was talking to his comrade next to Hakim. Dylan walked up to him and gestured at the air conditioner with the list.

"I need to get the parts to fix the air conditioner."

He nodded at him and gestured to follow him. Hakim looked up when they passed his desk.

"Leaving us here in this heat?" he asked Dylan with a grin on his face.

The guard behind him reacted immediately. With his flat hand, he slapped Hakim against the side of his head. Afraid of more punches Hakim held his hands up around his head, while looking back at the guard, who yelled.

"No, talking!"

Dylan was pushed outside before he could say anything. They escorted him all the way through the underground parking garage up to the storage place with discarded equipment. It was hot, and Dylan had difficulty breathing up here. He immediately started searching through the old equipment, as he preferred to limit his time in this heat. An hour later, he had found everything he needed. He looked at the two guards, who clearly had a hard time coping with the heat as well. Soaked in sweat, he signaled to them that they could go back.

Back in the computer room, he was surprised to see that most people had left. Only Hakim was still sitting next to the Asian man. He nodded at Dylan as he passed and continued explaining something. Dylan got to work in the back. He looked around the room while replacing a part in the air conditioning. He noticed that the nearest computer was still on and the screen was not protected by any password or screensavers. For a second, he contemplated using the computer to go online to find a way to send a message out. But a loud yell pulled him abruptly out of his thoughts.

"Work! No looking!"

Hakim noticed the whole thing and glanced at him from the corner of his eye. The guard who was standing behind Hakim had walked to the door to get some fresh air. Hakim waved at the guard next to Dylan. He walked up to him and Hakim asked,
"Could we get something to eat and drink? Everybody is having lunch, but we're also hungry."

The guard looked at the Asian man as if he wanted to check it with him. He got a nod back, and the guard walked toward the door. Dylan did not hesitate for a second. He got off the stepladder and pretended to pick some tools out of the toolbox. Bent down, he moved closer to the computer. He opened the internet browser and typed the internet address of a global mapping site. His heart was pounding in his chest. He searched their current location while glancing anxiously at the door. The guard was standing with his back to them and spoke to someone outside.

He saw on the map they were located on the westside of the city of Oran in Algeria. Tensed, he copied the latitude and longitude GPS coordinates. Then he opened the mail program on the computer and pushed the 'compose email' button. He typed Elizabeth's email address into the 'to' field, pasted the coordinates in the mail, and typed 'help' in the 'subject' field. He pushed the 'send' button and glanced back at the door. Someone outside handed two bottles and some food to the guard. As fast as he could, he moved to the 'sent items' folder and deleted the email he had just sent out. Subsequently, he moved to the 'deleted items' folder and deleted the email permanently.

A loud yell startled him. He dropped onto the floor, pretending to look for something. The adrenaline rushed through his body when the angry guard ran over to him.

"Don't touch computer!"

Dylan looked up at him. On his knees, he lifted a screwdriver up and showed it to.

"I dropped my screwdriver."

The guard looked at him skeptically. He still didn't trust it and stared at the screen, but saw nothing suspicious. With a distrustful and puzzled look on his face, he handed a bottle of water and a candy bar to Dylan.

"Thank you," Dylan said nervously.

The man, who had been working on this computer before, returned and the guard spoke to him in Arabic. He pointed at Dylan, and they looked at him. The man immediately checked the computer and the mail program. A few seconds later, he replied to the guard in Arabic and shook no with his head. Meanwhile, Dylan got back on the stepladder and continued his repair work. He relaxed slowly, as it seemed he had gotten away with it. From the corner of his eyes, he noticed Hakim peering at him. He didn't dare to return his look as he saw the guard was staring at him with suspicion, so he continued working.

A while later, he got off the stepladder and tested the air conditioner. Most people had returned to the room, and it was really warm inside. It felt like a gift from heaven when the cold air blew in his face. The man working at the computer next to him looked up and smiled. He held his hands together in front of his chest and bent forward to show his appreciation. He gathered all the tools and folded the stepladder. The guard approached and raised his hand in front of the air conditioner.

"Good! Follow me!"

Dylan followed him, and when he passed in front of Hakim, he blinked. They escorted him all the way back to his cell.

49.

That night, Dylan woke up in the dark. He heard voices around him, but couldn't understand what they were saying. He felt several hands grab him and lift him from his bed. He tried to see who it was, but it was pitch-dark and he could only distinguish dark shapes next to him. He heard a door open and felt them take him away. They carried him like that for a while until suddenly they dropped him on what felt like a hard table. He felt his hands and feet become strapped to the table.

In an instant, a bright spotlight went on and a muscled, broad-shouldered man stood in front of him dressed in green surgeon clothes. He had a shaved head and grinned at him. On the other side of the table, a tall man with long, dark hair in a tail and a mustache lifted Dylan's shirt up at his shoulder. The man with the shaved head approached now with a razor-sharp scalpel in his hand. The light of the lamp reflected in the knife. Then he made a long and deep incision in his shoulder and blood started gushing out the gaping wound. First a small stream of blood, but the stream got larger and wider. Blood gushed over his whole body and over the table. Dylan screamed frantically and looked terrified around him. He saw the two men wading through a pool of blood. The blood sprayed out of the wound into the air, and everything turned red around him.

Abruptly Elizabeth woke up, soaked in sweat. Another restless night. She tried to fall back asleep, but she kept on twisting and turning in her bed.

Later that morning, she was sitting at her desk in her office and sipped from her coffee. She tried to concentrate on her work, but after another horrible night, she felt exhausted. It drove her nuts that she didn't really know what to do to find Dylan. Every time a phone rang, she was hoping for some news about the search, but was disappointed when it was for ordinary work issues. When Hawkins finally called later in the afternoon, she wasn't sure what to expect anymore.

"Morning, I just came off the phone with my contact at the Europol task force."

"And?"

"Good news. The fourth man, Romano de Luca, was seen in a shop in Granada in Spain. The local police tried to arrest him, but he got away after a heavy shootout. Two policemen were severely wounded and they believe that Romano de Luca got shot. He got away in the white van that was stolen from the farm in Figueres."

"They got away?"

"Yes, but the good news is that the shootout made it onto the news. Soon after, an old lady called to report that she had seen the white van with several men entering the parking lot next door to her house. The police are preparing a large raid as we speak. My contact in the Europol task force has promised to call me back later tonight to tell me how it went."

"Okay. Well, I hope they succeed."

"Yes, me too. If we can interrogate those men, we might be able to find out more about what has happened to Dylan and Hakim."

"Let's hope so. Well, let me know when you hear something. You can call me day and night."

"I will. Talk to you later."

She hung up and stared out of the window next to her desk. Overlooking the field in front of the vast premises of the Enviro complex, she couldn't help hoping that maybe this raid would be the breakthrough they had been waiting for. She continued working hard for the rest of the afternoon until exhaustion hit her at some point.

She stretched out and looked around. Most of her colleagues had gone home already. Time to go back to her apartment, although she disliked her lonely evenings at home. She turned off her computer and walked back to her apartment. She entered the empty living room, wondering when Hawkins would call her back. She turned on the news to break the silence. Again, they were talking about the disaster on the Mars colony.

The last few days, the tragic events in the Mars colony had been big news. Two-thirds of the three hundred inhabitants had died from alien bacteria, which seemed to have infested the local food supply. The bacteria multiplied so aggressively inside the human body that they ate their human victims from the inside out. This happened so fast that twenty-four hours after initial contamination, only the bones of the victims remained.

The surviving inhabitants destroyed the complete food supply and isolated all infected victims. They were starving in an isolated part of the Mars complex, surviving only on water. The less than hundred survivors desperately tried to restart food production in the isolated part, but yesterday, the colony suffered a major setback. A powerful dust storm destroyed large parts of the complex. Dozens died, and many were injured. Their situation looked dire, and everybody was following the horrible developments closely. After investing a fortune into this mission, it shocked most people that this colonization of Mars seemed to culminate in this tragic fiasco.

After dinner, she cleaned up the kitchen. She returned to the living room with a cup of tea. She turned on her laptop to check her email. Several of her friends were asking for updates about the abduction. She took her time to answer. For the rest, only some commercial emails of little interest. Every day, she hoped there would be some message from Dylan. She was sure that if he could, he would try to contact her. Unfortunately, again no such email in her inbox. She was about to close her laptop when she thought it might be worth checking her spam folder.

It was filled with junk mail. Many from companies trying to sell her something. She carefully went through the long list of emails until her attention was drawn to a specific email. The subject was 'help' and it was from a sender she did not know. She clicked on it and there were only numbers in the email. She was about to delete the email when she realized that the strange sequence of numbers looked like GPS coordinates. Her heart started beating faster in her chest. Would this be the message she was hoping for? Only one way to find out.

She copied the numbers and opened a global mapping program. Then she pasted them into the program and pushed the 'enter' button on her keyboard. A map opened up and zoomed in. She couldn't believe her eyes as she was looking at a suburb of the city of Oran in Algeria. This couldn't be a coincidence. He must still be alive. Thank God. Excited, she grabbed her phone and called Hawkins.

"Good evening, Mr. Hawkins, sorry to disturb you this late, but I believe I've just received a message from Dylan."

"A message from Dylan?"

Elizabeth explained all the details to him. He insisted on coming over right away. Ten minutes later, she opened the door for him and showed him the message. They looked at the map together.

"Mmm, that fits well with the conclusions from the Algerian police."

"Now that we have a clear signal and location from Dylan, we should be able to do something, right? Maybe they can send a unit of the European army into the area and organize a rescue mission?"

"I wish it could be that simple. I fear no European politician would dare to approve a mission in a foreign country like Algeria. Don't forget, the Algerian government is at war with the militia group controlling that region. I don't think Europe will risk getting involved in a regional conflict like this."

"But who's going to save Dylan then!?"

"You know what, let me address it with the Europol task force. I will also debrief Jeff Tusk, our CEO. Maybe he can use his contacts to get things moving. But I can't promise anything. I mean, I doubt they will launch a rescue mission and risk getting involved in an interior war."

"Let's try. He needs our help!"

"I'll start working on it right away. Could you forward me the message?"

Elizabeth turned back to her computer.

"Done!"

"I'll call you as soon as I've got some news."

He rushed out of the door, leaving Elizabeth between hope and desperation. She heated some water for her tea. Then she sat with her teacup behind her laptop and contacted Matteo on her video call program. She explained everything, and he reacted enthusiastically.

"That's great news! Now we can finally take action."

"Well, I'm not sure. Mr. Hawkins doubted Europe would approve a rescue mission, as it might drag them into a regional conflict."

"Ah, yes, I see what he means."

"Don't you think we should go over there together and try to rescue him?"

"Elizabeth, that's a war zone. No way I let you go into that. But yesterday I met with my buddies at my Special Forces Command unit. I told them that the police thought they took him to militia-controlled territories. We've even discussed a rescue mission, and they seemed enthusiastic about the idea. I think they would be willing to help us."

"Really? What are you thinking of?"

"We should probably wait until we get a formal answer from Mr. Hawkins to see if they'll start a rescue mission, even though I doubt it. But I'm more thinking of a covert rescue mission."

"What do you mean?"

"Well, I have five of my buddies from the Special Forces Command unit who I think would be willing to join me. With or without approval, we could fly to Algeria and execute a secret rescue mission to free Dylan."

"Would you do that? That's quite dangerous."

"Yes, but we've been yearning for a good mission like this. We've already started brainstorming and now with these coordinates we can finally go ahead."

"Wow, that would be great."

50.

Elliot walked through the lush gardens of the dome. Most trees in the orchard were blossoming. Nature flourished, showing off its stunning beauty. He was shocked that his father had sent his brother away like that. He understood his father's changed behavior after that night better now. He could only imagine what went through his mind and led him toward his act of ultimate despair. He wished his father had spoken to him about all this instead of leaving him behind guessing. But he also felt delighted. Apparently, his twin brother was alive and had come looking for his family. This triggered something in him. He knew what to do next.

Deep in thought, he passed through the vegetable gardens until he arrived at the eggplant section. He had promised Elsa to cook for her that evening and wanted to prepare her favorite dish. He picked two eggplants. Then he continued further and climbed the stairs in the greenhouse. He climbed all the way up to the fourth floor. Several minutes later, he arrived panting. The sweet smell of strawberries filled the surrounding air. Elsa's favorite desert. With his bag filled with strawberries and vegetables, he strolled homewards.

Back in his apartment, he prepared dinner until the doorbell rang. He opened it for Elsa and they kissed at the entrance. He loved the sweet smell of her skin. She really was a pretty woman. Since his father's death, he felt closer to her, as she had been a genuine support to him. He poured her a drink and continued preparing dinner, while telling her about his meeting with Conan. She listened attentively.

The moment they sat down at the table to enjoy their dinner, she said,

"I still can't believe your twin brother showed up here at the dome's entrance. Nobody else has ever succeeded in that. Quite impressive, that brother of yours."

"Yeah, unbelievable, isn't it? I mean, when I went outside last time, I remember all the drones flying through the air and there's like a whole army base in front of the dome. He literally risked his life to see his birth father. I wonder if he actually knows he has a twin brother or not?"

"Maybe you should try to find out?"

"What do you mean?"

"Well, you could try to contact him."

"Easier said than done. You know the Council doesn't allow contact with the outside world. Only in exceptional cases do they allow it and even then, strictly monitored and limited."

"I think your case is quite exceptional."

"Yeah, but I think they mean that it has to serve the greater good of the community of the dome."

"I didn't say it would be easy, but do you think it was easy for your brother to get to the dome?"

"I see your point. You're right. I should just try. Maybe I should contact Abe, since he told me at the funeral I could if I needed anything."

"What do you've to lose?"

Next morning, after Elsa left for work, Elliot thought about their discussion. It had done him good to talk to her about his twin brother and his father. He slowly processed and accepted his father's death. The amazement he had felt from the entire story had now triggered an insatiable urge in him. He had to find his twin brother.

After a pleasant stroll through the gardens, he descended underground and continued to his office. He greeted his colleagues and got himself an espresso from the coffee corner. At his desk, the first thing he did was to look up Abe's phone number. He took his seat and dialed it. His secretary responded.

"Hi, this is Elliot. I'd like to schedule a meeting with Abe."

"What is it about, and how much time do you need with him?"

"Well, at my father's funeral, he told me to contact him if I needed any help. I need to ask him for a favor. I guess fifteen minutes of his time should be enough."

"Okay. Let me see. I've got some space on his agenda at ten past four in the afternoon. Would that fit for you?"

"Perfect. I'll be there."

The rest of the day, he worked hard to catch up on his work. He was working with his team on an extensive project that intended to boost the efficiency of the nuclear fusion reactors, a challenging project. The more energy they could squeeze out of the same reactor, the more they could use to feed the climate plants to capture more greenhouse gases. An important step in this enormous effort to reduce the amount of greenhouse gases accumulated over more than a hundred years in the atmosphere, a daunting task.

He took short breaks from time to time. During his breaks, he looked for anything he could find out about his twin brother. It did not take him long to find information about him. He quickly found out that he worked at the Environmental Technologies division at Enviro in Denmark. He learned he was a lot like him. They had both received a technical university degree. He deducted his brother must be as passionate about fighting climate change as he was.

He found the phone number of Enviro Technologies online and he wished he could just pick up the phone and call him. But he knew it would be no use. The information security network in the dome made all external communication impossible. Any external contact was only possible after an official authorization from the Council. He remembered how his father had been in contact with external companies he wanted the community to invest in. He had explained how he always needed prior approval. Even after getting it, the internal security department monitored closely all conversations and email contacts.

Later in the afternoon, he left his office and walked through the underground maze of corridors toward Abe's office, on the other side of the dome. He thought about everything he wanted to ask and how to formulate it convincingly. He knew how difficult it would be to convince him and get this permission. The closer he got to his office, the more nervous he became.

He arrived at the entrance door to the Central Administration and stood in front of the reception screen, which illuminated automatically. After reporting to the reception, the heavy metal door slid open with a hiss. A humanoid robot appeared in front of him and escorted him to Abe's office. The humanoid told him to wait in the reception area next to the office.

Ten minutes later, Abe welcomed him in and sat down behind his desk.

"Take a seat, Elliot. What can I do for you?"

"At my father's funeral, you told me to contact you if I needed any help. Well, I need a special favor. I'd like to get approval from the Council to contact my twin brother."

Abe looked dumbfounded at him, and Elliot explained all the things he had discovered since his father's death. Abe listened attentively. He told him what he had found in his father's belongings and about his discussion with Conan. Abe had received and read

Conan's report already and was aware of what had happened at the dome's entrance. Elliot looked full of hope at Abe.

"I guess with all that has happened, you can understand that I'd really like to talk to my twin brother. I hope you can make this exception for me."

"Elliot, thanks for explaining everything to me. I understand how important this must be for you. But you know that we only allow contacts with the outside world that benefit the community."

Elliot had a bad feeling about where this was going and already let his head down. Abe noticed.

"Your father dedicated his life to our community. I remember this painful discussion we had with him now more than twenty years ago. Your parents were overwhelmed when they found out they were going to have twins. They had paid for three places in the dome, and suddenly they needed four. Your father practically begged us to make an exception and allow the twins inside. The Council was divided on this subject. I was in favor of making an exception, nevertheless the proposal was vetoed by another Council member. This had been one of the most heartbreaking decisions in my time as a Council member. Elliot, I'll have to discuss this in the next meeting, but I promise you I'll do my utmost to get you this approval. I believe the dome owes this to your family."

51.

Inspector Javier Morales tied the laces of his black combat boots. He sat up straight and checked out his men as their van swirled through the streets of Granada. Everything had gone so fast since he had received that distressing call. Two of his men had been shot down at a local store. Both were severely wounded. They had been tipped off that a fugitive on Europol's most wanted list had been spotted at this store. They were just doing their duty and now both men were fighting for their lives in the hospital. Javier felt angry and eager to avenge his wounded men.

Shortly after, all the local new channels broadcasted images of the fugitive and the white van that he used to flee the scene. Almost immediately after the broadcast, they received a call from an old lady who had seen the van and several suspicious men entering a small house next to hers in a neighborhood at the edge of Granada. Javier mobilized twenty of his finest men, all heavily armed. They were on their way with several police vehicles.

He gave instructions to his men while driving over there. They split up into two groups, each entering on a different side of the street. The sun had set, and they drove through the darkness toward their destination. Javier peered through the window at the two other police vehicles that were turning left while they continued straight. Almost there. Everybody was busy preparing their weapons and gear. Concentration mixed with excitement.

Five minutes later, they entered the street where the target house was located, just to stop several hundred meters farther. They blocked the entire street with their vehicles. No car could get in or out anymore. They took their arms and waited for Javier to give them the go ahead. He contacted his colleagues on the other side of the street.

"Alfa, we're in position. Are you ready?"

"We're all set, Bravo."

"All right, everybody be careful. These men are armed and dangerous. Let's move in, Alfa."

Javier lifted his gun in the air and waved at his men.

"Let's go!"

They opened the back of the van. One by one, the armed policemen filled the street. It was still very warm outside. They lined up, holding their automatic rifles, ready to engage. Javier led them toward the target's house. It was quiet, and they only heard their own footsteps and breathing while approaching the closed gate. Javier looked at the other group on the other side of the gate. He spoke in a low voice into the walkie-talkie on his arm.

"We're in position. Cut the power."

Several seconds later, the lights went off everywhere in the street. Javier moved his night vision visor over his eyes. He gestured his men to move in. First, they tried to open the gate by hand, but when that didn't work, two men forced it with a battering ram. It opened and the other men moved in. They first peeked inside the white van that was parked on the inner court in front of the house. It looked empty. They continued toward the house.

One of his men tried to peer inside, but the blinds were all down. A line of policemen formed in front of the door. You could almost feel the tension in the air as they advanced quietly. When Javier made a signal with his hand, the two men in front of the line rammed the door open with the battering ram. They rushed in and with the light on top of each rifle aimed in front of them, shining through the dark corridor. The agents in front checked the first room. They looked inside, but it was all dark. They checked the entire room. There was no one there. The rest continued further into the kitchen. Carefully, they glanced inside. The kitchen was dark and empty. Only the dirty plates and empty bottles betrayed someone had been there before.

Now the men went stealthily upstairs, carefully checking every room. They continued like that throughout the entire house until it became clear to them that there was nobody inside.

"No one here, boss."

"Yes, it seems we've arrived too late."

Javier moved his mouth to the walkie-talkie on his arm.

"All clear. No one inside. Turn the power back on."

The lights went back on. The men looked at him, awaiting his orders.

"All right. At ease. Let's search the place, while I contact our friends at Europol."

52.

With his wife and son, Ebo rushed to the makeshift house they had been living in for the last couple of months. Their long-awaited moment was about to happen. Filled with hope, excitement, and fear, they packed their bags and went outside. Together with a large group of other people, they followed the armed guards. They walked upward along the parking ramp. Ebo turned his head and looked back at the many who remained in their makeshift houses. He wondered if they would follow soon and why they were not coming with them.

As they continued upward into the underground parking garage, it became warmer and warmer. It reminded him of the horrendous trip they had made to arrive here initially. The heat during the day was unbearable. There were stories of people staying out too long who suffered severe burns, dehydration and heatstroke. Too long outside during the day would almost certainly lead to death. The sudden departure dumbfounded most of them. Some walked in silence upstairs, while others mumbled to one another. They followed the ramp upstairs, swirling higher at the end of each corridor until they reached the highest floor.

The air was much warmer up here and fell like a blanket upon them. Ebo looked at the ramp and noticed the barriers in front of the entrance. The guards continued further toward the exit. They entered the street, and the first thing he did was to look up at the dark sky above him. Right after, he noticed the long row of trucks parked on the road in front of the underground parking, where several armed guards separated the large group into smaller ones. Every time they counted a certain amount of people and sent them to another truck. Ebo did not want to be separated from his wife and son and held on to them as they queued in the long line.

Anxiously, he waited until they arrived in front of the line. The guard indicated to the people in front of him to continue toward a specific truck. He touched the shoulder of everyone passing behind to keep track of the count. Ebo moved his wife and son in front of him and, to his relief, they could stay together. Only a few individuals followed him as the guard started sending the rest to the next truck. They rushed, and he helped his wife and son climb inside. The cargo hold was packed with people, and they tried to find a free spot. Everybody bumped into each other.

Then a guard showed up and closed the backdoor. Suddenly, it was pitch dark inside. His wife and son held onto him tightly. A while later, the truck started moving and turmoil arose among the people. Everybody tried to sit down to avoid falling with the swirling movement. They sat down as well, and he held his wife and son close. Eventually, the truck stopped turning and continued straight.

It became even warmer inside, with everyone sitting packed together like sardines. His face turned all sweaty, and he wiped it with his sleeve. He still couldn't believe they were finally going to go. He had waited so long for this day. It also terrified him, since he was not sure if they could actually make it alive. But at this point, he did not have any other choice than to wait and hope.

53.

Cheng proudly explained to his boss what he had accomplished. Abdul listened attentively and realized that what Cheng had programmed could actually work. He challenged him several times, but he had thought of everything. He had worked round the clock with his team until he finished everything. They went through the whole plan together, and it impressed Abdul. Cheng had already taken the liberty of sending instructions to Marco and his team. Abdul looked at Cheng in admiration while he showed him the instruction manuals that he had sent to them.

Their cooperation went back more than five years. Abdul met him when he raided the office of a crime lord, called Mukami, in Mombasa, in Kenia. Abdul paid Mukami for years for his hacking services. Until one day the poor soul thought he could make even more money blackmailing Abdul with information that would link him to several international crimes. It didn't take long before Abdul reacted. He located the culprit and raided his offices with twenty of his most loyal men. He butchered Mukami with a machete, and they ransacked his office, killing many of his men. However, when Abdul ran into Mukami's team of hackers, he offered them a job instead. Cheng immediately accepted, like most of his colleagues. Abdul made his offer sound like something they were free to turn down, but after separating the people who refused from the ones who accepted, he ruthlessly executed the ones that had refused.

He appreciated Cheng more and more over time. He showed initiative and did not hesitate to give his opinion. He was extremely loyal to Abdul. He was one of the few hackers who dared to speak up even when it would be a message Abdul would not like to hear. He based the current plan on an idea from Cheng. Even though the plan was complicated and had taken him years to execute, he believed he had made the right bet. He was going to find out soon enough.

"You did a good job, Cheng," Abdul said while tapping him on the shoulder.

"Thanks, boss."

"Did you send the additional instructions to Marco?"

"Yes, I did."

"Perfect. Ahmed, how far are we with our transportation arrangements?"

"Last week I bought another two. We've got more than enough space now to fit everybody."

"Great, start moving everybody to our launch site."

"All right, boss. We've started preparing already. I've calculated we'll need to drive about three times back and forth."

"Perfect."

Ahmed left, and just when Abdul wanted to continue talking with Cheng, he coughed. He put a handkerchief in front of his mouth while he continued coughing. Cheng immediately passed him a glass of water. He took it and drank a bit. His coughing calmed down. He closed the handkerchief to hide the blood in it and tucked it away in his pocket.

"Okay, Cheng. Time to go ahead with our genius plan. Prepare your department for departure and we'll pick you up later."

Abdul left the room and rushed to his office. He took the seat behind his desk and typed an email for Marco to inform him about the latest progress. He urged him to make all necessary preparations as quickly as possible. Then he walked toward his private quarters, further down the corridor. As he entered his living room, he felt all excited and energetic, spurred by the good news. He walked to the corner where a heavy punch bag hung on a hook. At first, he punched it a few times, but soon after, his thoughts took him back to the reason that had triggered his grand plan: Jabari Saad, the man responsible for his parents' death. Then the punches followed each other faster and faster.

His eyes filled with rage, and he exploded with his fists against the punching bag. He was finally going to get his revenge. The wheels were in motion. He was about to move closer to his target. While punching the bag, he could almost imagine Jabari's face in front of him, even though he had never met him. After their lethal visit to Tony Gamal, it had not cost them much effort to find Jabari's home address. He had constructed a large, private, so-called 'climate-change-ready' compound on the terrain where their parents' apartment had once been.

One night, after observing the compound for several weeks, they figured out the perfect way to enter the heavily guarded premises. At that time, Cairo suffered from a plague of rats. Due to problems with the trash collection, the streets were filled with trash. The rat population grew exponentially, infesting the streets and houses. The city council acted by hiring an army of pest control services to clean up the city. They passed through the streets and went from house to house to check for rats and to terminate them if they encountered any.

Dressed in white uniforms and with a van marked 'Pest Control' on the side, they went to the compound. At the door, they explained they came for an inspection. Abdul showed some forged papers, but the guard at the door only glanced at them. A moment later, they walked through the large compound. Inside, it almost looked like a palace, richly decorated and well-furnished. Almost immediately, they sensed something was off, though. A guard escorted them through the different rooms inside. After seeing more boxes piled up, Abdul looked at the guard.

"The owner, Mr. Jabari Saad. Is he in today?"

"No, sir. Master Saad has moved out."

"What do you mean, moved out? They moved out for good?"

"Yes, sir."

"But this place is all new? Where did they move to?"

"They moved to Europe."

"Where in Europe?"

"Sorry, sir, but that's private information. I'm not allowed to tell you."

"Did you spot any rats on the premises?" Maheer changed the topic as the guard seemed to get suspicious.

"No, none."

They continued going through the building, and they pretended to look for rats, searching carefully throughout the house. When they arrived in what looked like an office, Maheer gestured at Abdul to point his attention at the boxes piled up in the corner. Maheer talked to the guard to distract him while Abdul inspected them. They were all labeled, and on the label, there was an address in Berlin. He sneakily took a picture when the guard looked the other way. After inspecting all the rooms, they left.

In the following days, they checked if they could travel to Berlin. Unfortunately, the tickets were so expensive that they could not afford them. In addition, it would be difficult to get the required special visas to travel to Europe. They had no other choice than to park their plans to go after Jabari Saad. Meanwhile, they expanded their criminal activities and started making more and more money.

By the time they had accumulated enough to pay for a trip to Europe, they got caught and convicted for several minor offenses, making it even more complicated to get visas. After their release from prison, they adapted and became more careful, staying behind the scenes in their drug dealing activities. They continued expanding their organization into other activities like robbery, human trafficking, prostitution, blackmailing, and kidnapping.

Despite their attempts to stay in the shadows, they eventually had to leave Egypt, because the police were suspicious. They became wanted criminals in Egypt and moved to neighboring Libya. The country was in a state of anarchy. Militias ruled large parts of the country. Abdul and Maheer felt like a fish in water there. They expanded their criminal activities internationally, and their organization grew further in power and reach. The downside was that they could not travel legally to Europe anymore. They were condemned to a life in hiding, surrounded by armed guards.

After punching the bag for about thirty minutes, Abdul felt tired. He drank some water and continued to his bedroom. He thought of his brother. If only he had been patient enough. He should have been here with him now to enjoy this exciting milestone together. Thrilled, he started preparing for the imminent departure.

54.

Several days had passed now since his meeting with Abe, and the waiting drove Elliot nuts. He wanted to call back the day after, but Elsa advised him to wait. She thought it could be counterproductive to disturb a Council member too often. Abe had promised Elliot to get back to him, so she said he would just have to wait until he did.

Meanwhile, he had difficulty focusing on his work. Elias, his boss, noticed it when Elliot walked by his desk.

"What is wrong with you, Elliot? You seem absent minded today."

"Yes, it's because of all the things I've found out since my father passed away."

Elias had always been quite close to Elliot. Often, he filled the gap his father had left even when he was still alive. Now he looked puzzled at him, and Elliot explained everything he had learned since his father's death.

"Wow, a twin brother!? Who would have thought!? I've known your parents for a long time and they've never told me about it. I even saw your mother during her pregnancy. She had a big belly, but they never mentioned they were expecting twins."

"At least I've got a better understanding now about what drove my parents to their desperate acts. I guess it will help me find peace with it."

"This explains a lot. I never understood why they were so unhappy and depressed after entering the dome. Most people were ecstatic and felt privileged to live here. I always assumed they had some issues in their relationship, although I never really understood what was wrong. And your father was not the type to talk about these things."

"I know. That was part of the problem. But I guess you can imagine now why I can't wait to get in touch with my twin brother."

"Definitely! Especially now that you know what risks he took to find your parents."

"So, do you think I could check with Abe to see if they've reached a decision already?"

"I think you have to be patient, Elliot. Abe is a man of his word. He will discuss it with the Council on the first occasion he has. Knowing him, he'll get back to you right after. I wouldn't disturb him again. It could annoy him."

"I guess you're right. Thanks, Elias."

Elliot returned to his desk and continued working on his project. The conversation had done him good and calmed him down. Even though he didn't like it, he had no other choice than to wait.

In the evening, he used his spare time to find out more about his twin brother. On the website of the Swiss Federal Institute of Technology in Lausanne, he found Dylan Myers on the honorable list of students that graduated Summa Cum Lauda. His brother was a bright man and the more he read about him, the more curious he became. Dylan had earned a Master's degree in Environmental Sciences and Engineering. They clearly shared many interests. It drove him crazy that his brother had been so close, right at the entrance of the dome, without him knowing about it.

A few days later, he finally received a call from Abe's secretary.

"Hi Elliot, Abe would like to schedule a meeting with you in his office at three thirty. Does that suit you?"

"Yes. Did they decide anything?"

"I don't know, he didn't tell me."

"Okay, I'll be there."

Later that afternoon, he rushed to Abe's office, full of anticipation. He was hoping to get permission to contact Dylan. He believed he should get it, because this was an exceptional case. Still, he had many doubts running through his head. They were very strict on limiting contacts with the outside to the bare essential, essential being what benefits the greater good of the community. His father had pounded those rules in him over the years. The closer he got to Abe's office, the more he worried. Why did he not tell him about the decision over the phone? That could only mean that he wanted to explain it and elaborate on the reasons why they have made this decision. He feared that the decision was going to be negative, because Abe wanted to tell him in person.

He followed the humanoid robot to Abe's office and there he greeted his secretary. He was five minutes early.

"He's still in a videoconference. Please have a seat."

Elliot sat down on the couch in the corner of the reception area. He felt anxious and had clammy hands. He tried to remain positive, but doubts were racing through his head. The secretary asked if he wanted something to drink and he took some tea. Maybe it would calm him down. He sipped his tea while waiting. About twenty minutes later, the door of Abe's office opened.

"Sorry to keep you waiting, Elliot. My meeting ran over. Come in, please."

Elliot got up and entered his office. He was quaking in his boots.

"Take a seat, please."

"I've discussed your request in the Council meeting. I can tell you that your unusual request has caused quite a heated debate between the Council members. There was considerable controversy during our long discussion, and I'll spare you the details. We've weighed all the pros and cons deliberately..."

Elliot listened attentively, though he couldn't stop his legs from shaking.

"... and we have reached a decision that we did not take lightly. We will exceptionally grant you permission to have contact with your twin brother under strict conditions."

A broad smile appeared on Elliot's face, and he sighed in relief.

"Yes! Thank you! Thank you! This means a lot to me."

Abe had not finished talking and was dumbfounded to get interrupted. But Elliot's enthusiastic reaction touched him.

"Elliot, I didn't finish."

"Ah, of course. Sorry for interrupting."

"We'll monitor all your contacts closely and under no circumstance can you say anything that could harm the dome. You also have to make clear to Dylan Myers that he has to protect the secret of the dome at all costs."

"I will! I will! Thank you! Thank you so much. You can't imagine how much this means to me," Elliot answered with tears in his eyes.

He left Abe's office and rushed back home as fast as he could.

55.

Right after closing the gate, Marco opened the sliding door. Romano lay in a pool of blood on the floor of the van. He held his hands on the wound in an attempt to stop the bleeding. With a look of despair and agony, he glanced at Marco, who said,

"Shit, Romano. That doesn't look good."

Farid tried to explain what had happened, but Marco quickly understood and interrupted him.

"James and Farid, we have to be quick now. Go and get us another van. We have to leave as soon as possible. I'll take care of that wound."

Farid and James nodded and rushed out of the gate. Marco climbed into the van and took a first-aid kit from one of the wooden crates. With a pair of scissors, he cut open the right pant leg. He tightened the belt around the leg and cleaned the wound with some water. He inspected the wound, then he looked at Romano.

"You're lucky. It's just a graze. The bullet just passed through the flesh."

"Well, it's bloody painful."

"Don't worry. I'll take care of your wound. At least there's no need for a doctor."

Marco covered the wound and wrapped a long bandage around his leg. He gave Romano a painkiller and a bottle of water. Then he climbed out of the van and helped him to get out. He put his arm over his shoulder and supported him while Romano hobbled toward the door of the house. Inside, he helped him to lie down on the sofa.

Marco left him in the living room and hastily started packing all their belongings.

At dusk, Farid and James arrived with a dark green van. They parked it with the sliding door facing the gate to facilitate the transfer of all their equipment. They immediately started carrying all the crates, equipment, and tools to the new van. Marco joined them with the luggage from the house and they filled the van as quickly as they could. It was getting dark already, and Marco kept pushing them to hurry. When they finished, Marco walked back to the house.

"You two. Check the house and the van to ensure we left nothing behind. I'll carry Romano to the new van. Let's try to leave within five minutes."

Farid checked the van while James rushed inside. Marco supported Romano and helped him hobble to the dark-green van in the twilight. He put him in the back and rushed back inside. He returned with a mattress, which he put on the floor of the van.

"Here, Romano. You lie down here, this way your leg can rest."

"Grazie, Marco."

Marco took the driver's seat and waited. Farid came out of the house and told James to hurry. Farid sat next to Marco and a few seconds later, James closed the gate and jumped into the back of the van. They drove away immediately through the dark street. At the end of it, they turned right onto the main street. Marco noticed two black vans approaching at high speed. At the moment they passed them, he could distinguish two police officers in front. He looked at Farid, who had seen it as well, and he nodded back at him.

"Just in time."

They left the city as fast as they could and took the highway westward. Later, they turned south toward Malaga. They drove non-stop. After passing Malaga, they continued all the way southwest along the coast.

Three hours later, they arrived in Algeciras. They drove through the small town and continued south toward the sea. Farid looked at his phone.

"We're almost there. It should be next to the road along the beach."

Marco continued driving over the small interior road. It was a dark night, but they could distinguish the ocean on the horizon. The road was empty. Ten kilometers farther, Marco slowed down as they approached the designated location on the map. On their left, they could see the surf of the sea. They both peered ahead until Farid pointed in front of them.

"I think it's over there on the right."

Marco saw it as well now and drove a bit further. Then he parked next to what looked like a thick, high pole. He turned off the lights, and they both got out of the van. It was dark and there was only some light on the horizon from the nearby Algeciras. One could hear the infinite sound of the breakers not so far away. Marco opened the sliding door on the side of the van. He took a headlight from a bag. Then he took off his wig and put the adjustable headband with the headlight attached to it on his bald skull. He turned the light on and gave another headlight to Farid. Then he looked at Romano, who looked tired.

"How are you holding up, Romano?"

"I'll be fine, boss."

Marco continued unpacking and passed a laptop to Farid. He took one of the bags from the van while Farid opened a document on the laptop.

“All right, let’s make sure we take everything with us. Let’s see. First the toolbox.”

James passed it to Marco, who put it on the ground next to the van.

“Check!”

“Electrical wire.”

James passed a roll of wire to Marco, who tucked it into the bag.

“Check!”

“Circuit board.”

“Check!”

They went through the entire list until they had everything they needed. Marco and Farid carried the bag and the toolbox toward the thick pole outside.

“James, you stand watch. Anything suspicious, you let us know!”

“Okay, boss.”

They continued toward the thick pole. It had a diameter of more than two meters and they disappeared out of sight behind it. Marco unscrewed the panel on the backside and removed it completely. They both peered into the pole, which was filled with electronics, fuses, and wires. Farid checked another document with a technical drawing. Together they went through the instructions they had received earlier on from Cheng. They adjusted the electronics inside the pole accordingly.

An hour later, they had finished everything. Farid did a last check, and Marco looked over his shoulder at the laptop.

“And?”

“We have a connection.”

“Perfect. Let’s go.”

They closed up the pole and returned to the van. They opened the side door. Romano was sleeping on the mattress. While they put everything in the back, he turned on his other side but did not open his eyes. James joined them next to the van.

"Ready?"

"Yep, all set. Let's go to the next one."

They all got back inside and drove away. They continued further over the road along the beach. Farid spotted the next pole about fifteen minutes later, and they parked next to it. They could see the lights from a small village not too far ahead of them. They gathered everything they needed from the van. Farid and Marco walked toward the pole and James stood watch.

It was a quiet night, and the road was deserted. James strolled toward the beach and the light sea breeze made the warm night more bearable. While walking back to the van, James noticed two headlights approaching on the road in front of him. He turned his head in the direction where Farid and Marco had disappeared. He could only see the thick pole. He took the safety off his gun and tucked it back into his trousers. The lights came closer and he could distinguish the shape of a car. He hid behind the van as it approached.

The car slowed down while passing the van on the other side of the road. For a moment, James thought it would be okay, but then the brake lights of the car went on. It stopped. Then it drove backwards until it was next to their van. James quickly kneeled next to the tire of the van.

"Problemas con la camioneta?" the man asked from the car.

"No, speaka Spanish."

"Ah, turistas. Car trouble?" the man asked in English with a strong Spanish accent.

"Yeah, I think I got a leak in the tire."

"Do you need any help?"

"No, I'll be fine."

But it was too late. The man stepped out of his car and came toward the van. James noticed he was wearing a uniform and carried a gun in a holster on his hip.

"Are you from the police?"

"Yes, I just finished my shift, and I was on my way home when I noticed you over here."

"That's a relief. I am always a bit wary of strangers in the night."

"I understand. You're all alone out here?"

"Yeah, just on my way to my hotel, when it felt like one tire was empty."

The policeman looked at the tire next to James. When he stood next to him, he turned and looked toward the thick pole. Then he noticed the lights behind it and put his hand on his holster.

"What are those lights over there?"

Before he could turn his head back, James had already taken a knife from his pocket. He grabbed the man from behind and slit his throat with the razor-sharp blade. Blood gushed out of his neck like a tap. He looked in disbelief at James before collapsing on the ground.

James did not waste a second. He walked over to the man's car, stepped inside, and started it. He turned and parked it next to the lifeless body. He popped the trunk and got out of the car. He dragged the heavy body and lifted it inside the trunk. He pushed the man's arms and legs inside and closed it. He looked around and noticed the giant billboard about five hundred meters farther. He got back in the car and drove over there. Next to the billboard, he drove off the road onto the dirt ground and parked the car behind. He got out and walked back. He turned his head to check. The car was out of sight.

Marco and Farid were waiting for him next to the van. They looked baffled at him.

"Where did you go?"

"I got rid of a problem."

They all got back in the van and Marco drove to the next spot about ten kilometers farther. They continued working until they finished everything early in the morning and left for Tarifa. Marco drove to the north of the town into a quiet neighborhood. They entered a small street and stopped in front of a white gate. Farid got out and opened it. They parked inside and closed the gate. James helped Romano get inside of the house. He put him on the couch and then he climbed the stairs and dropped exhausted on a bed in one of the rooms.

Farid took the laptop into the kitchen. He checked something on his screen. When Marco joined him, he looked over his shoulder.

"Are we ready?"

"Yep, everything seems to work. What do we do now?"

"We wait."

56.

Elizabeth woke up early in the morning and felt even more restless than the days before. Since she received the message from Dylan, she could not stop thinking about him. The urge to do something after his cry for help became unbearable. She didn't want to wait for the bureaucrats to get back to her. They would probably tell her that a rescue mission was too risky politically.

After breakfast, she went to the office, although she was in no mood for work. She stared at her computer screen while she thought about Dylan. She thought of what her brother had proposed and slowly became more and more convinced it was the best option. After trying to get some work done for a couple of hours, she felt she was collapsing. She got up and made her way to the main exit of the Enviro building.

As soon as she arrived outside, she allowed the tears to run down her face. The stress was getting to her, and she could no longer stay in that confined office space. She looked at the forest on the other side of the terrain while she walked away from the building. As she got closer to the trees, she thought back to the practice runs she had done with Dylan on a terrain not too far from there. His persistence and drive to get to the dome at all costs had impressed her. Her love and respect for him had only grown further since. She missed him so much. There was not a moment in the day she did not think of him and fear for his life.

The stroll calmed her down, and she returned to the office. When she walked through the main reception, she noticed Hawkins crossing the large hall. He had not seen her and almost disappeared in the corridor on the other side. She called his name, and he turned his head.

"Miss Muller!?"

"Any news?"

"Well, yes, and no. I talked to the head of the task force this morning again. He doesn't want to start any rescue mission without approval from the head of Europol."

"Did he ask for it?"

"He did and apparently, the head of Europol has discussed it in the European Council. They prefer to first go through the diplomatic channels. They're going to contact the Algerian government and discuss the matter."

"But I thought the Algerian government had no control over the area where Dylan is?"

"That's correct and probably they won't do much."

Elizabeth sighed and glanced at her shoes in desperation.

"I know it's frustrating, but this is what I was expecting."

She looked back at him with a determined look in her eyes now.

"Okay, well, at least it's clear to me now that I don't need to expect much from Europol. No need to wait any longer."

Steve Hawkins looked confused.

"What do you mean? What are you planning on doing?"

She hesitated for a moment, but then explained.

"My brother is planning a rescue mission to get Dylan out of there."

"He's planning what? That's extremely dangerous. He could get killed."

"I know, but he's highly trained. He's an experienced Grenadier in the Special Forces Command unit of the Swiss army."

"Really!?"

"Yes, and he found five friends and colleagues willing to join him on a mission."

"Wow. That could work."

"I hope so."

"You know what? Let me discuss this with our CEO, Jeff Tusk. The bureaucratic reaction of Europol also frustrated him. He feels responsible for his two abducted employees."

"You think he could help?"

"Possibly. I'll get back to you as soon as possible," and Hawkins rushed away.

Elizabeth returned to her desk, slightly more hopeful than before. She was even able to get some work done. When she got back from lunch with her colleagues, her phone rang. It was Hawkins. She listened while he explained everything to her.

"That's wonderful news! I'm thrilled to hear that."

"When do you think your brother can go?"

"I think he has been preparing everything already. I'll check, but I got the impression he could leave almost immediately."

"Great, could you send me his details? I will contact him."

"Sure. Thanks again, Mr. Hawkins!"

As soon as she hung up the phone, she dialed Matteo's number.

"Hi, sis. Any news?"

"I've got great news, actually."

"Tell me."

"Well, it looks like Europol isn't going to do much. I mean, they're first going to try the diplomatic path. But then I mentioned to Hawkins that you're planning a rescue mission yourself, and to my surprise, he was all for it. He addressed it with Enviro's CEO, Jeff Tusk, who offered his help."

"Help? In what way?"

"Well, it looks like you're going to fly to Algeria in sheer luxury in first class. He's offering the corporate hydrogen plane of Enviro to fly you and your team to Algiers."

"Wow, that's great!"

"Wait, that's not all. He'll take care of all the permits and paperwork for you and the team. On top of it, he's going to provide you with several of Enviro's newest high-tech military gadgets to use during your mission."

"Great! My buddies are going to love this. Enviro's military technology is state-of-the-art."

"When can you leave?"

"Well, I think we're ready to go."

"Perfect, I'll pass your details to Hawkins and he'll contact you to arrange for the plane to pick you up in Lausanne."

57.

After the guards escorted him back to his cell, Dylan felt exhilarated. Unfortunately, he could not really share it with anyone in the cell, since the only people present were the two Arabic men. He had tried to communicate with them several times before, but he did not know how to explain what he had done using sign language only. He waited for Hakim to return to the cell to share his excitement.

His patience wore thin, as Hakim did not return for quite a while. When the door finally opened, Dylan turned his head to look, but was disappointed to see a guard entering with water bottles and candy bars. After he left, Dylan went to lie down on his mattress. He thought of Elizabeth. Would she have read his message already? Would she understand it came from him? Would she send help to save them?

Hakim returned to the cell late in the evening. The guards pushed him inside, and he looked exhausted and pale. He still had not completely recovered from his infection. Though the moment he noticed Dylan, he seemed to perk up. He first turned his face to check if the guards had closed the door before a grin appeared on his face.

"And? Did you succeed?"

Dylan showed a triumphant smile.

"Yes, I've sent our coordinates to Elizabeth."

"Great! I was afraid that guard would hurt you, but I guess he wasn't completely sure what you had done."

"Let's see if we get some help now."

"I sure hope we will."

"They've kept you quite late today?"

"Yes, they seemed to be in a hurry. Anyway, I got the impression they've finally got what they were looking for."

"Ah, really. I hope they still need us though, otherwise they might decide to dispose of us."

Hakim shrugged his shoulders and drank some water. Then he went to lie down on his mattress and fell asleep soon after.

The next day, Dylan woke early. The two Arabic men were awake already, but Hakim was still deep asleep. He drank some water and ate one of the candy bars. With every day that passed, he longed more and more for some elaborate food other than these dry bars. He thought of Elizabeth and the delightful meals they used to have together. He really had to get out of this place.

Hakim woke up several hours later. He looked slightly better than the day before. He finished the last candy bar and drank some water. They talked and tried to pass the time, relaxing and playing some mind games from time to time. At the end of the afternoon, they both felt something was wrong.

"That's weird. Normally, the guards pass three times every day. They've not shown their faces at all today. Did they come while I was sleeping?"

"No, I haven't seen them yet, and I thought I still had to fix several air conditioners."

"Strange."

They waited, but no one came. Later in the evening, they really started to worry.

"I'm getting hungry. I guess we should try to call them."

"Yes, I agree. This isn't normal."

They knocked on the door and started yelling.

"Hello? He! Ho! Anyone!? We want some food, please!"

They waited and listened at the door, but it remained completely silent. They looked at the two other men in the cell, and they also seemed concerned. They banged the door harder now and screamed out loud.

"Hello!? Help! Help! HELP!"

They waited for a moment to listen at the door. The silence after made them anxious.

"No one. Maybe we should try to get out of here?"

"Let's try."

They banged against the door with their shoulder. Nothing happened. Dylan gestured to the two other men to help them, and together they tried to kick the door open. It didn't move an inch. Hakim looked around until his eyes fell on the bed in the corner.

"We should use the metal frame of that bed as a battering ram."

"Great idea!"

He turned toward the others, but they seemed to have understood as they were walking toward the bed already. They removed the mattress and lifted the bed frame. They carried the frame upright together and prepared it in front of the door. They walked backwards first to enable a running start. Hakim looked at the others and counted down.

"Three, two, one, go!"

They ran as fast as they could and rammed the metal bed into the door. A loud bang echoed through the cell. One of the Arabic men bumped into the side of the door at the moment of impact. The heavy metal door didn't move an inch. It stayed shut.

"Shit! That didn't work. Let's try one more time."

They went backwards again and rammed the metal bed another time into the door. Besides a few scratches, there was no damage. It remained shut.

"Mmm, that door is too strong. Let's wait a moment, maybe someone will come now after all the noise."

They waited for several minutes, but didn't hear any sound outside. No one came. Disappointed, they tried one more time, but this time Dylan hurt his arm. The door still didn't bulge an inch.

"This doesn't work. Maybe we should try to detach the legs from the bed and try to stick them in the side of the door and use them as levers to crack the door open."

"Okay, let's try."

The legs of the bed came off easily. The side that was attached to the bed frame had a sharp edge. The four of them stuck it into the side of the door at different heights.

"Okay, on the count of three, we try to use the legs as a lever to open the door. Three, two, one, go!"

They tried with all their force. It seemed to move a few millimeters until Hakim's metal leg bended. The metal was not strong enough.

"That doesn't work either."

They took a break and drank some water from the remaining bottles. One of the men kicked the door out of frustration. It stayed solidly shut. Dylan looked at the remaining water and realized it wouldn't last more than a day. If no one showed up, they would be in deep trouble.

58.

Matteo felt the powerful thrust of the hydrogen jet as it pushed him backwards in his chair during take-off. The ultra-luxurious plane had room for twenty people. With only six passengers onboard, it felt like the royal treatment to Matteo and his friends. After receiving the good news from his sister, he immediately called his friends to prepare to leave early in the evening for the rescue mission. He drove to Lausanne airport with Leon, who picked him up with a driverless taxi. Leon was much taller than Matteo, but just as muscular, which made him an imposing figure. No one messed with him. They met the rest of the group at the airport. After carrying all their luggage and equipment on board, they took their seats in the plush leather chairs inside. They took off feeling like kings.

About an hour later, they landed at the New Houari Boumediene Airport in Algiers. Half of the city of Algiers, including the old Houari Boumediene Airport, had flooded ten years ago as a result of the rising sea levels in the world. They built the new airport about ten kilometers south of the old one. The plane taxied all the way to a special section of the airport reserved for private airplanes. They disembarked as soon as the plane came to a halt. The sun had just gone under, but the heat still fell on them like a warm blanket. The air quality was poor, and they all wore their respos. A brown, heavily armored truck drove toward the plane and stopped in front of them. A neatly dressed gentleman stepped out.

"Mr. Matteo Muller?"

"That's me," Matteo replied while raising his hand.

"I'm Peter Townsend. I work for Enviro Technologies and Mr. Tusk asked me to provide you with this state-of-the-art army truck for your mission, including several of our newest military weapons and equipment."

"Nice!"

"Let me give you a brief instruction," Peter said while opening the back of the truck.

They listened carefully and asked him several questions. They were all quite excited. The special treatment and support of Enviro added to the total experience. Some of his friends were listening to the instructions, while others unloaded their luggage. After the instructions, Peter handed the key of the truck to Matteo. He thanked him and then said to his friends, "Let's go! Everybody in the truck!"

Peter drove with them to help them pass smoothly through customs. After the formalities, they left the airport and dropped Peter off at a nearby hotel. Matteo and Leon discussed the planning, while the others entered a local shop to stockpile food and water. They carefully planned the whole route and checked all the information from Enviro. This included important information, like the coordinates of the military checkpoints west of Algiers gathered through satellite observation.

As soon as the others returned with the supplies, they drove off westward. The outside air was cooling off now the sun had set, making the heat more bearable. The aim was to accomplish the entire rescue mission during the night to avoid the blistering heat during the day. They estimated that the drive west to Dylan's coordinates would take them about four hours without stopping. There and back would take eight hours. The sun would rise around six in the morning. Leaving them with less than two hours during the night. Not much slack, thought Matteo.

On the first leg of their journey, they passed through a long stretch of poor suburbs. Almost the entire population lived in the coastal region, as the rest of the country was the Sahara Desert. After a while, they left the suburbs behind. The long stretches of dry arid land in between subsequent towns became longer the further they went westward. The road in between the towns was not lit, and they drove through the darkness most of the time. After two hours they passed the town Chlef, named after Algeria's longest river, which had dried up entirely as the result of climate change.

"That was the last large town in government-controlled terrain. Soon we'll enter the no-man's-land zone before entering the militia-controlled western part of Algeria," Leon explained from behind the steering wheel.

"All weapons are loaded and ready, but we still have to activate this new magic gadget from Enviro," Matteo said, while getting out of his chair.

In the back of the truck, there was a large, square metal box. Matteo took something from the side that looked like some sort of hand scanner. First, he aimed it at his own face and his face lit up in the red light of the scanner. Then they heard a voice coming from the metal box.

"Scan approved. Matteo Muller registered."

Now he walked over to Leon. He pointed the scanner in his face while he was trying to concentrate on the road.

"Hey! I'm driving. What's this anyway?"

"This box is one of Enviro's latest gadgets. It'll protect anyone who has been registered as a friend."

"Scan approved. Leon Baumann registered."

"Now you're a friend as well," Matteo said with a smile on his face.

He continued scanning the faces of the others until everyone was registered. From a bag he took what looked like watches. After pressing some buttons, he gave everyone a watch.

"If you're in trouble, you just press the red button on the side together with the screen and this magic gadget will check out what's wrong and will react appropriately."

"How does it work?"

"It uses a complex artificial intelligence program, which basically assesses your situation and chooses the most appropriate response. Peter didn't explain everything, but he emphasized that it could save your life."

"Well, as long as I've got my buddy here, I should be fine," Rafael, a broad-shouldered man with short blond hair, joked as he patted the handgun hanging on his hip.

"Guys, we're approaching the first checkpoint. Could you hand me our travel documents, Matteo?" Leon interrupted the laughter.

Matteo took the papers from his backpack and handed them to Leon while he watched the road in front of them.

"Here they are. Is it a governmental checkpoint?"

"According to our intel, it should be. Look at the flag on the door of that army truck."

They approached the checkpoint, which was illuminated by streetlights like a lit beacon in the darkness around. A barrier blocked the road. Army vehicles were parked on the left and right of it. Next to the barrier, there was a small guard post constructed out of sandbags. Above the sandbags, they saw a piece of heavy artillery sticking out. They slowed down, and an armed guard came closer. They opened the window, and the guard addressed them in Arabic.

Leon replied in Arabic. Matteo did not understand a word of what they said. Leon handed over the papers. They continued talking in Arabic and after checking the documents, the guard gestured that they could pass.

A moment later, Matteo grinned at Leon.

"I didn't know you speak Arabic."

Leon grinned back.

"Some of us do more than just train their muscles."

About five kilometers farther, they ran into another governmental guard post. This time, there was a whole military base next to it. And a bright searchlight followed their truck as they approached the barrier. Leon showed the documents and spoke for a while in Arabic. The guard pointed in front of them, as if he was trying to show something. He gave back the documents, and they opened the barrier to let them pass.

"This was the last governmental post. The guard explained that this is the border between government-controlled and militia-controlled territory. From here on, we are on our own."

The further they drove, the worse the road became. There were potholes everywhere and often the difference between the sand next to the road and the road itself was no longer clear. Matteo carefully studied the map and their intel.

"There should be another checkpoint in about ten kilometers controlled by the militia. Probably it's better to avoid it. There's an exit to a village one kilometer before it. We'd better get off there and continue on this small interior road."

"Yeah, let's do that. I prefer to avoid those militia guys," Marc, with his shaved head and square face, commented from the back while he played with his handgun.

At the exit, they left the main road and continued driving northwest, toward the coastal route to Oran. This road was in even worse condition, and the truck ride became rougher. They passed through a small village, lit only by a couple of streetlights in the middle. After passing through, they continued into the dark night. They passed several similar villages while driving deeper and deeper into militia-controlled land.

After leaving another small town, they continued driving westward on a small road. Suddenly, two headlights appeared behind them. Initially far away, but they caught up with their truck quickly.

"We have visitors," Matteo told the others while he peered into the mirror at his side.

When the two headlights came close enough, they could distinguish the shape of a large truck behind them. The truck continued to come closer until it drove close to their bumper. Too close.

"What does this guy want?" Leon said anxiously, looking into the rear-view mirror.

They drove through another tiny village with not a soul on the street. In between the buildings, the truck continued to drive behind them, glued to their bumper. Leon peered into the rear-view mirror and the truck started working on his nerves.

"This truck is about to hit us."

At the end of the road, they noticed what looked like a gate at the edge of the village. A large truck drove up behind the gate, blocking the way, and a large searchlight turned in their direction. The truck behind them backed off from their bumper now.

"Roadblock!" Rafael yelled from the back, and he took an automatic rifle from the rack in the back. Everybody prepared their arms as they approached the truck. Two men carrying automatic rifles gestured them to stop.

"They're all armed. Hold your weapons. Let's first try to negotiate our way through. I understood that these militia guys are quite sensitive to money," Leon said.

"I agree. Let's try to avoid a shooting," Matteo added.

Leon slowed down and opened his window as they approached the armed men. A man with a dark beard said something in Arabic. In his mirror, Matteo noticed that the truck that was following them before now stood right behind them. They had no way to go with both ways blocked. Leon continued talking to the bearded man. Suddenly, the man yelled something in the direction of the truck blocking the road. Another bearded militia man wearing a black beret and a light brown uniform stepped out and answered. Leon turned his head to Matteo.

"He asked us what we're doing here. I told him we're on our way to Oran to pick up a friend. He says we can't go to Oran without their permission. I asked him where we can buy a permit and he told me to talk to his boss. He wants us both to get out."

"All right, let's see how much he wants," Matteo replied.

Matteo and Leon stepped out of the truck and walked toward the man with the black beret. The bearded man followed them closely, pointing his automatic rifle in their direction. Leon said something in Arabic. The man with the black beret replied, and after a short discussion, Leon turned to Matteo.

"It'll cost us ten thousand dinars to pass. Could you hand him the money?"

Matteo nodded and took the money out of his pocket. While he was counting it, he got kicked behind his knee from behind. An armed man pushed him hard on the ground, just as the bearded man did the same to Leon. Matteo looked back toward their truck and noticed that several armed men were stepping out of the truck behind theirs. Matteo got pushed further down on the ground by the barrel of a rifle against his head until his face was touching the sand. He heard someone shouting in Arabic, after which Leon yelled, "Everyone has to get out of the truck with their hands in the air, otherwise they'll shoot us!"

For a moment, nothing happened. Rafael discussed anxiously with the three others if they should do as told or come out shooting. The adrenaline rushed through their bodies as they watched the armed men approaching. Matteo waited on the ground and worried that his friends might attack the militia men. They would shoot him and Leon, for sure. He did not want to wait and yelled, "Rafael, don't plan anything. Do as we're told or they'll shoot us for sure!"

The back of their truck opened, and their four friends stepped outside with their hands in the air. Several armed militia men appeared from behind and pushed the four in the direction of their boss. They put them next to each other and forced them to kneel. Matteo peered at his friends from the corner of his eye. They all had the barrel of a gun against the back of their head. He could hear a man yelling in Arabic from the back of their truck.

A moment later, the man with the black beret shouted at Leon and kicked him in his ribs. Moaning, Leon answered. Their conversation became more hectic and sounded aggressive to Matteo. Then Leon addressed Matteo in a low voice.

"This is not good, Matteo. They think we're mercenaries hired by the Algerian government. I tried to convince them otherwise, but he didn't believe me. I think they're going to kill us."

59.

As soon as Elliot arrived at his apartment, he rushed to the table in the living room. He still had difficulty believing the Council had granted him permission to contact his twin brother. He sat down at the table and started up his computer. He had gathered all the information he could find about his twin brother online. He searched for a moment until he found the mobile phone number of Dylan Myers.

Elliot dialed the number, full of anticipation. He listened to the dial tone and waited anxiously. After ringing four times, a voicemail message started, and Elliot heard his brother's voice for the first time.

"Hi. You've reached the voicemail of Dylan Myers. You can leave a message after the beep."

"Hello, Dylan. This is Elliot, your twin brother. I'll try to call you back later."

He hung up the phone, slightly disappointed. He would try again later. It was too late to return to work. Elsa was coming for dinner that evening and he preferred to prepare everything early on. He had promised to prepare an Indian dish for her. He checked if he had all the ingredients and noticed he was missing spinach. He took a basket and rushed out the door.

Upstairs in the gardens, he walked all the way to the back until he arrived at the spinach field. He took what he needed and walked back. The sun was shining above the glass roof of the dome. He glanced up for a moment and thought about his twin brother, who was out there somewhere living in this inhospitable world. The world his parents had sheltered him from while leaving his brother behind.

Back in the apartment, he started cooking. Elsa rang the doorbell just as he was finishing.

"I've got permission to contact my brother," Elliot said immediately after opening.

"That's fantastic!"

They kissed and moved to the kitchen. Elsa looked impressed at the neatly set table.

"Mmm, that smells delicious. You've prepared everything already. What a pleasant surprise!"

Over dinner, Elliot told her about his meeting with Abe and the phone call to Dylan. He tried to call him another time after dinner, but he got his voicemail again. Elsa noticed his disappointment.

"Does he have another number where you could reach him? Where does he live?"

"He lives in the compound of Enviro Technologies in Ikast in Denmark."

"Is there a general number you could try?"

Elliot searched online for a moment.

"Here I've found the general number of Enviro in Ikast."

Elliot looked at the clock.

"We have a four-hour time difference with Ikast, so it's ten thirty there now. They must be closed, no?"

"Just try, Elliot. What do you've got to lose?"

He nodded and dialed the number.

"Good evening, Enviro Technologies. How may I help you?"

"Hi, this is Elliot. I'm looking for Dylan Myers."

"Dylan Myers, let me see. Ah, let me put you through."

He waited for a few seconds while Elsa sat down next to him, full of anticipation.

"Hello, Elizabeth Muller speaking."

"Good evening, this is Elliot. I'm looking for Dylan Myers, is he in?"

"What? Dylan? Uh, no, he isn't there. Where do you know Dylan from?"

"I'm his brother."

"Is this a joke? He doesn't have any brother."

"Well, he does. A twin brother, actually. Could you turn the video on your phone on, please?"

She hesitated for a moment, still in disbelief about the whole story, before switching on her video. She looked flabbergasted at the screen. Besides a different haircut, Elliot looked exactly like Dylan. His skin looked slightly less tanned than Dylan's. The shape of the face, the chin, the eyes, the nose, everything resembled. It freaked her out.

"Jesus, you're a spitting image of him."

"I know. I guess he's not even aware he has a twin brother, since I only found out recently as well. Last year, Dylan met my father, I mean our father."

"What? You're living in the dome?"

Quickly after the line got interrupted, and Elliot heard a voice.

"Please do not discuss the dome or the line will be disconnected."

Slightly stressed, Elliot continued the conversation.

"Sorry, I'm not allowed to discuss that, but I would really like to talk to him."

"I'm sorry, but that won't be possible."

"Why not?"

"He has been kidnapped."

"What!? Kidnapped?"

Elizabeth explained what had happened. Elliot could not believe his ears. He had just learned about his twin brother's existence, and now he had been abducted. He offered to help, but Elizabeth explained that her brother had gone to Algeria to rescue him. At the end of the conversation, they agreed to stay in touch and he gave his email address to Elizabeth.

60.

Martin had been analyzing the three months of video footage thoroughly for several days. His boss was right. Hakim Sayed had stolen confidential information. It was perfectly clear to him now how he had done it. He had bypassed the stringent security system, which was supposed to safeguard Enviro's confidential data. It was time to inform Hawkins. He was even afraid it could be too late already. He called his boss.

Hawkins showed up at his desk five minutes later. Martin gestured to come and sit next to him in front of his computer screen.

"I've checked the video footage, and you were right. Hakim copied confidential information."

Martin fast forwarded a video until they saw Hakim sitting at a workstation. He looked around first and then he held his phone in front of the screen.

"Ah, that's how he copied the files without the system registering it," Hawkins said while glaring at the screen.

"Yep. I've checked all the footage, and he copied lots of files over several weeks."

"Were you able to find out what he has copied exactly?"

"Initially, I stopped the footage and zoomed in on the screen to see what he copied. This took too much time, of course, so I marked down the date and time he took pictures of the screen and on which workstation. I matched these data with the log file from the server with records from all the files accessed. This way I was able to deduct which files he copied."

"Okay. And?"

"Well, look here. He copied a list of files with drone operating software. But when I looked further, I also found this."

Hawkins approached the computer screen to have a closer look.

"Oh shit. That's not good. We should warn our colleagues at border protection at once."

Hawkins grabbed his phone and dialed a number. Martin looked anxiously at him.

"Hi, this is Steve Hawkins from Security speaking. We've just found out that crucial, confidential information about the border protcction system has been stolen."

He continued explaining what had been stolen exactly and asked them to run some tests. He hung up and looked with Martin at the rest of the stolen information until his phone rang.

"Hi, Mr. Hawkins. We've just run an extensive test on our system and I fear we have a breach."

61.

The man with the black beret put his heavy army boot on Leon's face, who moaned from the pain. His mouth got pushed into the dirt of the road and he had difficulty breathing. He tried to say something to the angry man, although with the boot on his face, the sound of his voice got smothered. The man yelled something in Arabic and reloaded his gun. Matteo looked at him and knew it was a matter of seconds now. The militiamen could kill them at any moment.

As he was lying face down on the ground, he could not look around much without drawing attention. A guard still held the barrel of the gun against Matteo's head. He had his arms flat on the ground above his head and slowly he tried to move his left hand closer to his right hand. The man with the black beret continued to yell at the others in Arabic. Suddenly, he heard how the soldier holding him down cocked his gun. In a split second, Matteo reached for the watch with his left hand and pushed the red button on the side while simultaneously pushing on the screen.

Maybe he was too late. It looked like they could kill them at any moment. He felt the barrel of the gun against his head. At that instant, the man stopped yelling as he heard a high-pitched buzzing noise above him. The soldier who was holding him down moved the rifle away from his head as he looked up at the sky.

The sky was dark and there was nothing to see, but they could hear the high-pitched noise spreading around them. Matteo tried to look up without attracting attention. The militiamen surrounding him shouted in Arabic, their voices in distress. The noise confused them. One of them fired his automatic rifle in the air. Several seconds later, the high-pitched noise seemed to intensify. Right at that moment, several explosions all around them lit up the sky. Matteo covered his face.

There was a loud explosion right above his head. The gun of the armed soldier above him fell on his back. He felt the man collapse on his legs. He opened his eyes and heard a beeping noise in his ears. He tried to get up in a haze. Through the cloud of dust, he noticed the man with the black beret lying on top of Leon. His friend had blood splattered all over him and did not move.

Matteo pushed the heavy body off his back while turning around. He pushed the man on his shoulder and got startled. The top of his skull was blown away. There was blood everywhere. When he got up, he wiped what he thought was sweat away from his face. But his sleeve was all red, soaked in blood. He pushed the dead body away and got back on his feet. Next to him, Leon started moving.

"Are you all right, Leon?"

Matteo pushed the dead man off Leon's back and he slowly crawled up.

"Ouch…I guess…," Leon mumbled.

A bit further, his other friends were also crawling back on their feet. Matteo looked around at the bloody massacre. The militia men lay scattered around the street with their heads blown away. Blood was spattered everywhere. There was a horrible smell of burned flesh.

"What the hell was that?" Rafael asked as he approached Matteo.

"Remember this metal box, this gadget, we got from Enviro. I pushed the button to launch it. Those micro drones eliminated all the militiamen."

“Nice gadget. It saved our lives.”

“Everybody, all right?” Leon asked.

“We’d better get moving before they send reinforcements,” Matteo replied when he saw all his friends were back on their feet.

“I’ll move that truck,” Rafael said while walking toward the truck, blocking their way.

They moved some bodies out of the way and climbed back into the truck. Leon started the engine and advanced through the street. He stopped to let Rafael jump into the back. They continued and drove out of the village onto the deserted dirt road westward. Matteo cleaned his face with a wet towel. He hoped they would not encounter more trouble like this, otherwise they might run out of gadgets to save them.

“I thought we were trying to avoid the roadblocks?” Rafael said.

“Well, we’re trying, but I guess they must have seen us. Maybe someone in one of those villages warned them,” Matteo replied.

“With our headlights on these dark roads, they can see us from kilometers away,” David commented from the back of the truck, while he was still cleaning his face.

“He’s right. Our headlights make us sitting ducks. Leon, maybe you should turn them off and try to drive using the night vision visor?” Matteo suggested.

“Great idea!”

Leon pulled over and switched off the headlights. They vanished in the surrounding darkness.

“Could you pass me my helmet, Rafael?”

Rafael handed it to him. He flipped the night vision visor in front of his eyes and it automatically switched on.

“I can see the road. This might actually work.”

Leon started the engine and drove away into the darkness. He could vaguely distinguish the road through his visor. The electrical engine barely made any noise and the low drumming noise from the tires was all you could hear. They drove further westward while avoiding the roadblocks. From time to time, they passed through a village, all deserted and asleep.

Almost two hours later, they arrived at the edge of the city of Oran, deep inside the militia-controlled region. Here in Oran, the streetlights were faintly illuminating the road and darkness no longer kept them out of sight. Leon flipped his night vision visor up and turned the headlights of the truck back on. The streets were deserted. No one in sight. Matteo studied the map while the system continued giving directions.

"We're almost at the location indicated by the GPS coordinates. Let's gear up. We should assume that the kidnappers of Dylan and Hakim are armed and dangerous."

They all started preparing their weapons and putting on their helmets. Matteo tightened his bulletproof vest and checked his shoe laces. After twenty minutes of driving through Oran, Leon slowed down. Matteo pointed at the street on their left side.

"It should be a bit farther in this street."

Leon turned left. He heard the others in the back loading their guns. The street was empty and faintly lit. Matteo looked again at the map on the screen.

"It should be two hundred meters farther on the left side. Try to go slowly until we have a visual of the building."

The truck advanced slowly through the street until Matteo pointed to a building.

"There! It should be there in that driveway."

"That looks like an underground parking garage," Leon commented.

"Yep, I don't see anybody anywhere. Strange. Maybe we should pass in front one time to have a look."

They drove slowly further and passed the entrance of the underground parking. There was no one in sight, but as the driveway of the parking sloped down steeply, they could not have a good look inside. Leon continued and a few hundred meters farther, he turned around and stopped.

"Maybe we should use one of those reconnaissance drones from Enviro. We could send it ahead before entering the parking. This way we can explore how many men there are and where," David suggested from the back.

"Right, let's do that," Matteo replied, and he climbed in the back. He opened a crate and took out a black drone.

Rafael opened the backdoor. Matteo stepped outside and posed the drone on the ground. He took the controls and started it. It took off above them with a high-pitched noise. Matteo stepped back inside, observing the screen carefully. He flew the drone toward the parking entrance. A moment later, it disappeared inside and they watched the video footage on the controls to have a look inside the parking garage.

The drone passed the barrier and descended along the driveway. The garage was empty, except for a few old vehicles. To their surprise, they did not see anyone. It was dark, and the drone switched to night vision. Sea containers occupied most parking spaces. It continued to the end of the parking garage, where the driveway swirled further down. It flew further down to the next level. The spaces on this floor were filled with old equipment, like fridges, air conditioners, and electronics. There was a small guardhouse, but no one was visible inside.

"The first two floors look safe. I suggest we go in. Marc and Burke can patrol ahead of the truck by foot. Then Leon and me follow with the truck and David and Rafael can go by foot watching our back. Put one of those half dome security guards at the entrance of the parking to watch out for unexpected visitors," Matteo said.

"Yep, will do," Rafael answered and took a black, half dome shaped bowl out of a crate and turned it on with the switch on the bottom.

"Let's go then!" Leon said while starting the engine.

They all flipped their night vision visors over their face. Rafael attached his phone to the sleeve of his army suit and checked the screen to open the footage from the half dome bowl.

"It works. I'll place it at the entry and turn on the guard function so that we'll get a warning if anyone enters the garage."

Leon stopped about ten meters before the closed barriers. Leon and Matteo stayed inside the cabin while the others stepped out. Immediately after, Leon advanced at full speed into the parking garage's driveway. The truck rammed through the barrier, which snapped off instantly. He stopped inside and waited for the others to follow. Rafael placed the half dome bowl at the entrance and they moved inside. Marc and Burke walked in front, and David and Rafael followed about ten meters behind the truck. They all kept their automatic rifles ready.

Leon followed the two red shapes of Marc and Burke and scanned the surroundings for other red shapes, but there was no one else at this level. Driving at a walking pace, they moved further. Matteo checked his screen. No one in sight. At the end of the parking garage, Marc and Burke walked down the ramp, which swirled downward to the lower level. It was completely silent inside, besides the humming noise from the truck.

"No one in sight on this level," they heard Marc say through their headsets.

The truck followed them downstairs.

"No one behind us either," Rafael said through the radio communication.

They cautiously continued further into the underground parking garage. Level after level, they moved downward. At some point, they heard Marc say, "No one on this level either, but it looks like lots of people have been here. The parking garage is filled with makeshift houses. There are beds and mattrasses everywhere. Strange, there's nobody. It almost looks like they all left in a rush."

Leon descended another level, swirling down over the driveway. Now they could see it with their own eyes. Matteo even stopped looking at his screen. Makeshift houses left and right all abandoned. Discarded mattrasses and a lot of debris everywhere.

"Spooky," Leon commented.

They continued and saw the same thing on the levels below.

"Looking at all those makeshift houses and beds, you get the impression that hundreds, if not thousands, of people used to live in here. Makes you wonder where they all went. It looks like we arrived too late. Probably Dylan and Hakim have been taken with them," Matteo said.

The further they continued, the more Matteo had a bad feeling. They were too late. Everybody had left. They descended to the next lower level. Again, the parking lot was filled with abandoned makeshift houses. Then they arrived at a strange heavy metal door in the wall. It had been left open. It looked like an entrance with a desk in front of it. They stopped and got out of the truck. First, they sent the drone in to check if anyone was present.

When it did not spot anyone, they entered and continued through the gray corridor. In the end, they could only go to the left or to the right. Matteo, Leon and Marc went right, and the others turned left. They passed many open rooms, all of them deserted. Most with debris scattered all over as if everybody had left in a hurry. They communicated with the other three through their headsets, but it seemed they also found empty rooms.

Further down the corridor, they found a room that looked different. It was relatively dark. Walls painted burgundy. In the middle there was a large wenge desk with wooden ornaments. Matteo entered first, and when he turned his head to the right, he noticed a large wooden frame. It looked like a frame from a painting, but the painting had been removed. He walked over to the desk and searched through the papers that were left behind. He read several documents and then said,

"It seems this is the office of a certain Abdul Jabbar. If you ask me, probably the big boss around here."

They took some papers with them and moved on. They checked every cupboard and looked behind every door. The inhabitants had abandoned the entire complex in a hurry. They returned through the corridors, calling out Dylan's and Hakim's name. No answer though, just silence. Back in the underground parking garage, the others were waiting next to the truck. Matteo looked at them.

"No one here. Let's continue further down and search everywhere for any trace of Dylan or Hakim."

At the lower levels, they found more of the same makeshift houses. When they finally arrived at the bottom level, they slowly returned up, still calling out Dylan's and Hakim's name, pausing and listening once in a while. They searched every space and every corner and opened every closed door to check what was behind it.

They found absolutely no trace of Dylan or Hakim. At some point, they found a closed door opposite a small guardhouse. Marc yelled their names once more.

"Dylan! Hakim!"

This time, they heard a faint voice behind the door.

"Help! Help!"

Matteo listened at the door.

"Dylan!? Hakim!?"

"Yes, help us!"

Matteo felt a wave of relief. They had found them at last. Marc tried to kick the door open, but this one was different. It was solid and did not move an inch. Matteo tried another time. Still, nothing happened. Burke took a battering ram from the truck and, together with Marc, they rammed the door open. Matteo rushed inside. There he was, lying on a mattress. He looked into Dylan's eyes. At last, he had found him. He looked weak and had lost weight.

"Dylan! Thank God you're still alive!"

"Matteo! I'm so happy to see you," Dylan replied in a shaky voice as he tried to crawl up, but he felt too weak to stand.

"Do you have water?"

"Guys, bring some water for everyone!" Matteo yelled.

Meanwhile, Hakim also sat up straight and looked at the armed men in disbelief. Dylan drank water and ate some of the food Leon had brought with him. They were starving.

"We didn't have any food for several days and yesterday we ran out of water," Dylan explained.

"The place looks completely abandoned," Matteo replied.

"Abandoned?" Hakim asked, joining the conversation.

"Yep, like they left in a rush."

"I was afraid of this," Hakim said as he looked at Dylan.

"We should warn the police immediately," Dylan said.

"We will! But let's first get you all out of here. This is still a region controlled by militia, so we better get out of here as soon as possible."

They helped the four men back on their feet and supported them to the truck. As soon as everybody was inside, Leon drove off. Swirling upward through the parking garage, he hurried to the exit. It was still dark outside, but the sun would rise in an hour, and they wanted to return to government-controlled territory as fast as possible.

62.

After driving all night uncomfortably cramped together with everyone in the truck, Ebo and his family arrived at another underground parking garage. He helped his wife and son to climb out of the truck, and they felt overwhelmed by the noise. Thousands of people sat packed together. The chatter of all those individuals in this underground space was deafening. The guards escorted their group toward a marked space inside the parking. They ordered them to sit on the floor and distributed bottles of water to everyone. The guards were pointing their guns at anyone who disobeyed. A man who did not stay in his assigned space got knocked down by the back of a gun. He crawled back to the assigned space.

Frightened, Ebo moved his family to the back of the marked space. They drank some water. He did not dare move or approach the guards in this tense atmosphere. They just stayed there and waited. Time seemed to pass slowly. They tried to sleep a bit. Ebo's wife and son were exhausted and fell asleep quickly. But Ebo couldn't sleep. He was too afraid to close his eyes. He wanted to watch over his family and protect them. He dozed off from time to time, but with the slightest movement around him, he woke up again.

The whole day, they stayed confined in this underground parking garage. The guards distributed food bars only one time that day. His son complained he was still hungry, yet they did not dare to ask for more food. At least they had enough water. The only thing that made the waiting bearable was the prospect of leaving soon. A Somalian man told him that he overheard the guards talking about it. They were going to leave that evening right after sunset.

In the afternoon, his wife and son were more rested and Ebo was finally able to sleep a couple of hours. He woke up when the surrounding chatter increased. People were getting up, trying to see what was happening. He also got up and looked at the crowd. He noticed all the way in the back they were instructing people to go outside. It looked like they were going to leave. Ebo grabbed his wife and son by the hand while they were waiting.

An hour later, it was their turn to leave. They followed the guards along the driveway inside the parking garage. When they arrived at street level, the guard yelled they should all enter the truck as quickly as possible. The sky was magnificent. A beautiful sunset provided them with a kaleidoscope of vivid colors. They followed the group and climbed into the truck. It drove away once full. With the brisk movement of the truck, he fell against someone next to them. Some people got stuck and yelled. His son started crying.

They felt relieved when the truck stopped half an hour later. The guards opened the back door and yelled that they should all get out. In the twilight, Ebo climbed outside and helped his wife and son get out. It looked like they were in an immense industrial harbor. There were enormous cranes and large walls of containers on the dock. The guards guided them toward a pier. Many boats were waiting. He noticed several trucks delivering more people. They moved toward the pier and many were already boarding the ships.

They queued in front of a large boat. He observed how they guided the people in front of him below deck. It looked like more than two hundred people were getting onboard. They all had to walk over a gangplank. Before they were allowed to board, a guard scanned their neck. At some point, they stopped sending people to the lower deck and guided the rest to the upper deck, which was open on the sides. Ebo was happy he did not have to go into the lower deck. The idea of being locked up below without the fresh outside air did not appeal to him. The guards ordered them to sit down. As soon as they filled the boat with people, the guards detached it from the shore. They steered away from the pier and set course to open sea.

After leaving the harbor and entering the open sea, they slowed down. Ebo noticed a dozen boats waiting. He peered at the shore and noticed how the empty spaces on the faintly lit pier got filled quickly after by other ships. The buzzing crowd on the waterfront reminded him of an anthill. Streams of people boarded the ships and filled the decks. They moved slowly further away from the coast into the open sea, forming a long line. More and more boats joined them. Eventually, he could not see the lights of the shore anymore, but only the lights from the other boats.

Even now during the night, it was still warm, and sitting all packed together made it quite uncomfortable on board. He did not dare let go of his wife and son. Too afraid to lose them out of sight in the crowd in the darkness. There was a clear moon in the sky and they could see several faint stars. He wiped the sweat off his neck and felt the bump from the chip they had injected under his skin. He still remembered that day when they arrived in Oran. It shocked him to see how many people were living in the underground garage. So many had chosen to leave their home country, just like him. After paying upfront for this trip, the guards told him they had to inject a chip into his neck.

Not that they gave him much choice. The guard explained that without the chip, they would not be allowed on the boat. He asked what the chip was for. The guard told him that it would protect him against the drones on their voyage across the Mediterranean Sea. They injected the chip under the skin with a strange-looking metal pistol. Initially, the chip annoyed him and his neck was painful. But several weeks later, he got used to it. All the refugees had one, and later he even noticed that all the guards had them as well.

The noise of the ship's horn pulled him out of his thoughts. The boats on his left and right blew their horns one by one. He started counting them, but at some point, he lost count. He figured there were at least thirty that were moving in a long line formation. On his left, he could see the lights of many boats as far as he could see and the same on his right side. The noise stopped, and they seemed to increase their speed. Excitement filled his head. They were leaving.

After hearing all the stories of refugees who tried to cross the Mediterranean Sea to get to Europe, he had felt desperate. All of them died trying. The drones destroyed their boats. None of them ever made it alive. He had asked so many people if there was someone who knew how to cross safely into Europe. When he heard about the great Jabbar, he was skeptical at first. But the more he heard about him, the more he believed that this man might be their only hope to get into Europe safely.

They were finally going to cross the Mediterranean Sea after all those months of waiting. If everything went well, they would be in Spain later that night. The more they moved north, the more afraid he got, though. What if this was all a big hoax? What if this great Jabbar was a fraud? No one had succeeded since this border security system had been installed. Up to now, it was all a promise. Doubt filled his mind, and he held on tight to his wife and son.

An hour later, someone yelled in the crowd.

"A drone! A drone!"

People started pointing up at the sky. Ebo looked up, but saw nothing. He could feel the fear spreading through the crowd. Some people started praying. Some screamed and some cried. A man next to him yelled and pointed up. He looked in the same direction. Now he saw it as well. The dark shadow of a drone flying through the sky. It was coming toward them.

Panic broke out in the crowd, and they started pushing each other. He saw the fear in his son's eyes and grabbed his wife and son. He held them close to his chest. The adrenaline was rushing through his body. He turned his head and looked back up at the sky. He could see the drone clearly now. It was much closer. Anxiously, he touched the bump in his neck as if he wanted to check whether the chip was working. His heart pounded in his chest while his son started crying on his lap. His wife whispered a prayer.

63.

So far everything had gone according to plan, and Abdul felt thrilled as he boarded the modern yacht in the cargo port of Tangier Med in the north of Morocco. Located in the Strait of Gibraltar, it was an ideal point to cross the Mediterranean Sea and enter Europe. All the other boats were already in open sea waiting for him. After all these years of careful planning, it was finally going to happen. He climbed the stairs and entered the modern bridge of the yacht. His crew waited for him inside.

The cabin on the bridge was equipped with a modern climate control system. He immediately noticed that the filtered air inside was so much cleaner and fresher. What a pleasure after all this time living in polluted air. The captain greeted him and asked him when he wanted to leave. Abdul looked at Ahmed, who just entered the bridge.

"So, how far along are we with boarding all the people?"

"We have just boarded the last boat. The guards checked the underground parking garage and I think we've got everybody."

"How many are we in total?"

"We've scanned seven thousand three hundred and twenty-three people. Spread out over thirty-five ships."

Ahmed answered a call on his phone. He spoke for a moment and then addressed Abdul.

"The last one has left. Everyone has boarded now; we're ready to go."

"All right! Captain, let's go!"

Ten minutes later, they left the port of Tangier Med and steered to open sea. Abdul noticed the moon and thought of his brother. If only he had been more patient. He noticed a long line of faint lights from left to right on the horizon. The closer they got, the more impressive it looked. Thirty-four boats all moving in one line formation. They quickly caught up with the formation, as he had made sure that their yacht was the fastest. He figured that if his plan would unexpectedly fail, at least he could try to make a run for it and see if he could make it through, even if the others wouldn't.

The captain steered the yacht to the middle of the long line formation. Abdul looked to the left at the long line of lights from the boats. Then he looked to the right. He felt proud of his fleet. This would make the headlines all around the world regardless of the outcome. If they fail, it would be the largest refugee massacre on the European border in decades. If they succeed, it would send a shock wave through the global community. The prestigious and impenetrable European security border would have failed. It would baffle the international press.

Although, for Abdul, failure was not an option. He was running out of time. He had to continue what he and Maheer had strived for all that time. This was his chance to get to Europe, and it was now or never. He looked at the radar screens in front of him over the shoulder of the captain. He could clearly see the Strait of Gibraltar on the electronic map and the long line of boats gradually approaching the border. The zone in which the drones were operating was clearly indicated by a red bar on the map. He thought about how his brother had died in the open sea, and a wave of anxiety hit him. He looked around him and saw Cheng sitting behind a computer screen.

"Everything ready, Cheng?"

"Yes, boss. We're all set."

"Take me one more time through the whole system, Cheng."

"Sure. We use the security system in the way it has been designed. Any boat or trade ship that wants to cross needs to get a formal permission from European customs. When it is granted, the system registers the unique identification code of that ship. As soon as it approaches the border, a drone scans the ship's unique identification signal. It is then verified with the central system on shore. If the code matches the list of approved codes, it will let the ship pass."

"Reaching the European security border in ten minutes," the captain announced on the bridge.

Cheng looked at the captain and then back at Abdul.

"To verify a code, it communicates with the nearest system poles on the European shore. Marco installed an extra module on all the system poles along the Spanish coastline in the Strait of Gibraltar. The drones will soon scan the identification codes of all our thirty-five boats. It will instantly compare them with the ones in the system poles on shore. We've added all through the extra module. Our codes are now on the list. We bypassed the central system and should be able to cross safely."

"Only five hundred meters left until the border," the captain announced.

Abdul turned his head and looked outside. He peered at the sky. He distinguished a dark shadow flying through the sky.

"A drone is coming our way," Ahmed announced as he looked at the sky through his binoculars.

Cheng looked nervously at his screen. Abdul glanced at him. Let's hope he has made no mistakes, he thought to himself. They advanced further, and he could see the drone getting closer. He noticed several other ones flying through the sky above the long line of boats on his left. He looked to his right and noticed the same sinister spectacle. If this did not work, then within minutes he would witness a massacre around him and end up like his brother.

The boat continued, and he peered straight up at the drone above the yacht. He held his breath as they passed underneath. On his left and right, he saw the rest of the fleet advancing with the drones now all above the fleet. The moment of truth was there. It was silent on the bridge. He could feel the tension in the air. The captain steered the yacht and looked at the horizon. He looked anxious and was sweating. Abdul felt nervous as well. More than seven thousand souls put their trust in him, the great Jabbar. His heart pounded in his chest as they sailed further through the calm ocean. Cheng broke the eerie silence.

"Boss, I think it worked!"

"Yes!" Abdul yelled enthusiastically, and threw his fist up in the air.

He looked at the captain, who was visibly relieved. Abdul took his phone and dialed a number.

"Marco, we passed! Is everything ready on shore?"

"Everything is ready, boss. Congratulations!"

"Thanks! See you soon."

He hung up and addressed the captain.

"Order the fleet to go full speed ahead to their destination. Everything is in place."

The captain smiled and blared the announcement to the entire fleet through the radio communication system. A loud cheer echoed from all the surrounding boats as the passengers realized they were now safe and Abdul felt a surge of pride filling his soul. He had succeeded.

64.

Hawkins rushed to the operating room of the border security. A breach had never happened before. There had been many attacks by hackers, but they never gained access to the actual drone security system. The European government had outsourced the system's operating activities to Enviro. All European custom departments had access to it. He was entering the operating room when his phone rang. It was Matteo Muller.

"We've just passed the first checkpoint and have now returned to governmental controlled terrain with Dylan and Hakim."

"Congratulations! Are they okay?"

"Yes, they're malnourished, but for the rest they are fine."

"Good to hear."

"We're also calling to warn you. Hakim believes his abductors are trying to cross the Mediterranean Sea to reach Europe at this very moment."

"Thanks for the warning. We've already identified a breach in our system and are looking into it right now. Any idea where they're planning to cross exactly?"

"No, I'm sorry."

"No problem. I'll have to go now. Safe trip back home!"

The operating room manager was gesturing at him, and Hawkins rushed to his desk.

"We've found a breach in our system. There are inconsistencies in the identification codes for permitted entries between the central system and several local transmitters."

"Can you show me which local transmitters have been breached?"

The manager opened a map on the screen. Hawkins looked at it, baffled. All local transmitters along the coast from Tarifa up to Algeciras were breached. This was simply unbelievable.

"The Strait of Gibraltar, of course! Call the Spanish Customs immediately! Maybe they can still get there in time!"

65.

The yacht outpaced the rest of the fleet, leaving them farther and farther behind. The long line of lights became fainter and moved out of sight behind them. In front of Abdul, it was all dark on the horizon. They advanced at high speed through the relatively calm sea. After their successful crossing of the border, he was wondering if someone had already noticed their trick. If so, it was most likely that the Spanish customs would come searching at sea or would wait on the shore. They had passed a first large hurdle, but they were far from safe.

Abdul approached the captain and looked over his shoulder at the large control panel in front of the steering wheel. There on the radar screen he could clearly see their own boat, followed by an impressive line formation of vessels behind them. For the rest, there were no other boats in sight. So far, so good. Still, he was nervous as they moved toward the coast. He called Marco again.

"Hi Marco, we should arrive in less than thirty minutes. Everything all right on your side?"

"It's calm out here. I haven't seen any boats or cars, besides our own trucks."

"Good! See you soon."

They continued further and lights appeared on the horizon. Looking at the map, he figured that the brighter lights on the left were from Tarifa. The ones on the right were fainter. It could be the southern suburbs of Algeciras. The yacht set course right in the middle between the lit areas where all was dark. The captain navigated straight toward the coordinates they had given to him.

Twenty minutes later, they could finally see the coastline through the darkness. Lit by the moonlight, they could only see a vague line far away. A light blinked three times from the shore. The agreed signal from Marco and his men. The coastline slowly became more visible. Cheng peered at it until he noticed something.

"The pier! It's over there on the right."

"Yep, we should be there in less than five minutes," the captain said from behind his steering wheel.

"All right! Everybody, prepare yourself to leave this yacht in five minutes. We have to be really quick on the shore, since the Spanish customs could show up at any moment," Abdul announced through the intercom of the boat.

The buzz on the bridge increased, and they could see how people on the deck were gathering their belongings to disembark. Abdul looked at the pier and noticed the two vehicles on the road in front of it, a large truck, and a luxury coach. He followed the road with his eyes. There, he noticed a long line of trucks as far as he could see. All of them had their lights switched off and were parked in complete darkness. Now he turned his head to the other side and there he saw the same spectacle, a long line of trucks, waiting in the dark. Marco had done a superb job preparing all this, he thought.

As they slowed down to dock at the pier, Abdul looked at the radar. The other thirty-four boats were closing in and would soon reach the shore as well. Still no sign of the Spanish customs anywhere. He most certainly hoped they all would make it, as they were a crucial part of the next phase of his grand plan. Although he was not going to be there when they arrive. He would be long gone by then. The captain ordered his crew to prepare for mooring. Abdul looked at the pier, which was really close now. They had reached the shore in one piece. He felt euphoric.

He stepped onto the pier shortly after and walked toward the road. They had made it and entered Europe. This alone was an enormous accomplishment. It was going to shock the European community. Their high-tech border security system had been breached. The largest successful arrival of refugees in Europe in the last decades. He marched confidently toward the road. Marco waved at him. His men carried his luggage and crates with everything they had taken with them from Oran.

Marco greeted him enthusiastically. Abdul embraced him and slapped his muscled shoulders.

"My friend! Glad to see you!"

"Welcome to Spain, boss! Let's get on the bus. We should leave as soon as possible. The Spanish customs could arrive any moment."

They rushed toward the bus. Ahmed, Cheng and all the men who belonged to Abdul's close circle joined them. The rest loaded all the goods into the truck next to the bus. They drove away ten minutes later. Abdul glanced one more time at the sea, and on the horizon, he could see the lights of the other boats. Their bus passed dozens of trucks waiting for the others to arrive. Then he turned his head back to Marco.

"My compliments. This army of trucks is impressive."

Marco smiled back.

"We involved our entire European organization in the preparation. We've got transportation for all refugees. Tonight, we will drive them all driven to safe houses. We'll spread them out all over Europe as discussed before."

"Perfect."

As they entered the highway, Abdul stared out of the window. Looking at the Spanish signposting, he grasped what they had accomplished. If only his brother could have been with him now. An unprecedented breach into the European security border. He confidently looked forward to the next phase of his plan. This was only one step toward his goal. Nobody could anticipate what was about to come. Europe would never be the same again.

66.

Petrified, Ebo looked up at the sky, holding his wife and son close to his chest. The dark shadow of the drone terrified everyone on board. They waited, holding their breath, and peered up at the dark shape. It slowly passed over them as they moved further through the calm water. When the boat left the drone behind, a loud cheer erupted on board. They had passed the high-tech security border. What a relief.

"Thank God. Mr. Jabbar kept his promise," Ebo said as he was observing the cheering crowd around them.

He looked up one more time, but the drone had disappeared out of sight. They had passed. On his right, he saw a modern yacht leaving the line formation. It was much faster and the distance between them increased quickly. The great Jabbar rushed ahead of them, he figured. He wondered if he would ever see him again. The euphoric feeling of passing the border faded. He worried about the Spanish coast guard. They still had to make it on shore and get away without getting caught.

At the time when he paid that hefty sum to the man working for Jabbar, the deal was that they would help them pass the border and bring them to a safe house somewhere in Europe. But now that the yacht of the great Jabbar was moving out of sight, he was not so sure if they would keep their word. On the other hand, he thought, with this enormous number of refugees hitting the shores at once, they could never catch them all. The numbers worked in their favor.

The boat vibrated more than before and he had the impression they were going faster. He looked around and noticed several boats were going even faster than theirs, but also several were lagging behind. It was clear that they had broken off the strict line formation they had sailed in before. A moment later, he noticed the faint lights of a city on the horizon. He whispered in his wife's ear, not to wake up his son.

"We're almost there, my love."

She hugged him and glanced into the distance. The shore got closer and their anticipation grew. They could see the first boats arriving before them on the shore. They stayed at a relatively large distance from one another. On his right, he saw the modern yacht moored onto a pier. The great Jabbar must have arrived a long time ago. Some boats continued sailing until they got stuck in the sand. People climbed off and waded through the water toward the beach. Other larger ships stopped before and with smaller boats, they brought the people on land.

The shore was really close now, and they were slowing down. The captain announced everybody should get ready to disembark. The guards instructed them to climb down the ladder onto a smaller boat that would take them to the beach. Guards yelled instructions to guide the large group in an orderly fashion toward the ladders. A man disobeyed, and a guard hit him with the back of his rifle against his ribs. The man moaned and fell on the deck. Some other people helped him back on his feet and they continued moving to the smaller boats.

After helping his wife and son down the ladder, they all took a seat crammed in between the other people. The boat moved up and down with the waves and as soon as it was full, it left for the shore. They all got soaking wet from the splashing waves. The moment they touched solid ground, everybody rushed out of the boat. Ebo carried his son through the water, walking closely behind his wife, too afraid to lose her out of his sight. There were several armed guards on the beach, guiding them toward the large trucks that were waiting in the street.

There were so many trucks parked, it was an impressive sight. Several of them looked modern and strange to him. It was as if there was no cabin in front. More like containers on wheels, surreal and frightening. To his relief, the guards guided them toward a traditional truck. They instructed everybody to climb into the truck that looked almost full. Ebo helped his wife and son to climb in the rear. But when he wanted to climb on himself, a guard pushed him back. The guard pointed at a driverless truck further on.

"Full. Get on the other one!"

"But my wife and child are on this one. I can't be separated from them."

His son started crying and his wife begged the guard to let Ebo climb in the rear, but the guard wouldn't bulge.

"It's full. Now move it. To the other one."

Suddenly, a man climbed out of the rear and jumped in front of the guard.

"He can take my place, sir. I'll go with the other truck. Families belong together."

The guard accepted with a grim face and gestured Ebo to enter. He quickly climbed inside and hugged his wife and son. Two guards climbed inside as well and sat next to them. The guard closed the tailgate. Ebo's son stared anxiously at the automatic rifles. They started moving and drove away over the road. He could see through an opening in the back that some trucks drove off in an opposite direction. They turned quickly after onto a small dirt road away from the coast. Still no sight of the police or the Spanish customs.

The shaking of the truck promptly decreased as they left the dirt road and continued on a paved road. Ebo was about to doze off when they slowed down abruptly. The guards instructed everybody to be quiet. Through the radio on the guard's uniform, Ebo could hear the driver talking to the guard next to him in the cabin.

"A police car is blocking the road. Everybody, silent!"

The people in the back turned completely silent. His son held him tightly. Then they heard through the radio.

"Good evening, officer. An accident?"

"Yes, a driverless taxi had a blown-out tire and crashed into that tree. The passengers were dead on impact. What do you have in the back?"

"Furniture. We've got to make a delivery in Seville."

"Okay. My colleague is going to have a look."

"No problem. You can have a look in the back," the driver said in a louder voice.

The guards in the back prepared their automatic rifles. Ebo felt his heart pounding in his chest as they heard footsteps getting closer. The guard next to him aimed his rifle toward the rear flap of the truck. A moment later, a policeman opened the back and looked into the frightened eyes of the refugees. Apparently, he did not see the armed guard hiding on the side. The policeman took out his gun and pushed on the radio on his shoulder.

"Alfons, come and look over here. The truck is filled with refugees."

The guard next to Ebo fired his rifle through the rear flap. A deafening noise sounded throughout the truck. They all covered their ears. A hail of bullets killed the policeman on the spot. They heard a shot in front. Immediately after, the engine of the truck went back on and they started moving. Through the radio, they heard the voice of the driver.

"All clear, we'll continue our route."

Ebo felt his son shivering with fear against his chest. He held him and his wife tightly and couldn't help thinking of those unfortunate policemen. What scared him most was the emotionless face of the guard next to him, who fired the shots without hesitation. His family's long and dangerous voyage had still not ended. Nobody dared to talk for a long time. He wondered where they were taking them. In Oran, they had explained that they would send all refugees to different locations all over Europe and that they had no choice in their destination. All he hoped for was to arrive safely and sound wherever they were going. The start of their new life.

67.

Dylan said goodbye to Matteo and his friends at the Lausanne airport and boarded the private hydrogen jet. He tried to relax as he sat in the lush luxury chair. Hakim fell asleep almost immediately next to him. Besides for the pilot and a flight attendant, they were all alone on board. It all had gone so fast. That morning, he had still been locked up in his cell. They had run out of food and water and tried everything to get out of there. He had given up all hope and mentally prepared himself to die in there. They couldn't believe it when they heard someone calling out their names. Dylan yelled with his dry and painful throat as loud as he could to respond.

Later, in the army truck, he felt a sense of relief mixed with a surreal feeling. But it was only when they entered government-controlled territory that he finally felt secure. He was a free man again. At the airport in Algiers, he briefly spoke with Elizabeth on the phone. She was in tears during their call. They were flying back the same day, and he was really looking forward to her embrace.

The private hydrogen jet took off and set course for Midtjyllands airport in Karup. This was a small local Danish airport close to Ikast. He thought back to the refugees in the underground parking garage. There were so many of them. He wondered if they had made it to Europe. All those people desperately fleeing away from their own countries in the idle hope of finding a better life elsewhere. Climate change unleashed a massive global stream of refugees. The richer countries closed their borders, unwilling and unable to cope with the massive stream. Other countries had no choice and many of them ended up in anarchy and chaos under the overwhelming weight.

He fell asleep halfway through the flight. An hour later, the hydrogen jet landed in Karup. Only now, after touching Danish soil, he woke up safely back in Denmark behind the European security borders. It was warm outside, though nothing compared to the blistering heat in Algeria. He felt much better breathing through the respo than he felt during his captivity. The heavy feeling in his lungs had gone away.

He passed through the security check and a wave of joy and happiness overwhelmed him the moment he saw Elizabeth. They hugged and kissed. He was so happy to see her he got tears in his eyes. Hakim joined them in their driverless taxi back to the Enviro compound. He noticed that Hakim was avoiding eye contact in the taxi and staring at the floor. He seemed down and uncomfortable.

"What's wrong Hakim? You're not happy to be back home?"

"I'm happy to be back. I'm just worried about what will happen to me. I mean, I stole confidential data. They could send me to prison."

"Ah, yes. I understand. Well, we'll just have to wait and see. There are mitigating circumstances. You were blackmailed, they threatened to kill your sister, and they abducted you. Maybe things will turn out better than you expect."

"I hope so," he replied and stared out the window.

A moment later, they arrived at the Enviro premises. The taxi stopped right in front of the main entrance. There were several people waiting for them inside the large reception area. Olav Sorenson, Dylan's boss, came to greet him, as did Hakim's boss, Jack Rowling and Steve Hawkins, and several friends of Dylan and

Hakim. Even Jeff Tusk, the CEO, was there. After greeting and talking briefly to everyone, Dylan approached Hawkins.

"Any news from the Spanish customs about Abdul Jabbar and the refugees?"

"I just got off the phone with my contact at Europol. They arrived too late. The Spanish customs caught only one boat with more than two hundred refugees on board. Apparently, it ran into engine trouble and could not reach the shore. They found thirty-four abandoned boats along the coastline east of Tarifa, but no refugees. They estimate that between seven and eight thousand refugees reached the shore. This is the largest refugee arrival in Europe since the installation of the European security border system. The breach is a disgrace to Enviro and our biggest priority is to fix it and upgrade the security."

"Wow, seven to eight thousand refugees. That's a lot of people. I saw a large crowd in the underground parking garage where they kept me prisoner, but that is much more than I thought. Maybe they had more people at other locations."

"They've started an extensive investigation and Europe has asked Algeria and Morocco for their help, so let's see what they come up with."

From the corner of his eye, he saw how Hakim was escorted away by several security people. He looked ashamed and stared at the ground.

"What will happen to Hakim?"

"I don't know yet. First, he'll be interrogated and there will be an investigation."

"Will he go to prison?"

"I don't know. Enviro has pressed no charges yet. I wouldn't be surprised if they cut a deal with him since he is the most qualified person to help us fix the weaknesses in the border security system."

"I feel sorry for him. I mean, they had threatened to kill his sister and abducted him. I don't think he's a bad person."

"I agree, Dylan, although for now we'll have to wait and see."

Most people had left at some point, and Elizabeth approached Dylan with a big smile on her face.

"I still have a surprise for you."

"A surprise? Tell me!"

"Well, let's go to our apartment first."

She looked at the time and then they strolled home, hand in hand. He was so happy to be back. She opened the door for him and they entered.

"So, what's the surprise?"

"When you were away, someone contacted me."

"Who?"

"Your brother! Your twin brother, to be exact."

Dylan stared at her with his mouth open in disbelief.

"Say what?"

"You have a twin brother. His name is Elliot, and he lives in the dome. He promised to call me at seven o'clock tonight."

Dylan looked at the clock, still baffled by the news.

"But that's in forty minutes."

"Exactly, that leaves us just enough time to have dinner."

Elizabeth told him all about her conversation with Elliot. He listened, fascinated. Dylan talked about his abduction and all that had happened since. He felt excited and slightly nervous when the phone rang, even though Elizabeth tried to comfort him.

"Don't worry, he's just like you."

They answered the phone and when they turned the camera on, Dylan couldn't believe his eyes.

"Hi. This is weird. It's like looking in a mirror."

"Yeah, it's strange, although I'm thrilled to meet you finally, Dylan."

"I really did not expect this. I mean, after going to your place and that disappointing meeting with my biological father last year."

"Speaking about my father, I mean our father…"

Elliot explained all what had happened to his father. It shocked Dylan to hear about his suicide. Dylan explained about his daring trip to reach the Dome and his brief meeting with his father and how he had left abruptly. They talked about their mother. They had so much to tell each other. Late that night, they agreed to call again the day after.

That night when Dylan was lying in bed, he contemplated all the things that had happened to him lately. He felt overwhelmed, and meeting his twin brother touched him deeply. All his life, he had felt something was missing. As if he was connected to something without knowing what it was. Everything fell into place now that he had met his twin brother. It felt like a new phase was starting in his life.

BY THE SAME AUTHOR

R*ejuvenation* is a gripping scientific thriller of a journalist's investigation into a promising new drug, which is about to change the human race forever.

ISBN: 9789464007329 (paperback)
ISBN: 9789464007336 (hardback)
ASIN: B082MR9SV5 (eBook)

T*he Dome* is a riveting thriller about a young man's quest to find his biological parents in a world ravaged by the catastrophic consequences of climate change. The first book in the Dome series.

ISBN: 9789464007343 (paperback)
ISBN: 9789464007350 (hardback)
ASIN: B08NFCFSQC (eBook)

Lightning Source UK Ltd.
Milton Keynes UK
UKHW020956291121
394778UK00011B/1057